THE INDOCTRINATION

Works by K.L. Bone

Rise of the Temple Gods Series
Rise of the Temple Gods: Heir to Kale
Rise of the Temple Gods: Heir to Koloso
Rise of the Temple Gods: Heir to the Defendants
Rise of the Temple Gods: Heir to the Prophecy (coming soon)

The Black Rose Series
Black Rose
Heart of the Rose
Blood Rose
Shadow of the Rose
Silver Rose (coming soon)
Princess of the Rose (coming soon)

Tales of the Black Rose Guard Series
Daughters of the Rose (coming soon)

Other Works
The Indoctrination

See www.klbone.com for more.

THE INDOCTRINATION

K.L. BONE

The Indoctrination Copyright © 2013-2017 by Kristin L. Bone
ALL RIGHTS RESERVED.

Cover Art © 2013 by Skyla Dawn Cameron

First Edition: August 2013
First Paperback Edition: January 2014
Second Edition: January 2015
Third Edition: July 2017

All rights reserved under the International and Pan-American Copyright Conventions. No part of this book may be reproduced or transmitted in any form or by any means, electronic or mechanical including photocopying, recording, or by any information storage and retrieval system, without permission in writing from the author.

This book is a work of fiction. Names, characters, places and incidents are either the product of the author's imagination or are used fictitiously, and any resemblance to any actual persons, living or dead, events, or locales is entirely coincidental.

DEDICATION

The story is dedicated to my family for their love
and support and to my long-time writing mentors
Pam, Lili & Kate.

Prologue

"Do you swear to tell the truth, the whole truth, and nothing but the truth, so help you God?"

"I do," I replied.

"State your name for the record."

"Dehartra Chrissalynn Kasar, highest-ranking military commander, and Setian Empress."

"Empress Dehartra, you have been charged with ninety thousand counts of murder, multiple counts of rape, and high treason. How do you plead?"

"I plead guilty!" I shouted so my voice would carry above the crowded room. "Guilty to more murders than I can recall. Guilty to multiple counts of rape. But never, never in my life have I ever committed treason!"

I paused as the courtroom was shocked into silence at this unexpected confession. Taking a breath, I continued, "My only real crime is fulfilling my designed purpose; being what I was made to be. Forced to serve the empire, why not rule it? Why not enjoy the rewards, and bask in the pleasure of power? All I have done is defend what I am.

"The Setians took over the universe. I destroyed their council, and claimed leadership for myself. I am the most preeminent military leader in existence, and ascended to a position of ultimate power. You think I am evil? You charge I am a terrible, wicked person? Listen to my story as it is meant to be heard, and hear it well, for I will only tell this once, and you shall never hear its like again."

My first memory is not of grand parties or mass destruction, but of a day far more ordinary.

When I was five years old, my father took me out for a special trip, just the two of us. My mother stayed home with my younger brother, who did little more than sleep and cry at what I recall were the most annoying of moments. We left early that morning, and I watched the blooming sky from the passenger seat of my father's red Camaro as we drove down the California coast. The sunrise revealed perfection normally found only on a postcard. Gray emptiness faded to an elaborate array of pinks, reds, and oranges before finally changing to a beautiful cerulean blue as the blazing sun rose to warm the sky, chasing back night's inky hold for another day.

He took me to the beach, a beautiful spot difficult to find, but worth it once you were there. We had to scramble over jagged rocks, and down a narrow, overgrown trail. Not another soul in sight, the sand stretched ahead in a smooth slope, seemingly untouched.

Throwing my sandals to the wind, I ran to the ocean with my father close behind me, kicking sand in every direction. Reaching the gentle shore break, ocean waves tickled my bare feet; the breeze whispered in my ears as though welcoming me home. I put my hand in the clear water, delighting in the coolness, and soft tug of the currents. We took a few steps back, but not far enough to leave the wet sand completely.

"Will you build a castle with me, Daddy?"

"And what would you do with a castle, my dear?"

"I would be a princess!"

He laughed. "You would, Chrissa, and someday you will be."

"Really? A real princess?"

He smiled as I scooped the sand to build my castle and gazed into the glistening blue water. "You were meant for far more than this." He looked back at me. "Someday you shall be a princess, the most powerful and beautiful in all the land."

I smiled with unblemished trust in his promise, and he laughed before leaning down to assist me in my construction. Twice waves from a passing ship came in closer, and twice we pulled back, trying to get the castle high enough it would not dissolve into the water. With his big, smooth hands, my father dug a wide trench around the now lop-sided fortress to better protect it.

"I need some sea shells," I told him, "to decorate with."

Daddy stopped piling sand and walked the beach in search of the perfect adornment. He returned a few minutes later. "Here you are, my princess. Five shells for you."

As I stood there staring at my castle, seeing a far grander structure that what we'd actually achieved, I surveyed the gifts carefully arranged in his palm. "This one," I held up a yellow shell with a streak of a surprisingly bright blue, "will be my captain." I put the first piece by the hole I had made in the castle's base. "He will be my friend, and do whatever I ask of him."

"Will he now?" My father chuckled.

"Yes," I replied with a confident smile. "This one," I picked up a shiny black piece of a mussel, "will be the lord of the castle. He will love me and protect me from all danger." I placed the sharp-edged piece at the top of the castle, by a hole serving as a window overlooking the vast sea.

Selecting two more shells from his hand, one pure white, while the other had a black base striped with white, I put these on the top of the castle. "The prince and me," I declared boldly.

"And what about this one?" my father spoke of the last remaining shell in his hand.

"This one?" I picked the piece up to examine it. "Umm..." Jet black, smooth to the touch, it had a tiny splash of red in its center. As I stared, the red splash seemed to form the shape of a tiny rose.

I handed it back to my father. "Here, Daddy, this shell is for you."

"For me?"

"Will you keep it safe?"

He smiled warmly as he assured, "Yes, Chrissa, I will keep it safe."

The castle finished, my father and I walked along the water's edge, allowing waves to wash over our toes. He kicked tangled bundles of seaweed aside, and I'd squeal in delight as hermit crabs scrambled for new cover.

"Oh my girl, if you had any idea of the things you will one day see! The world is so much more than you imagine."

"Will you show me these things, Daddy?" I asked in youthful ignorance.

"Yes, my darling, I will. You will see it all, and I will be there to show you."

I laughed and, for one magical moment, we were the only two people in a beautiful world.

But like all moments, this one came to an end. Two weeks later, my father was dead. He had gone back to the sea, on a fishing boat with a couple of his friends. A sudden storm had shredded the boat, and though a search was conducted, his body was never recovered.

After he died, my mother changed. She gave up all will to carry on with her life and responsibilities.

Despite this shattered childhood, I remember my sixth birthday with crystal clarity.

My mother woke me early and carried me into her bedroom, where she presented me with a new dress, a blue frock with flowers down the front that twirled prettily in the mirror.

I was too young to understand what was about to happen. Couldn't possibly have predicted the coming events.

A few hours later, my mother woke my baby brother and told us we were going on a trip.

I remember how beautiful she looked behind the wheel of the car. A plain, blue cotton dress perfectly accented her feminine form. Her long, black hair flowed loose around slim shoulders, trailing to end above her thighs. Her lipstick, which she'd not worn since Daddy's death, a bold red against light skin. But most of all I remember how her blue eyes held a sadness my six-year-old mind could not understand.

"What's wrong, Mommy?"

"Nothing, honey." Her only reply.

She drove up to an ugly green building, surrounded by a wooden porch. As I stepped out of the car, a woman with non-descript brown hair rose from a chair and came to greet us. She smiled at my brother, James, before shaking hands with my mom. They stepped aside, and whispered for what seemed like hours, as my brother and I entertained ourselves on the porch.

Finally, the lady walked to where my brother and I were playing. She told us something I will never remember, because when she finished, I looked back toward my mother, who was in her car.

I looked in confusion as my brother cried, "Mommy?"

"Where's she going?" I didn't hear the answer over the engine roaring to life.

I stared hoping, waiting, trusting she would wait for us. Mommy always waited for us.

Without even a glance in our direction, my mother put her car into drive and moved onto the road.

I called, "Mommy? Where are you going? MOMMY!"

The car disappeared.

That was the last time we saw her. Eventually, the nice lady took my brother's hand and walked him into the orphanage, promising him a cookie.

I stood on the sidewalk, confused tears streaking my face, whispering, "Mommy?" Wondering what I'd done wrong. Promising I'd be good if only she'd come back. It would be the first of many nights I would stand outside waiting for her to return; she never did.

A few months after we arrived, a young couple, Jill and Barry, came to meet with us. After only three visits, the couple petitioned for, and was soon granted, guardianship. We were whisked away to their home in the country, which sat in the center of fifteen acres. Their two-story crimson house was surrounded by a stone wall, and a simple wrought-iron gate served as the entranceway. We were given separate rooms on the upper floor, and allowed to share a third as a playroom.

Barry and Jill were traditional, with kind but firm expectations. They had taken the liberty of painting our rooms; one pink and one blue. All of the remaining rooms were either a sky blue or off-white.

Comfortable, if not affluent, Jill was a teacher at the local middle school, while Barry was a defense attorney for one of the town's law firms. When Jill's grandparents had died, they left the house and land to her. We were treated well, and received everything we needed throughout early childhood. Because of Jill's profession, education was a high priority, and I developed a love of knowledge. I escaped in novels, and could often be found lying on my bed, allowing stories to transport me to different worlds.

As time went by, memories of my old life faded, but the dream of my mother one day returning burned like a flame. I suppose it is the dream of every orphan.

James, younger when abandoned and burdened with only foggy memories, adjusted well, while I struggled with feelings of being a lost child in a world where I did not belong.

As I reached middle school, and the conflicting emotional chaos of puberty, I found myself an outcast, who never seemed to find common ground with any group. Despite my adoptive parents' attempts to push me toward a more social life, and sports, including my mother dragging me to occasional parties for the children of her neighborhood friends, their efforts were to little avail. Belonging nowhere, I sat alone at a corner table in the back of the lunchroom, or invisible under a tree at parties.

My heart longed for the fading promise my father had made on the far-off beach, which now existed only in my dreams.

Chapter I

SOMETIME AFTER MY TENTH birthday, I was alone in my bedroom, sprawled out on my white bedspread embroidered with light pink roses and green petals. Barry and Jill had gone out for the evening. A young woman named Claudia was watching us, and had brought a greasy pepperoni pizza when she arrived.

Tummy full, I was thoroughly engrossed in a Star Wars novel when a strange, high-pitched sound made me put down the book. I lay still, listening intently to the following silence.

Shaking my head, I picked up my book. *Screech!* The sound came again, this time loud enough I covered my ears. The metallic whine lasted thirty seconds, followed by another eerie silence.

This time I jumped from the bed and moved quickly to my desk. Reaching over the cluttered surface, I threw back the sheer pink curtains and opened the window. Cold winter air raced into the warm room as I cautiously looked outside. The night sky was filled with blinking red lights, outlining a round blue and brilliant white vast shape; an aircraft but unlike any I had seen before. My eyes, adjusting to the glare, detected black with silver streaks along the side, and bright lights in the front.

Fear engulfed me as I ran to my brother's room, calling his name. I found him standing by the bed. I struggled to think of what to do, where I might be able to hide him, but never got the chance.

Armed men, with strange guns, entered the room. Eight in all, wearing matching shirts with a circular symbol on the front. Tucking James protectively behind me, I asked what they wanted, but the men remained silent.

Another man entered, wearing a more-familiar business suit. Black slacks accompanied a white, long-sleeved shirt under a black jacket.

"Who are you?" My voice came soft and unsteady. "Are you going to hurt us?"

The strange man smiled. "I would never dream of harming you. If you promise to come with me, quietly, I will agree not to harm your brother, and leave him be. Do you understand?"

Tears came to my eyes, but I nodded yes. "Who are you?" I asked again. "Have I done something wrong?"

The man gave a soft laugh. "Amazing, the mind of a child. How I have missed…" He paused. "Come, child, all will be explained in time."

The suited man nodded to one of the others, who lowered his gun as he walked toward me. He took my hand and led me out of the bedroom, down the stairs. We walked out the front door, where the ship had landed. Massive, it covered the lawn as far as I could see. At our approach, a doorway slid opened, lined by more armed men in red jumpsuits.

I stopped, terrified, and tried to step back.

The guard tightened his grip on my arm, firm but not painful. "No one will harm you. You have the word of Lord Nicholas Kasar."

I took a shaky breath and allowed myself to be directed down the isle of armed men, through a doorway that must have been twenty feet high. At odds with the screech of their arrival, the ship was completely silent, and the men did not make a sound. *Why is it so quiet? What do they want with me?*

The last questions I would ask standing on my home planet as an innocent young girl.

Once aboard, I was led down a series of hallways with solid black walls. Everything looked identical, until the guard escorting me opened a door where there had been no sign of one moments before.

Left alone, the only light came from scattered bulbs, small and dim like the nightlight in the bathroom, surrounding a bed. By the time I reached it, fear and shock had me physically shaking. Didn't help that the room was cold, so I fumbled with the covers and wrapped them securely around me. Curled into a fetal position, I lay there for many hours before falling into confused dreams.

When I awoke, the low lights around my bed had been replaced by bright ones above, revealing the walls to be a light pink, and the bedspread I'd wrapped around myself was a darker pink satin, lined with white lace at the edges. On the opposite wall appeared to be a fireplace, complete with red brick, but no fire burned within. Instead, what looked like glass pebbles glowed in shades of blue, yellow, and orange, emitting a steady heat that coaxed me into unwinding myself from the bed covering.

As I scanned the room, I noticed a young woman with shoulder-length brown hair stood patiently against the far wall. "Hello, young mistress," she said. "My name is Monica. I'm your maid, and am here to ensure you receive everything you require. I have taken the liberty of preparing your bath. Please follow me."

I tried to ask her where I was, but she silenced me with, "Your questions will be answered soon enough."

Unsure how to respond, I followed her into the next room. Expecting something more utilitarian, the opulent, normal-looking bathroom surprised me with its spaciousness. Mirrors, bordered in gold, lined the walls. In one corner, stood a marble bathtub, with a gold inlaid faucet, filled to the brim with water and sweet-smelling oils. When Monica left, I shed my clothes and sank into the soothing heat.

When the water cooled, I dried off with the provided towel, and went back to my room, where an elaborate gown waited upon the bed. More light pink silk, but with jewels lining the top, flowing sleeves, and a short train. I ought to let someone know pink isn't my favorite color.

Once dressed, the maid transformed my hair into an elaborate updo with tons of curls, and fastened a gold necklace with pink diamonds around my neck.

When I found the courage to again ask where I was, she replied, "Kasar wants to tell you himself."

Monica escorted me into a large room. The air was warm, and filled with a pleasant aroma I could not place, but caused my stomach to remind me I'd not eaten since pizza last night. I was led to a rectangular table, and seated across from a man who introduced himself as Lord Nicholas Kasar.

"Please, sir, why am I here? What do you want?"

"You," was his answer. "Word of you has come to me from afar. The moment I saw you, I knew I'd been right in my choice."

"Choice?"

As I asked, a creature that should not exist walked through the door. It had four legs and a horse's lower body, but its upper torso looked humanoid, and the entire form was covered with bright red fur. On its head were two eyes, a nose, and a mouth all very similar to a human's. Reminded me of the centaur I'd seen depicted in mythology books, though this one appeared decidedly scarier.

"He is a Lorid," Kasar revealed, noting my curious stare. "One of over a hundred species which you have never seen, nor heard of."

Kasar rose from his chair and walked around the table. He took my hand and led me to the window, where he revealed an unbelievable, wondrous, and terrifying truth. As I looked out, only the blackness of space greeted me.

"Most of the creatures on this ship are not of your world," Kasar explained. I stood in silence as he continued, "Lorid are our enemies. Horde, and Slith are one with the Setian Empire."

With that, another creature approached, standing seven feet tall on two legs, with two eyes, a pig-looking nose, and a slit for a mouth.

"A Horde," Kasar said.

Beside the Horde slithered a creature, about three feet long, with twenty legs, six sets of arms, blue spiky fur, six eyes, and the ugliest mouth I had ever seen.

"A Slith."

As I gawked in open-mouthed shock, Kasar explained, "These creatures' entire races belong to the Setian Empire. I am one of the few humans, and the seventh-highest-ranking member.

"Your question, my dear, is why you are here. The answer, is to make you my princess and heir. You will be indoctrinated in our ways and, in exchange, your every desire shall be met."

Over a meal, which included foods I'd never seen before, but were mostly delicious once I got past the odd textures, I asked questions for what must have been hours—I'd lost all sense of time. Kasar answered each one patiently, sometimes with an odd twinkle in his eye. By the time Monica returned me to my chamber, I had learned more than I'd ever imagined.

Chapter II

Learning about the different species and planets was a lot to take in.

For starters, there are approximately four hundred planets capable of supporting life. We traveled at speeds faster than light, and visited hundreds of exotic and strange locations throughout various galaxies. Of the life-supporting planets, only one hundred support intelligent species. And of these, only eleven qualified as major races.

The most powerful of these species were rivals, the Lorid Sovereignty, and the Setian Empire.

As with Earth, each government dealt in various titles, and positions, with varying degrees of influence. The highest among the Setian ranks were councilors, followed by the military leaders, known as Setian lords. When a leader achieved these ranks, they were also granted the right to choose a name different from the rank they were assigned at birth. Being raised by Lord Nicholas Kasar, I was treated as the daughter of a very powerful man.

Kasar had ordered that I be treated as his beloved child. None dared disobey, or ask for a higher authority on my wishes. My personal staff included maids, two tutors, and three additional servants whose sole job was to serve my every whim.

A few months after my abduction, we attended a convention on one of the Markata Moons, deep inside Setian space. During these assemblies, leaders of rank could be found in attendance, along with a supporting entourage of ships, troops, servants, and allies. The moon thus hosted a grand social gathering, protected by an impenetrable fortress.

Meetings were held inside a glass dome, which had various lecture halls to host the different conferences. A center complex housed various vendors, who came from all parts of the galaxy, hoping to sell their treasures, or edible treats, to tired attendees. While walking from a conference on the Horde movement, to a meeting concerning the current Lorid battlefront in the Korid system, I happened upon an unusual creature displayed in one of these booths.

With alert eyes and a flicking tail, it reminded me of a cat, only it had six legs and four eyes. Black stripes ran down deep green, bright blue, and on one animal, hot pink fur. While the other two slept, the pink one made curious eye-contact with me, one of its paws stretched out between the cage bars, as if begging for my touch.

"Is it a kitty?" I asked the man who seemed to be in charge of them.

"They are called *semnas*," the man answered. He towered above me in his crude Horde form.

"From the planet Palta?" I asked, putting my recent classroom knowledge to the test. "They're pets, aren't they?"

"Yes," he replied, turning from me as the next customer approached.

"How big do they get?"

Focused on the more lucrative prospect, a woman dressed in adorned layers of fine cloth, he did not answer my question.

From what I recalled, semnas grew to be about twenty pounds, a large housecat. "How much is the pink one?" I asked again, determined. I reached out to carefully stroke the soft paw with one finger.

He turned back to me. "Expensive," he replied, not bothering to hide his annoyance.

"How expensive?"

"Extremely expensive."

"But how much is expensive?"

"I'm busy! Why don't you head down to the *zerka* stand? I hear they are good at helping little girls with stupid questions."

Upset and confused by his rare rudeness, I walked toward the Lorid battlefront conference. When I arrived before the black metal door, two guards stood at attention on either side.

I pulled the plastic badge draped around my neck from under my dress and showed it to the guard on my right. The bright red color gave me top-level clearance, but the name on the badge caused the guards to bow before opening the door. They nodded to a man inside, who raced to escort me to a prime seat.

"Chrissalynn Kasar," he said as we moved to the front of the massive lecture hall. "An honor to have the child of our esteemed Lord Kasar with us today."

I took a seat.

"May I get you anything? Food, drink, a fan, or heater? A computer to take notes for you, perhaps? Anything at all?"

"I would like a *krepta*," I said, naming a fruity drink I'd recently been introduced to. "And did you say a computer would take notes *for* me?"

"Of course." Two minutes later, I sat with my drink in one hand, and a computer taking notes behind me.

When Kasar arrived, he took his seat beside me, and the lecture commenced. I settled into the pillows as voices droned on, and endless charts were projected of places you shall never see.

New to the galactic perspective, the political details were confusing, but occasionally they would post pictures of colorful places, and creatures I had recently come across in my studies. Many were allies to the Lorid Sovereignty, and I found great interest in learning the various connections between different species.

The lecture switched to battle strategy, which was beyond my youthful comprehension. I shifted in my seat, struggling not to fall asleep in my chair before the lecture ended.

"How're you doing, Chrissa?" Kasar asked me as the crowd dispersed.

"Okay, I guess."

"These lectures can get boring, but I assure you the information will prove useful in time."

I nodded.

"Have you visited the center complex yet? There are usually some amazing finds amid the numerous vendors. They bring the best and rarest the empire has to offer."

Shame flooded my cheeks with warmth, and I looked down in an attempt to hide what I feared to be a childish reaction.

"Is everything all right, Chrissalynn?"

I looked up, and finding Kasar's gentle glance, admitted, "I asked a Horde about this pink semna, but when I asked for a price he…" I paused and Kasar prompted me to continue. "He called me a little girl with stupid questions."

Kasar's eyes widened. "Stupid," he repeated. "He said 'stupid'?"

I nodded, embarrassed tears brimming.

Kasar turned and called three guards to his side before asking me, "Chrissa, could you point out this vendor to me?"

I nodded again. "It's near here, the only one I saw with a pink kitty."

"Show me."

A hopeful bounce in my step, we walked out into the crowded complex. After a few minutes, I spotted the semnas, and pointed the Horde vendor out. Kasar walked slowly toward the booth, flanked by his personal guard, as I trailed a few steps behind. The dealer bowed low as Kasar approached.

"My esteemed lord," the Horde greeted. "To what do I owe this unexpected visit?"

"What's your name?"

"Septa 5487."

"Tell me, Septa 5487, do you know my name?"

"Of course. You are Kasar, a lord of the Setian Empire."

"Very good." Kasar paused and motioned to me.

The guards parted as I stepped forward. "Tell me, do you recognize this girl?"

Septa 5487 glanced up enough to look at me. His skin flushed. "I do not recognize the girl," he stuttered.

"Her name," Kasar informed him, "is Chrissa. However to you, Septa 5487, her name is Lady Chrissalynn Kasar; my daughter." His voice hardened. "I understand you were quite rude to my daughter today."

Silence followed before the Horde finally excused, "I did not know. I had no idea she was your daughter. If she had let me know who she was—"

"She tried and was ignored."

"I—"

"You called her 'stupid,' did you not?"

"I never meant—"

"Silence! This is my daughter. An insult to her is, by extension, an insult to me and insults," Kasar motioned to the guard on his left, "are not to be tolerated."

With those words, the guard raised his weapon toward the Horde and pulled the trigger.

A bright flash of light singed the air, and momentarily disrupted my vision with flashing spots. When my sight returned to normal, in the place where Septa 5487 had once stood, there was nothing. Only the light scent of burning served as evidence a living being had once stood there. It took me time to process. The Horde had been incinerated, without a single drop of blood touching the floor.

The noisy market had fallen silent, but no one approached to question Kasar's action. He walked to the cages holding the catlike creatures. "I believe you wanted the pink one, did you not, my dear?"

I gave no response. Kasar had killed him, over a minor slight. My mind raced with a million thoughts, though I seemed unable to grasp any of them.

Kasar gently placed the tiny pink semna in my arms.

I focused on holding the warm, soft ball of fur with care. Eagerly devoted as much of my attention as I could to the simple task. Anything other than consider my role in another's death. Kasar touched my shoulder and led me out of the complex, back toward our private ship.

"Someone find Septa 5488," I heard him say. "Congratulate him on his promotion."

The next thing I knew, I was back in my own room holding the catlike creature, who blended with the décor. So much for not liking pink.

Kasar gently stroked the head of my new pet. "Pretty kitty," he whispered. "What will you name her?"

Amid the whirl of conflicting thoughts and emotions, I managed to say, "Aurora."

"Ah, after the sleeping beauty princess. A lovely choice." He smiled before wishing me goodnight and exiting the room.

My maid helped me into a soft, satin gown and robe.

Content, Aurora purred softly as she curled herself beside me, and I eventually drifted off to sleep.

Chapter III

A few months later, Kasar declared I was ready to see an actual Setian.

"I've wanted to meet one for some time now."

He led me into a room with a raised basin. I walked to the pool and peered down into the clear, light-blue water. Inside I saw several creatures, clear in color, similar to Earth's jellyfish, but with no definite shape. They shifted from circles, to squares, to triangles, and many other forms as I watched. To my surprise, they had no eyes, mouths, noses, legs, or arms.

"These are Setians? These?" I asked in confusion. "How could a blind and deaf species be so powerful?"

"In this form, they are not. Setians are parasitic. They enter other creatures' minds and control them. Once in another being's mind, they have use of eyes, ears, legs, and arms. Everything they need to thrive.

"Now," he continued, "there is a restriction of sorts. When a Setian enters a body, they absorb certain chemicals unique to the host they are possessing. Therefore, in order to successfully change hosts, the Setian must be cleansed of these outside elements by re-entering the water."

"Which means?"

"Setians cannot transfer themselves directly from one host to another without entering a pool. They would kill themselves, and the host they are trying to possess if they did so.

"I am Setian," Kasar revealed, "but you, my dear, are special. You are destined to be the only empire leader who is not one of us. Yes, Chrissa, you will be one of us; the best of us." He laughed.

The implication, the possible ramifications, terrified me into dumb silence. I should have fought with everything I had.

"Traitor!" a voice called.

Eyes searched the courtroom, but no one took credit for the insult.

"I ask you," I responded, "what was I supposed to have done? Fifteen years ago you did not even know the empire existed. I was a child, a million miles from everything I had ever known. Men were killed before my eyes. Lives destroyed over the briefest of insults. Horrifying creatures that should not have existed walked through my everyday life." I paused, allowing silence to fill the room.

"Eleven years old. Your own court systems do not judge a child so young. My fate dictated by a powerful being; not asked, or given a choice, but told. Can you imagine my fear? The only piece of my life that seemed familiar was the man standing before me.

"This man, this creature, hated much of the world, yet for reasons I still don't understand, he loved me. Treated me like the beloved princess my father had promised I would be. I craved the love he gave so freely. I wanted to be safe, and his love was my lifeline in a world I was far too young to understand."

As I continued my testimony, Kasar's next words sounded timeless in my mind. *"Yes, you will be mine."*

Chapter IV

Several months later, I sat in my room, at an elegant table covered with a pink satin cloth. My human tutor sat directly across from me, fidgeting with a large paperclip. I had spent ten hours a day, every day of the last few months, in intense learning sessions, but it still seemed we had barely scratched the surface.

"Now tell me," Mr. Indigo requested, "about the history of the Setian Empire."

"The first form of written Setian history is dated at nearly eight thousand years ago. It tells of a species called Nemora, who were a race of rather simplistic creatures. They stood five-feet on average, had eight legs, three arms, and nine multicolored eyes. They often sported red, blue, and brown fur. These creatures formed a symbiotic relationship with the more intelligent Setians. The two species worked together to form the beginnings of Setian society.

"Nearly eight hundred years after these first records, printed writing became popular throughout the planet. Setian books prevailed, and common knowledge expanded exponentially. Education, medical fields, and technology advanced over the next three thousand years, when the Setian's first version of computers appeared on the scene.

"Two thousand years later, cities covered the planet. The Setians unified into an empire. Two thousand years ago, the first faster-than-light ships were engineered, and life on other planets was discovered shortly afterward. Setians traveled the universe in peace for nine hundred years before they came into contact with another powerful force."

"And who was that?"

"The Karmels."

"What do you remember about them?"

"Karmels were a technologically advanced race, who moved from one planet to another, destroying other species before repopulating conquered planets with members of their own race." I drew a breath. "May I have some water?"

"Of course." Mr. Indigo reached for the pitcher between us, and proceeded to pour into the glass on my right.

"Thank you," I said, as I took a drink of the ice cold liquid. I had been talking for quite a while.

Mr. Indigo's gentle brown eyes communicated patience while I soothed my dry throat, but the paperclip spun furiously between his long fingers.

"What happened next?" my professor asked, after I'd emptied the glass and set it back down.

"The Karmels moved toward Setianta, the Setian home world, expecting an easy conquest. Though unified, technologically advanced, and skilled in the ways of war, the Setians had few actual defenses. Further complicating organization, the planet was divided into thirteen sections, with thirteen different leaders, who together formed a ruling council for the planet. When these leaders discovered the Karmels were coming, they decided it would be more effective to defend themselves, and their people, if a single person were in charge for the duration of the battle to come."

"Very good. Do you remember whom they chose?"

"Dehartra, who created the first military force ever seen on the planet. Armed ships were built by the hundreds, and over half the world's factories began producing items intended for war. In the short five-week window, between when the Setians learned the Karmels were coming, and the Karmels actually arriving, the Setian home world became the equivalent of a military state."

"Tell me, has your other tutor, Mr. Bariom, shown you a replay of the battle yet?"

"No."

"Would you like to see it?"

I nodded.

"Computer, show us the battles of Karmel versus Setianta. The table will be fine."

The room lights dimmed, and as I watched, an image took shape in front of me. As a hologram of the Setian world appeared, I watched in fascination as ships slowly appeared around the planet.

I jumped as the computer announced, "For your convenience, the Karmel ships are in red, and the Setian ships are green." Speaking computers were something I still needed to get used to. I shook my head and watched the battle play out before me.

Red ships raced toward the planet, and green ships rose up to meet them. Shots were fired, and ships of both colors disappeared from the screen. The Karmels were better shots, as they were far more experienced, but the Setians had more guns. Expecting an easy victory over a peaceful planet, the Karmels had only sent fifty ships. The Setians had managed to assemble two hundred.

So while the Karmels were better fighters, they lost the battle by sheer numbers.

After a brief pause, the hologram continued, because nearly a year later, the Karmels tried again.

The Setians were ready, not only with more resources, but improved skills in using them.

Their victory over the Karmels turned the Setians into a major force on the universal stage. Within the next hundred fifty years, the Setians were challenged by, and defeated, both the Rotes and the Sliths.

At my tutor's direction, these subsequent battles played over the table in brilliant, three-dimensional colors. On occasion, the story would pause, and the computer would stop the simulation to analyze the battles, pointing out what had been done well, and key points of failure. Battle strategy would become an important part of my training.

"What happened to those species once they were defeated?" Mr. Indigo continued the oral quiz as the hologram faded and the room lights brightened once again.

"They were assimilated into Setian society, which in the next two hundred years became known as the Setian Empire."

"How was this empire organized?"

I rubbed my eyes, tired from the long exchange, and adjusting to the different illumination. "Thirteen leaders ruled different regions, but one, the emperor or empress, ruled supreme, above the others. Those skilled in war became more important as battles became more frequent and intense. A few hundred years after the Setians won their first major victory, they became a military society. Everyone, men and women alike, are required to join the military, and hold equal opportunity for advancement."

"How is the military divided?"

"Each Setian, when born, takes the name of their province and a number. At one time, the highest-ranking member of each province—number one—was placed upon the council. However over time, this changed.

"Today, once a Setian reaches the highest ranks of their province, they are given an opportunity for promotion to the rank of sub-harars. Promotions can come from the top rank of any province.

"There are fifty-two sub-harars, twenty-six harars, and ten top-ranking military commanders also referred to as Setian lords. Once promoted to lord rank, Setians are given the opportunity to choose individual names, as a way of marking the distinction earned. For example, the lord of this ship chose Nicholas Kasar as his name.

"Each lord is given their own ship. Those of lower rank are divided among the top-ten leaders, with the better ships, weaponry, and soldiers going to those of higher ranks." I paused, recalling the final level of advancement.

"Individuals fortunate enough to advance beyond a military rank are invited to sit upon the council.

"Of the thirteen council members, one is chosen to serve as emperor or empress. Their identity is known only to those of the highest ranks within the empire, so our enemies are never sure which councilor ranks above the others."

"Yes, good, good. You have learned faster than I expected. Kasar did well in choosing you as his protégée. We have done more than enough for one day. Why don't you go freshen up for dinner? I look forward to reporting your progress."

Chapter V

When I was twelve, Kasar was asked to monitor a battle in a nearby system. Since he was going as a consult, and no additional forces were required, he took only five ships, leaving the majority of the fleet behind. My studies continued in his absence, and I spent many hours in the archive room watching past military engagements, studying the various strategies used, searching for both successes and failures.

Walking back one evening, I was surprised to find a usually locked door to my left standing wide open. Curious, I approached and glanced inside. A rectangular table stood in the room's center, and at one end sat a woman I had never seen before. She stared intently at a deck of cards in front of her before turning to glance my way, where her expression changed to a warm smile.

"Hello, Chrissalynn," she greeted in a pleasant voice.

"How do you know my name?"

"You are Kasar's protégée, are you not? Everyone knows who you are."

I took a step into the room. "I've never seen you before. Who are you?"

"My name is Lysalie, and I work on the ship's computers, so I'm not surprised you have never seen me before."

"Oh. What are you doing?"

"Playing cards."

I had walked to the table without realizing it. "Which game?"

"*Hyst*," she replied. "However, if you would like to play, I am well-versed in a variety of games native to your home planet. Poker, spades, rummy, hearts, anything you want."

"Blackjack?"

"Sure." She smiled. "Please, sit down."

I took a seat across from her and waited for her to deal. To my surprise, the cards magically appeared before me, out of thin air. "Wow!" I exclaimed, to her amusement. "How?"

"They are holographic."

"How do I pick them up?"

"Like regular cards. Go ahead, try."

I reached for the first card tentatively, and to my further surprise, I was able to pick it up. I held it in front of me, running my thumb curiously over the textured surface. When I let go, it remained floating in mid-air. Where had this technology been when my small hands struggled to hold cards for a game of fish as a young child?

Tilting my head, I grabbed the card. Once again, it moved into my hand. I did this several times, experimenting with different numbers of cards, while Lysalie chuckled in amusement.

"So curious," she commented. "It is hard to realize you have not always been one of us. How common aspects could seem magical."

I offered an embarrassed smile before laughing myself.

"Shall we play?"

"Sure," I replied. "Hit me." Another card appeared and the game began. We played for about two hours, and talked about everything, from how I was adapting to life in space, to the kind of music she liked. When Lysalie announced she needed to go, she offered to play with me the next night, if I wished.

The next day I read some history between the Lorids and Setians. My favorite area of study left me in a wonderful mood as I slipped inside the blue-walled room as I had the evening before.

Lysalie was waiting. "Would you like to learn a few new types of poker?"

"Sure," I answered, shyly.

Seven cards, five cards, Texas hold-em…she knew them all. From that evening on, we played on a regular basis. Lysalie taught me rummy, poker, and called on computer players to teach me spades and hearts. After learning the Earth basics, she turned to games such as hyst, *krenton*, *jevrea*, and numerous others from all over the galaxy. The suits, letters, and numbers changed from one game to the next, but the basic concepts stayed the same.

Months of lively evenings later, my maid, Monica, came to announce Kasar's return. "He's hosting a fellow commander," she informed me, "and requests your presence at dinner."

I hurried through my studies, excited about the upcoming meeting. Kasar had never brought home another commander. I was curious to see what the other military leaders, whom I had been learning about in my studies, would actually be like in person.

When I returned to my room, I found a wondrous surprise. A deep scarlet dress with satin sleeves that shimmered in the light, and in a diamond shape that hung around my wrists, waited on the bed. Low cut, adorned with jewels around the neckline, and fitted at the waist with a full skirt. Roses covered the gown's bosom, and petticoats held the gown out, turning it into a sea of ruffles surrounding me. As Monica buttoned the gown, I couldn't believe how beautiful I looked.

Seated before a mirror, Monica curled my hair into a sea of ringlets that framed my face. To perfect her work, she added a few scattered jewels in my hair. The warm, pulsing light from the glass stone fireplace caused them to sparkle.

"Kasar also sent this." Monica handed me a black bag. I opened it and withdrew a note. "I've missed you. Here is a special gift for a special night." Signed simply, with an elegant, "K."

I reached in further and withdrew a gold necklace, lined with large stones the color of blood. As Monica secured it around my neck, the smile upon my young face was never-ending. The eyes staring at the golden-rimmed mirror were those of a child, but the face looking back belonged to a woman I'd never met. With a touch of rouge, mascara, and ruby lipstick the transformation was complete.

Enjoying the soft rustle of fabric, I walked slowly down the hallway, my gown trailing behind me, roses crawling up my body. The banquet room had been set formally. A wide fireplace on the back wall glowed with stones like those in my private room, and a crystal chandelier hung from the ceiling, reflecting rainbows, which danced across the walls. A table stood in the center of the room, covered in a silver cloth inlaid with gold lines, and elaborate rose designs. Crystal glasses were set beside white china plates with silver roses around the edges.

As I approached the table, two men rose to meet me. Kasar stood in a black suit with a crimson shirt, a perfect match to my elaborate gown. His shoulder-length black hair was pulled tightly back with a silver band, highlighting his blue eyes. I returned his smile as he stepped forward and slowly brought my hand to his lips.

Never breaking his mesmerizing stare, "I missed you," he whispered, swinging me gently in a swirl of ruffles and roses.

The second man was similarly dressed in a black suit, but wearing a white shirt. His hair was as blond as Kasar's was black, and his eyes were the light-blue of a clear Earth sky. I would have guessed he was about twenty years younger than Kasar, but with the Setians, age was impossible to tell.

"Chrissalynn, may I introduce my friend, Lord Kavra, ninth-ranking commander in the empire, and a former protégée. I taught him everything he knows."

"Or so he thinks," came the mischievous reply.

I had never seen anyone tease Kasar. To hide my surprise, I lowered into a curtsy.

Kavra's hand touched my left shoulder. "You are the daughter of my esteemed friend and mentor. If anyone should be bowing to a position of servitude, it should be me. Rest assured, from this moment, I shall be at your service." As Kasar had, he placed a gentle kiss upon the back of my hand.

"Careful, Kav," cautioned Kasar. "She's my daughter."

"All the more reason to charm her," he retorted with a grin.

Kasar laughed, motioning to the table. "Be seated."

Kavra helped me to my seat, before taking one across from me.

"How was the battle?"

"It went well," Kasar replied.

"We kicked their sorry tails from one side of the galaxy to the other." This cheeky answer came from Kavra, of course.

"Where have the servants run off to?" Kasar lamented. "I am evidently going to need a lot more alcohol to get through this dinner."

An array of seafood was presented, including lobster, shrimp, halibut, *natll, fedmish, reveny,* and a delicious selection of other dishes from various worlds.

Kavra and Kasar told tales of their recent battles, each playing off the other. As the wine flowed, stories became more embellished.

"Remember the time you drank too much at Councilor Valerisa's promotion ceremony?" Kavra asked in a teasing voice.

"Don't you dare!" Kasar scolded, unable to hide his laughter.

"Has he told you the story?"

I shook my head, a smile splitting my face as a servant appeared to take my empty plate.

"Well, you see, Valerisa had received a promotion, from commander to councilor, and Kasar decides to get drunk at the party. He accidentally stumbles into the new councilor's room and—"

"Kavra, stop right there!"

Kavra laughed and pushed his chair back, as through ready to sprint. "Valerisa walks in from a side door half-naked, while Kasar is sitting there drunk as can be, and says—"

"If you say one more word, I will tell her about the time you and Lydia got captured by the Scaltz."

"Not fair!" he groaned.

Kasar shot him a beaming smile.

Silence loomed, broken when Kasar suggested, "Anyone ready for dessert?"

Servants brought out a triple-layer chocolate cake, drizzled with a vanilla and cherry sauce, topped with whip cream and shaved chocolate. Chocolate, Earth's major contribution to the universal market.

Four days later, I was leaning back in one of the rocking chairs Kasar had placed in my room, reading a novel on Lorid history, when a knock sounded at my door.

"Come in," I called.

"Hello, Chrissa," Kasar said, a warm smile on his face.

"Hello, Kasar." I closed the book, setting it aside.

"I will be leaving tonight for the Utymphotra front."

"So soon?"

He sighed. "Yes, the work of a commander is never done."

"Oh…"

"However, you might be glad to know Kavra will be staying, for at least a few more days. There are a couple of special projects, which he has agreed to help me on, that can only be completed from here. So I'm not leaving you entirely alone."

When he added, "I'm sure he has at least one more story to embarrass me with," after a pause, I could not keep the smile off my face.

"Please be careful."

"Always."

Three hours later, he left for battle.

Chapter VI

THAT NIGHT, I AWOKE TO muffled sounds pulling me from the warmth of my dreams. I groggily forced my eyes open, asking for the time.

The computer replied, "02:18 GD," the Setian equivalent of AM.

I closed my eyes, but once again heard the strange noise. I sat up, pulling the satin sheets from my body. The chemical rock fire glowed bright, and the room was warm as I pulled an *akron* robe, material as thick as wool with the texture of silk, around my thin pink gown.

I opened the door to a dimly lit corridor. As I got closer to the sound's origin, I realized I was hearing deep, masculine screams.

"Hello?" I called.

Another muffled scream. Indistinguishable moans.

I should have gone and found Kavra, but some force propelled me forward.

Unlike most others, the door to this room was silver in color, a thick metal that should have trapped all sound within, but did not. I put my left hand against the cold threshold, and used my right to pull the robe tight, attempting to keep out the chill.

The door opened without a sound.

The room was white, stark walls lined with metal racks. All of my attention focused on the far left corner of the room.

There, lying on a black table, was a figure. Nude, he'd been tied to the surface with an elastic-like material pulled so tight it cut into his skin.

Straps across his upper chest, waist, and forehead held him fast to the table. Bands were also tied tightly around each wrist and ankle. His legs were secured to the table, but his arms were connected to a pulley attached to the walls. His hands were in gloves, which spread his fingers apart, encasing all but his fingertips. Three other men, and one woman, stood beside the table.

The restrained male, based on equipment revealed below his waist, was not human. He had two arms, and two legs, like humans, but twelve fingers, seven on one hand, five on the other. He also had two sets of eyes, one above the other, with no eyebrows. His top eyes were lavender, while his lower were yellow. Both sets were open wide in pain.

Streaks of blood ran in rivulets down both sides of his body, pooling on the floor as rain forms on a street.

Concerned, I stepped forward, trying to understand. My mind could not comprehend what lay so clearly before my eyes.

Two of the men standing by the prisoner finally noticed my approach and turned their eyes toward me. "Who are you?" one challenged.

"She's Kasar's daughter," came the reply.

My eyes never shifted from the writhing form on the table.

"Should she be in here?"

The man and woman by the prisoner's arms did not look up. As I stepped closer, I realized they were holding slender needles glowing red from what was surely intense heat. The needles were slipped under the nails of the man's restrained hands. The scent of seared flesh assaulted my nose. His chest was covered with thin cuts.

Someone spoke to me, but I could not hear them, my eyes glued to the poor creature. He screamed again, raw and agonized. I put my head down as I gagged on the grotesque smell.

The next thing I knew, I was outside in the corridor, held secure in Kavra's arms. I whispered his name and he paused to reposition me so I could slide my arms around his neck.

"Chrissa," he said softly, "what were you doing in there? You should be in bed."

"I heard screaming." I let my eyes close as I was carried farther down the hall. A couple of turns later and we were in my room, where Kavra laid me down.

He shifted me onto the pillows. "Lie still, take deep breaths."

My maid appeared and handed Kavra a cool cloth, which he placed on my forehead. I relaxed as Kavra sent her away with his thanks.

As my head cleared, I found my voice to ask, "What's going on? Why are they hurting him?"

He sat on the bed and reached for my hand, which he gently took in his. "Chrissa, he is a prisoner who knows about the planetary defenses in the battle Kasar is fighting as we speak. The torture is being used to force him to confess what he knows."

"Why not infest him if he is so important. I...I don't understand."

"His race cannot be infested; otherwise we would."

"If we cannot infest them, why are we fighting them?"

Kavra's eyes bore into mine, pleading for my understanding. "The Shalites, the species we are fighting, are allies with his race, thus forcing us to fight them both. They are also allied with the Lorids who, as you know, are the greatest challenge to our empire. A victory against the Shalites would be a huge step toward our final goal of defeating far more dangerous enemies."

"So you torture him?"

"A necessary evil." His eyes turned soft. "I am sorry you had to find out this way. I would have preferred you were older before you saw what takes place." He shook his head and took a slow, deep breath. "However," he continued, "since you have seen some, perhaps you should have it explained."

"What?"

"People fear the mysterious more than the known. When I was first introduced to torture, my tutor taught me what to expect."

I shifted to see his face more clearly. "You think I should learn...torture?"

"I believe perspective would help you better cope with what you saw tonight."

"He was screaming." I shivered. "Not sure I *want* to know more about that."

"Yes," Kavra replied, "but I assure you, though his pain was great, very little damage was done. Torture of valuable prisoners is carefully designed to maximize pain while causing minimal permanent damage."

"Why?"

"We want to force a confession, not kill him."

"What was the device on his hand?"

"A *clovis*. It protects the hand."

"Protects?"

"Yes. When the *neps*, or in your language needles, are slipped under the sensitive nail bed, it is quite painful. The prisoner will naturally attempt to pull his hand away from the heat. If he's tied with rope or chains, it is possible for the prisoner to jerk so hard he damages his wrist or arm, causing more injury than intended. The clovis holds his hand perfectly still so while the fingertips are burned, the actual hand remains unharmed."

"But the blood."

"Scratches across his chest and arms, very shallow. Similar to a paper cut. They do not cause serious damage, but they do hurt. The screams you heard were from the neps."

"Just from his hands?"

"Yes, a particularly sensitive portion of the body, especially for his species."

"He's a Gastiranta, right?"

"Correct." Kavra gave me his first real smile of the night. "Those cultural studies are paying off."

"My favorite class." I managed to return the smile.

Chapter VII

AND THUS MY ROUTINE OF HISTORICAL STUDIES, and battle strategies, continued hand-in-hand with my new education in torture. Three weeks later, Kasar returned to the home ship and called me into one of the *reftas*, which is much like a living room on Earth. Decorated in deep reds with glowing glass fires against two walls, a pair of sofas sat in the center facing each other, with a low table between them. Kasar sat across from Kavra, who was the first to notice my arrival.

"Hello, my darling," Kavra greeted playfully. "You look lovely."

I flashed a smile. "You called?"

"We did," Kavra replied. "Based on our location, Kasar and I could not help but notice that we're close to Jereitinal, and decided we simply could not resist."

"Jereitinal?"

"Sweets, my girl! Jereitinal is the sweets capital of the empire. Go to the table and make yourself a plate." He indicated the room's corner.

As Kavra had indicated, the table was covered with exotic delights I had never seen before.

"Be sure to get some *creta*," Kavra advised. "It looks like red cake. Kasar loves that stuff, so if you don't get some now, there won't be any left."

"Get the chocolate pudding thing too," Kasar suggested, "Kav's favorite."

"He lies! It's awful. Spare yourself and force me to eat it."

I laughed and filled my plate, ensuring I received plenty of both mentioned desserts. Kavra patted the seat beside him, which I took happily.

The two returned their attention to their cards as I glanced at the paper to my left, which tallied the score. Kavra was moving in for the win.

Reclining into the cushions, I watched the game as I bit into pieces of heaven. To this day, I have never tasted anything as sweet as the desserts from Jereitinal. When the game was over, and the requisite gloating accomplished, the men dealt the next round.

"May I play?" I asked around a mouthful.

After a pause, Kavra offered, "Well, sure. We can change the game."

Kasar nodded in agreement.

"Why?"

The two exchanged a look.

"What do you mean?" Kavra asked. "You are more than welcome to play."

"No." I shook my head. "I meant, why do we have to change games?"

"Oh, well this is a rather complicated game, and the cards are different from the ones you are used to. I would be more than happy to teach you sometime, but for tonight, I thought you might enjoy playing a game you know."

"It is *cectra*, isn't it?"

"What?"

"You are playing cectra. I like this game."

The men glanced at each other.

"Did you teach her?" Kavra asked.

Kasar shook his head.

Kavra turned back to me. "You have seen these cards," he held them up, "before?"

"Better, I'm getting really good at them!"

The two men shifted uncomfortably.

"Chrissa?" Kasar asked.

"Yes?"

"How do you know this game?"

"My friend taught me."

"A friend?"

"Yeah! We play cards all the time. She's taught me lots of games. I really enjoy the ones from Palta, though others are fun too."

"Does your friend have a name?"

"Lysalie."

He repeated the name in a voice full of surprise.

"Why?"

"Umm…" Kavra tried, and failed, to stifle his laughter. "Who do you think Lysalie is?"

I shrugged. "She's fun, and pretty." By now, Kasar had joined in the laughter. "What's so funny?"

"Lysalie," Kasar started, but had to take a breath to control his laughter. "Have you been playing cards with my protégée?"

"Yes, Kasar."

My eyes searched the room. She sounded close, but Lysalie was nowhere to be seen. "I don't understand."

"Lysalie, would you please enter the room, in whatever form you presented yourself to Chrissa?"

The door opened and in walked my tall friend with piercing blue eyes, in a white satin top and black slacks. She looked very professional, her sleeves locked tight at the wrists.

"May I assist you?" she addressed the two men whose laughter had finally died down to a brilliant pair of smiles.

"Do you know Chrissa thinks you're a pretty lady?" Kasar asked.

"I did not realize this form would be considered pretty. I am pleased to know this."

"What are you talking about?" I clenched my fists as my face flushed with an embarrassment I didn't understand.

Kavra wrapped an arm around my shoulders. "Chrissa, *lysalie* is a Setian word. It means computer." He could not hold back a broad smile. "Your friend is a hologram."

"What?"

"I am a computer," Lysalie explained. "I took a human form to please you."

"A computer?"

Both men were laughing again.

"Thank you, Lysalie," Kasar dismissed her.

She didn't disappear slowly, like light fading from a room. Instead there was a quick shimmer, and she was gone.

"I'm sorry, Chrissa. Sometimes we forget you've not been with us all your life. A Setian grows up around these things, from birth." He offered a heart-warming smile. "We'll show Kasar what it is like to come in last place."

"Last place? Never!" Kasar answered his challenge.

"There won't be a last place," I clarified.

"Oh?"

"You're both going to be so far behind, second place won't matter."

They yelled foul as the computer dealt the first of many cards played on that wonderful night.

Chapter VIII

I WAS STUDYING WITH MY tutor one day, shortly after my fourteenth birthday, when Kavra made an unannounced visit. I had been struggling through some aerospace mathematics, and getting nowhere, when I saw him walk through the door. A smile lit my face and I jumped from my seat at the welcome distraction. "Kavra!" I exclaimed. "Have you come to save me?"

"You must be studying math."

I groaned. "Inner-dimensional math of vercietiles must have been created by the devil."

He laughed.

"Please, please, tell me you are here to save me."

"How could I resist such a plea?"

"Really?"

"Yes," he replied with a wide smile. "Actually, I have a surprise for you."

"Oh, what is it?"

"Well, it actually has to do with your torture studies." His answer surprised me. "Our forces recently caught a group of un-infestible soldiers, who have allied themselves with our enemies on the outskirts of the Doverian system. We believe several hold valuable information, which may be the key to winning the conflict."

"I think I heard about this from Kasar."

"Yes, I figured you had. The prisoners are alive and enroute to the Setian system, to a moon of the home-planet. Our top physicians"—and by physicians, he meant torturers—"are standing by to begin the gathering"—he meant interrogation—"process.

"Your tutor has sent reports of your progress in interrogation studies. Kasar and I have agreed, if you feel you are ready, this would be an opportune time for you to begin your observation of actual, live torture." He paused for a breath before asking, "What do you think?"

Uncertainty overcame me. To witness on a hologram was one thing. But to witness such torture on an actual, live being.

"You will not be required to perform any task with which you are uncomfortable. You have my word."

I eyed him for a prolonged moment, then slowly nodded. "Okay, Kavra."

He smiled. "I took the liberty of having your maids pack a few clothes," he told me. "They are waiting in your room on my ship."

"Thank you."

We took a shuttle to where Kavra's ship waited, and I soon found myself walking through a vessel very similar to Kasar's, except for the color. While Kasar's ships generally featured walls of jet black or stark white, Kavra's held a world of color. Paintings depicting medieval stories lined the walls in elaborate gold frames against blue, red, and deep lavender walls. Elegant ladies gazed across the well-lit hallways in landscapes of places you will never see.

He led me into a room, and I was surprised to see more than my clothes had been prepared. The room was decorated in various shades of red and black; my favorite combination. Everything had a Gothic appearance, from the carving of the desk, to the shape of the bedposts, and the black, sheer canopy which hung from the bed. Sound asleep, tucked in between two pillows as though she'd always belonged there, a glimpse of pink fur made me smile. It could not have been more perfect.

"For you, Chrissalynn," Kavra said with a formal bow that was undermined by the twinkle in his eye. "Consider it my way of saying you are always welcome, and should consider this ship your second home. Anytime you wish to escape the seriousness of my old master, you need but to ask, and I shall come whisk you away." He paused before adding, "I trust the room meets your approval?"

"You know it does."

The next few days were spent exploring Kavra's ship, and for me, were far too short. We played cards and board games while Kavra told ancient tales passed down through the Setian Empire for centuries. "If you had been raised in the empire from infancy, you would know these by now," he said as he launched into the next adventurous story.

We eventually arrived at the Setian moon where the prisoners had been sent for interrogations. I was allowed to sleep in the next morning as Kavra completed the preparations for our arrival. We were deep inside Setian space, so security was of little worry as we prepared to land upon the moon.

Kavra had advised me to dress comfortably, so I opted for a simple red top and a comfortable pair of black jeans. A plain silver chain completed the casual attire, and after quickly tying my hair back with a thin silver band, I was ready.

I met Kavra in the hallway beside the outer doors. It would be only my second time in the home galaxy, and I was excited. The doors opened and Kavra offered me his arm, which I took gladly. A short walk, he escorted me from the ship into a building directly ahead.

Two suns filled the lavender sky, while rolling yellow grass hills bordered both sides of the narrow gray walkway.

The plain building we were about to enter stood eight stories high, with symmetrical windows set approximately five feet apart. At our approach, a man on the inside rushed to open the doors.

Holding my arm in a formal grip, Kavra whisked me through the entry to stand before the front desk.

One of the two guards who had accompanied us stepped to the man sitting behind the desk. "Lord Kavra, and Chrissalynn Kasar, here to see the high inquisitor, Verayt."

"Of course," the guard said as he ushered us into a lift to the fourth floor. After walking down two corridors, one of the guards opened a silver door, which we entered.

The room had yellow walls, and was filled with tables littered with various devices. Blades ranging in size from as thin as a strand of hair, to as thick as a man's thumb. Others were covered with vials of liquid, some harmless, while others I knew from my studies would prove fatal from a single drop. As I stepped farther into the room, my attention was drawn to the man who had risen to greet us.

He gave a low bow. "Lord Kavra. May I be of service?"

"Inquisitor Verayt, may I present my pupil and friend, Chrissalynn Kasar, daughter of Lord Kasar."

The other man's eyes went wide. "Nicholas Kasar?" He seemed startled.

Kavra nodded and Verayt entered into yet another bow. "Forgive me. I did not realize, else I would have greeted you far more properly."

"Thank you," I replied. "No apology needed."

"Perhaps it is you whom I should be addressing. What brings you to my humble office?"

"Actually," Kavra interjected, "Chrissalynn has spent the past few months studying various forms of torture in the technical sense, but has never observed an actual session. I heard a new batch of prisoners were brought here. I was hoping we might watch your technique, proceeding to the next step in her training."

"Of course." The man smiled. "Her first real session. How exciting! I would be honored to teach her how it's really done. You know how I love a *captive* audience."

Kavra chuckled.

"We might as well not waste your valuable time," Verayt said. "A room is prepared. I was about to begin work as I received word of your arrival. If watching is what you wish, he has not even begun to scream yet."

Kavra gave a slight nod. "Lead the way."

We accompanied Inquisitor Verayt down the hallway into a room similar to the one on Kasar's ship. In the center, tied to a metal table, was a creature I'd never seen in the flesh.

He had six limbs, two legs, and two sets of arms, with six fingers on the right hands and four on the left. A deep green complexion, he had five eyes spaced sporadically around his one head, but only one set of diamond-shaped ears. Set low on his head, a single mouth with light green lips pressed tightly together, mentally steeling himself for what was to come.

"Good evening, Dessa," Verayt greeted in an inappropriately cheerful voice. "How are you feeling today? Well-rested, I hope." He took a seat beside the trapped man.

"All right, you know how this works, but I am going to explain anyway. Hope you don't mind? You see, Dessa, today we are going to have a nice chat. If you answer my questions honestly, this will all be over quickly, and you can go home. If you don't, persuasion will be in order. Okay?"

Dessa did not say a word.

"Are you sure there's nothing you would like to say?"

When Dessa remained silent, the inquisitor reached over to the table beside him. From one of the various trays he withdrew a thin blade and moved his rolling chair beside Dessa's shackled arm. "If at any time you are inclined to share the information or numbers I require, please start talking. This will be a lot less painful if you do."

Verayt took the blade to the side of Dessa's arm and ran it lightly across his skin. Black blood rose from his parted flesh. Verayt made three such cuts before putting down the blade and reaching for a particular vial. After glancing at the label, the inquisitor grabbed a black cloth and carefully poured some of the clear liquid onto it.

"Are you absolutely sure, Dessa, there is nothing you wish to tell me? We could start with a few less significant details. Names perhaps?"

Silence followed, and the inquisitor maneuvered the damp cloth over the wound. Dessa gave a sharp cry at the contact.

The prisoner drew deep, ragged breaths with occasional moans he was unable to suppress.

"Wow," I whispered under my breath. On one hand, his pain was horrible, his grimaced face and tight expression hard to witness. Yet, on the other hand, I found it fascinating.

"Chrissa, are you okay?" Kavra asked.

"Yes."

"It isn't a man."

"What?"

"When you looked away, you were turning away from a man in pain. If you look at him," there was another scream behind me, "like a creature, instead of a man, this will be easier to get through." Two more screams echoed across the room. "Deep breath now," Kavra suggested.

I did, and it helped to clear my head. Gathering my strength, I turned back to face those screams.

Verayt had the cloth pressed against his captive's arm, which was the source of renewed and continuous cries. "Come now, Dessa. All I want are some names and a few numbers. Give me either and we can make all this pain go away. You want the pain to stop, don't you?"

The man's—no, the creature's—eyes finally saw me. "You *repheta*!" The equivalent of bastard. "You infest children now? My *gupta* you have sunk low."

Verayt looked puzzled and glanced my way. "Forgive me, Dessa," he apologized to the man he was torturing. "I forgot to introduce you! This is Lord Kavra. You've heard of him, I am sure."

He spoke in the same voice one might use with a dear friend out on a Sunday stroll in the country. "The girl isn't infested; she is the daughter of Kasar. She is here to learn, so please, try to put on a good show. In fact…" He motioned toward me. "Come here, if you will."

I glanced toward Kavra and he nodded. I stepped closer to the doctor.

"The chemical we are using is *sectra* 4-D12."

My eyes widened. "That's lethal."

"No," Verayt corrected. "Sectra 4-D7 is lethal, not D12."

"Oops."

"Perfectly all right. Once beyond general names, sub numbers are easily confused."

He re-soaked the cloth and surprised me by reaching for my hand. Instinctively, I pulled back in fear.

"Do not worry, it only burns when combined with blood. Upon your skin, it is harmless."

With this reassurance, I tentatively held out my hand and allowed him to pass me the cloth.

"Would you like to try?"

I glanced back at Kavra.

"Your call."

I stared at the chemically-soaked rag and tried to recall my teachings. *Visualize only your tool, and the section of the body you are working.* I closed my eyes. There was no person, merely an arm.

"I'll try."

Skin, only skin.

"Take the cloth and place it over the cut on his right arm. Squeeze and hold for about five seconds, then pull away."

I glanced back at Kavra for reassurance. He smiled and motioned me forward. I turned toward the bleeding arm with too many fingers strapped into the spreader. Black blood oozed from the wound. If it had been red, I might have balked, but the different color helped me pretend the blood was something else, anything except what it truly represented.

I placed the cloth above the bloody arm and took a deep breath, half-excited, half-terrified. Giving the rag a light squeeze, I lowered it to the wound in a fluid movement. I will never forget his scream; not because the scream was the worst I've ever heard. Oh no, I've heard better screams. But because this was the first time the scream was meant for me.

I removed the cloth and pulled back. We waited for Dessa to catch his breath.

He cursed at me after he stopped moaning.

"Tell us the names, and we'll stop. You can go home, if you tell us what we need to know." I sweetened my voice to the best of my ability as I whispered, "Come now, a few names won't hurt."

I spent the next twenty minutes speaking nicely to the trapped creature, whispering false promises, and offering an end to the pain.

Verayt approached with a syringe.

My eyes widened. "Is that?"

"Yes," Verayt replied. "The same potion, only this shall be injected directly to the veins. The agony will be exquisite, but no permanent damage will be done. Do you know how to administer injections?"

"I have practiced, but never on the living."

"No time like the present."

I put the cloth down and took the syringe from his hand.

With the torturer's coaching, I administered my first injection on a live subject. No sooner had the drug entered Dessa's veins, his body jerked violently as his screams rose to ear-splitting proportions while the burning surged through his bloodstream. When the cries ceased, and no confessions came forth, a new syringe was filled, and the drug was administered again. He endured two more sessions before passing out.

Later, as I sat with Kavra aboard his ship, he told me I had done better than expected, and that I had made him proud. "Bravo, Chrissa, bravo. We're going to be staying in this space for a few days. Verayt has recommended beginning your training on the art of cutting. What do you think?"

I looked at him, nervous, but said, "Okay."

The next day, Kavra escorted me back to the inquisitor's chambers. Verayt began the session, cutting a series of thin lines across his captive's arms and upper chest. The creature, a Nuphima this time, spilled bright green blood onto the table, which ran in streams down tethered arms.

Verayt handed me the knife.

At the first stroke, the sensation of the blade slicing into soft flesh made my stomach heave.

I handed the knife back to Verayt and walked over to a metal chair. Sitting abruptly, I placed my head between my knees.

Kavra walked to my side. "It's okay, Chrissa. Take a few breaths."

I reached for him and followed his advice until my stomach settled.

"Shall I continue while you watch?" Verayt asked.

"No, I'd like to try again."

"As you wish."

I walked back toward him, took the knife from his hand, and returned to my place beside the prisoner. Holding my breath, I drew the knife across a bare arm. Still disturbing, but I took a shallow breath.

Moving from his arm, I made a stroke on the left side of his upper chest. After barely scratching the surface, the knife hit bone.

The prisoner hissed and I drew back, startled.

"His race has a thick bone plate," Verayt informed me. "We don't want to cut into the bone at this time, so move the knife three inches down," he pointed to a location lower on the creature's chest, "and the extra bone disappears. Aim to cut two inches below the surface so that you lightly graze the muscle underneath, but don't slice too deeply or he'll bleed out."

Raising the knife once again, I drew the blade across the target section of the Nuphima's chest. I did this slowly, attempting to regulate the pressure. The flesh opened easily beneath my hands, enough that I feared I had cut too deeply, yet little blood rose.

"Not quite deep enough," Verayt explained. He stepped forward and took my hand in his. "Here, let me guide you."

With his hand atop mine, we moved the blade over a half-inch down from the previous cut and, once again, sank the blade into the Nuphima's chest.

"Feel that?" he asked.

Our subject groaned as bright green blood seeped to the surface.

"This is the correct amount of pressure."

I nodded, concentrating on the weight of my hand and the resistance of flesh. Coppery blood perfumed the air, filling my senses. One of the great universal mysteries; though blood comes in many colors, the smell is always the same.

Inquisitor Verayt removed his hand and invited, "Try again."

After a quick glance at Kavra, I turned back to the creature lying helpless on the table.

Moving over another half-inch to the right, I once again cut into the flesh, this time bringing bright green blood to the surface on my own.

The inquisitor stepped closer to examine my work. "Great!" he exclaimed, before pointing to another area of the body and advising me to continue at the same general depth.

As I continued working with the knife, I imagined myself as a great doctor, a surgeon, working carefully to cut out the truth from deep inside my victim's mind. Like a doctor, I had to be careful, because cutting more than necessary would kill the patient, and that was not my intention.

"Provide information," Verayt said firmly, "and I will tell her to stop."

The Nuphima groaned in pain.

I continued the careful cuts as Verayt took the creature's left wrist and inserted a needle connected to a bag of green liquid. "A *meferita*," Verayt used a word I did not recognize.

"Blood transfusion," Kavra translated.

As my blade kept slicing, my imagination formed pictures in the lines of blood and open flesh. I saw a horse, followed by a dragon with wings opened wide. Instead of a doctor, I had become a painter, creating a priceless work of art the likes of which has never graced any gallery known to man. I drew the blade up and my dragon gained a rider, soaring into the clouds. Another few strokes and a castle appeared in the distance, the dragon racing to its defense, or perhaps destruction. Stroke after stroke, I enhanced the simple scene into an elaborate work of art.

As I painted, Verayt checked the captive's vitals, administered transfusions of blood, and gave various drugs throughout the session to keep our subject conscious. For the most part, I remained silent, concentrating on my work. The inquisitor spoke to the captive, seeking answers, punctuated by direct application of substances to the Nuphima's open flesh.

The screams and moans caused by the chemicals were different from those caused by my blade. I cut deeper, scraping the bone protecting the creature's neck. This brought forth yet a different type of scream.

Thus the torture session became a game, between Verayt and me, as to which one of us could make him scream the most. Together we composed a type of music if you will, horrible yet not without a cruel form of beauty for, once again, these screams were created by the stroke of my knife.

I have no idea how long this went on, but eventually Inquisitor Verayt announced, "Enough for today."

Turning to put the knife down slowly on the table, I reached out and placed a finger in the blood accumulated on the blade. Now a dark green, nearly black, the liquid was thick and cold, congealed. Fascinated, I watched blood drip from the tip of my finger to splat in uneven blobs on the floor.

Kavra approached me and placed a white rag over my hand, wiping the blood away.

Accepting his offered arm, we walked back to his ship. Later, after I'd bathed, Kavra had me sit at my computer and dictate my version of the experience. "I find it helps to understand exactly how you feel after one's first experience with torture," he explained. "We will review it later on."

Two days later, we were scheduled to return when Kavra summoned me to one of the ship's communication rooms. As I entered, Kavra was seated in front of an ebony desk. He motioned me to take a seat in the chair beside him.

I sat and turned to find a holographic image of Kasar seated at an identical desk.

"Chrissalynn," Kasar greeted me. "Kavra has been updating me on your progress. I take it you are enjoying your studies?"

"Anything is better than interstellar math," I replied, bringing a laugh from both. I added, "Yes, Father, I'm finding this part of my studies interesting."

"Good to hear," Kasar said. "I've spoken with both Kavra, and the high inquisitor. They agree that as long as you're in Setian space, you may as well continue training. They have a particular task in mind, and I'd like to hear your opinion."

"Okay," I said.

"What we suggest," Kavra explained from beside me, "is for you to remain with me on the home planet for the next few months. Inquisitor Verayt will assign a captive to you, under his supervision. Your ultimate goal will be to break this prisoner into confessing whatever information Verayt informs you is sought."

"Wait. You want me to break him? Me?"

"Yes," Kavra replied. "Verayt has offered to hand-select your subject. The three of us think you'll benefit from breaking the prisoner using a more..." He paused, searching for the right word.

"Creative?" Kasar supplied.

Kavra nodded. "A more creative method. Technique will be entirely your choice, and we will provide you with literature to ensure you have an arsenal of strategies to choose from. You will have three months to do this, and when you are not working on your own subject, you will be allowed to watch the professionals work on other patients."

"Also," Kasar added, "it will be a good opportunity for you to spend time on the home planet. You're always asking questions about where we come from, and our history. This will be the perfect time for you to see relevant locations with your own eyes."

"Really?" My mind worked to process this change of plans. "You really think I am ready to be in charge of an interrogation session? Both of you?"

They answered in unison, "Yes, we do."

"Well, I have wanted to try more things on my own, and I really would love to see more of the home world. If you are both sure, I would love to try."

"Excellent," Kasar said.

"Wonderful!" Kavra exclaimed with a smile. "I knew she would prefer to stay with me!"

Kasar sighed at Kavra's banter. "She wants to stay away from her math tutor."

Both men laughed.

Chapter IX

I REMEMBER STANDING ON THE ship's balcony and viewing the planet, illuminated by its two suns. Setianta was more than twice the size of Earth. As the ship moved closer, into a purple-toned sky, I noted half the planet was covered with water, framing forests with individual trees so tall they were visible even from above.

Kavra moved beside me as I stared intently at the nearest floating city, trying to determine what held the massive structure, far larger than the ship I was on, in place. "Nearly a thousand years ago," he said, "cities filled the land, choking the natural beauty of the planet. After the Setian nations became an empire, and our security was established, citizens became strongly concerned with the planet's health, especially after centuries of war. Councilor Graybow put his head in the clouds, literally. Using the same power that keeps ships suspended, he built his house a half-mile above the ground.

"Soon after, entire cities were built in the sky, while ones on the ground were carefully demolished, their materials reused whenever possible. With scientists directing re-planting efforts, and careful waste management, the beauty of Setianta was restored."

"Amazing," I whispered. To this day, glistening buildings set amid puffy clouds in a jewel-toned sky is one of the most magnificent sights I've ever seen.

"Look." Kavra pointed. "The capital city, Dehart Kavas, named in honor of the first Setian emperor, Dehartra. Home to nearly two million Setians at any given time."

"How many cities are there?"

"Thirteen, one for each province."

"Which one are you from? Are you and Kasar from the same area?"

"Your father and I are both from the Dehart province. This city is our home."

"Two million people in a single city. And thirteen cities in all. That's more than I expected. Who's actually on the planet? I thought all Setians served in the military."

"Nearly all. For the most part, beyond council members, city inhabitants are either too young, or too old, to serve."

Inside Setianta's atmosphere, the city loomed over the ship. Kavra pointed to an elaborate structure near the center whose architecture was a cross between an Egyptian pyramid and a Middle Eastern palace. Its gold exterior reflected the two suns in blinding flashes of light. "Do you know what that building is?"

"The Setian Council Chamber?"

He nodded. "Yes, built to be a statement, no expense spared, of Setian power."

"Will I get to see inside?"

"Of course. We'll be staying nearby. Once our ship lands, we'll take an escort to a private resort for Setian lords. Normally we would stay in my apartments, but since you're here," he gave a sly wink, "we can upgrade to your father's suite. He has an indoor pool!"

I remembered from my teachings that each of the Setian lords was given a private residence on the home planet. The higher the rank, the more grand the encompassing resort. Excitement for exploration, and relaxation, caused me to nearly bounce in anticipation while we paused to receive security clearance, and officially entered the docking station.

After brief instructions to staff regarding our belongings, and Aurora, we quickly disembarked. Kavra and I boarded a shuttle, whose large windows provided a wonderful view of the tall buildings while we rounded corners and headed down various avenues. We stopped and exited the transport at a narrow street between two especially tall buildings. Approaching two armed Horde guards, who stood at the gate blocking the road, Kavra reached into his back pocket and pulled out an identification card.

As the one on the right perfunctorily glanced at the identification, he looked up and greeted, "Welcome home. Will you be heading to you *rtremture*," a Setian word for resort or house, "this evening?"

"Actually," Kavra replied, "we will be staying in Kasar's rtremture."

"Of course, Kavra."

"I heard you were promoted to sub-harars level?"

"Yes," he replied. "Sub-Harars 30."

"It is about time. Congratulations!" Kavra turned to me. "We were in training together, though I rose through the ranks faster than he did."

"Some of us weren't taken under Kasar's personal wing." He winked at Kavra. "Some of us had to do it on our own."

They laughed.

"Tell me," the sub-commander chided in a friendly manner, "have you completely forgotten your manners? Or are you going to introduce me to this lovely girl?"

Kavra reached for my hand and moved me to his side. "Sub-Harars 30, may I introduce you to the daughter of Nicholas Kasar, Chrissalynn."

Both sub-harars stared in shock for several beats before Kavra's friend came out of his stupor. "Allow me to be the first to welcome you to Setianta. I hope your stay will be a pleasant affair, and should you find yourself in need of anything, please do not hesitate to ask."

"Hey!" Kavra protested. "No one's allowed to charm her but me."

Sub-Harars 30 winked at me as our transportation arrived. He opened the door to what appeared very much like a white limousine. "We utilize vehicles from various planets," the sub-harars explained, seeing my expression.

I slipped inside, overjoyed at the surprise. I had never been in a limo before. After playing with the rainbow lights, I gleefully accepted a glass of white wine from Kavra. Unlike Earth's restrictions, they did not mind if I drank, provided one of them was with me to regulate the amount.

As I stared out tinted windows, more buildings and landscapes passed by, although at a slower rate of speed than the shuttle. Occasionally I would see others in front yards, or along the side streets, who stared as we drove by, probably wondering who had arrived in such luxury.

We pulled up in front of an old-fashioned castle gate. The gate rose vertically, allowing us to drive underneath into Kasar's domain.

"It's like a castle from a storybook!"

He smiled. "Let me guess...you were a *Snow White* fan?"

I shook my head. "*Sleeping Beauty.*"

"Ah. The peasant girl who was really a princess."

My mind spun, remembering my childhood. "Or the discarded orphan," I said softly.

"No longer," Kavra cut in. He turned in his seat to face me. "You are a child of the empire now. Kasar's, and mine." His voice was fierce.

"But why?"

"What do you mean?"

"Do you know why he chose me? I asked him once, and he wouldn't answer."

A strange look crossed Kavra's face. An expression I couldn't place at the time. In barely a whisper, he answered, "I only know he has always loved you."

To this day, I wonder if the words were a lie.

The car came to a stop, and Kavra climbed out before the driver could open his door. He held his hand out to me, which I took graciously. "Welcome to your castle, Beauty." I stepped out and found myself standing on a path of shiny black rock. "Careful, it's slick."

With that warning, I took a step in my heels away from him to view my surroundings. Flames burned brightly from torches along the walkway, reflecting off the black rock. At the path's end, two doors with carved handles. Statues of fallen angels stood on either side, their faces staring down, forever forbidden to glance toward heaven's light.

Kavra complained, "He always was old-fashioned. I mean, come on, would it kill him to use lamps instead of open flames?"

"Yes," I said fondly of my adoptive father's hatred of unnatural light. "Here, in his home, after months on a ship where there are no other options, I think it might."

Kavra laughed.

We approached the tall black doors, which were covered with vines that had wrapped themselves around obsidian handles. The doors opened wide, revealing two men dressed in black tuxedoes standing on either side.

A few steps behind them stood a third man in a crimson suit, resembling a costume from the Middle Ages with its frilly shirt and full tails. He bent into a deep bow. "Welcome home."

"Thank you," I replied, motioning for him to stand.

"I notice you didn't welcome *me* home," Kavra pouted.

"You mean you're staying? I've been advised of the kitty, but who said you could come? I didn't get any orders saying I had to deal with you."

"Chrissa, may I introduce Prestac 2, your less-than-humble servant for the next few months. Don't worry, if he gives you any flack, let me know."

"Could say the same for you," Prestac shot back.

Kavra ignored the comment. "Make yourself useful and show us to our rooms."

"Not unless you say please."

"I will do no such thing. I'm a Setian lord and you are not."

Prestac rolled his eyes. "He gets testy after extended flights, doesn't he?"

"That, and losing at cectra," I replied, liking Prestac instantly.

"One day," Kavra cut in, "I will get the respect I deserve. Why do you treat Kasar so differently?"

"Because *Lord*," he emphasized the word, "Nicholas Kasar would string me up by toes if I didn't."

Kavra and I looked at each other, and said in unison, "True."

The walls were deep reds and black. Hand-painted portraits, and gold-rimmed mirrors, lined the hallways. Chandelier-style structures, holding fifteen candles each, provided extra light, in addition to the actual wood-burning fireplaces found in every room, not the chemical reaction used on ship.

"So dark," Kavra muttered. "When Kasar was promoted, one of his first priorities was to personalize his manor as quickly as possible. He had the former house demolished and built from scratch. Once he adopted you, he added this suite."

Kavra opened a door and we entered a vast room. Crimson walls framed a black marble fireplace. Opposite the dark red flames, a gold four-post bed was covered with a red bedspread. Looking around the room, I noticed a painting in a gold frame hung on the far wall.

As I reached the portrait, I gazed into Kasar's familiar sapphire eyes. He wore a black suit from the Medieval period, the sleeves cinched tight with ruffles down the front of his white shirt. Posed on the bow of an ancient sea ship, black sails billowing, before him stretched an endless blue sea. An optical illusion of some sort, or some kind of moving picture, the waves rose to frothy white peaks, blown by an angry wind. Kasar's hair fluttered tidily to the side. "Wow," I whispered.

I turned and saw another portrait on the bed's opposite side, hung over a sturdy desk where no two drawers seemed to match. This man stood on a similar ship, only the sails were a deep burgundy. Behind him, twelve other ships followed, each bearing sails of a different color. In more-simple attire, his brown eyes stared at me as though he could see into my soul. "Who is he?"

"That," Kavra replied, "is Emperor Dehartra. The ships behind him represent the other first council members. Kasar insisted this painting be placed in your room. He thought you would find it inspirational."

"Kasar has told me many stories about him."

"Dehartra found eternal glory through defeating our first enemies. Kasar is convinced the man responsible for the ultimate defeat of the Lorids will be as immortalized. He dreams of being that man."

I moved closer to get a better look at the picture. "Emperor Dehartra had a human host? An Earth human?"

"Near the end of his life, yes. He was one of the first to acquire a human body, though yours was not a planet we considered worth our while for many years."

I turned to a third wall from which hung an empty frame.

"This," Kavra informed me, "will someday be for your portrait."

Not sure how to respond, I turned to survey the rest of the room. My reflection looked back from a mirror that covered what I assumed to be a closet door.

Framed by the black sheer canopy, a deep blue gown lay atop the red bedcover. Moving closer, I reached out to touch the satin material, running my hand along the clear sequins trailing down the front, which sparkled various colors in the warm firelight.

A simple note said, "Welcome home, Chrissalynn." As always, the missive was signed with an elegant "K."

"He buys you the most beautiful gowns," Kavra commented softly.

I nodded in agreement. What every princess dreams of.

"What do you say I get a maid to run your bath, and we call it a night? Tomorrow, I'll show you around Setianta, and provide you with some books to study. They should help you design a treatment for your prisoner."

"Sounds good."

A maid came in and started the bath filling with sweet-smelling oils and exotic flower petals. While the enormous basin filled, two Horde arrived with my luggage, including a carrier with an annoyed kitty, pink fur all standing on end. After freeing her to explore, I sank into the steaming water.

Thirty minutes later, I climbed out and slipped into the jade satin gown and robe that had been laid out for me. Kavra entered the room to find me sitting cross-legged on the bed, coaxing purrs from Aurora.

"I'm down the hall, two doors to the left, if you need me. Otherwise the servants are at your disposal."

"Thanks," I replied. "Goodnight, Kavra."

"Goodnight, Chrissa." He closed the door behind him.

Removing my robe, and draping it over a nearby table, I climbed beneath the covers, soothed to sleep by Aurora's content rumble and warmth.

Chapter X

THE NEXT MORNING I DRESSED comfortably and met Kavra in one of the many banquet halls. After a quick breakfast, the table was cleared, and he presented me with several books to help with my torture studies. Covering techniques from multiple planets, the stack included two from Earth, describing various ancient practices. I started with a book from Verost, which I had the computer translate for me when I got back to my suite.

Beyond general information, I was also given a subject profile, allowing me to study their species anatomy, physiology, and mentality; all deemed important for effective gathering by the committee of Practical Torture Standards (PTS).

A knock on my door made me look up.

Kavra walked in. "Ready to explore?"

I nodded, moved Aurora from my lap to the bed, and grabbed a black leather jacket, a favorite of mine on cool afternoons such as this one. We left the house and climbed into another limo, black this time, and headed toward the center of the floating city. I asked many questions about various buildings, and what different signs said, because while I was working to learn the Setian language, a few words and symbols still escaped me.

We arrived outside a building with no windows. "This is a national museum," Kavra informed me. "What do you say we go in?"

I nodded and climbed out of the car. We stood before a flight of white marble stairs leading to two vast golden doors. Words I did not recognize, divided with etched symbols, lined the doors.

"Only in death," Kavra translated, "lies eternal glory. Long live the Setian Empire."

Arm-in-arm we walked up the stairs. Golden doors opened before us as we stepped into a marble hallway.

A tall woman walked toward us, her heels echoing across the hall. She held out a hand in greeting. "Lord Kavra, Lady Kasar, glad you could join us. Would you like the grand tour, or would you prefer to explore on your own?"

"It is up to Chrissa."

"The tour!" I said excitedly.

We spent the next three hours walking through the museum, gazing at various artifacts from the many worlds that composed the empire. Our guide answered my countless questions as I attempted to absorb all I could concerning the different species and histories on display.

My favorite, of course, was the section on the Setian world. I got to see a preserved Ferdkin, one of the original species the Setians formed a symbiotic relationship with. Tall with brown fur, the species was all but extinct, the majority having been killed from a chemical virus spread by enemies of the empire.

We entered a narrow hall where the lights dimmed.

"The Emperor's Hall," Kavra informed me. "It contains portraits, and biographical information, of every emperor who's sat upon the mighty throne."

I entered the corridor, low heels echoing with each step. An unconscious reaction to the stories of ancient heroes, my breathing grew shallow as I read about Emperor Keithem who defeated the Hertias. How Emperor Fedmick initiated the first infestation of the Hordes, while Emperor Derickt completed the conquest. Emperor Keritn conquered the Slith nation, while Emperor Keverat signed the Treaty of Palta, one of the empire's strongest allies. Emperor Jeritam, who was famous for winning the first battle ever fought against the Lorids.

As we reached the end of the hall, one familiar portrait stood grander than those surrounding it, lit from all angles. A hallowed man whose power radiated above the others.

Like the image in my room, Emperor Dehartra was dressed in a jet black suit with a gold-buttoned shirt. However, instead of a ship, he sat upon a carved ivory throne. Twelve chairs stood behind him, six on each side, becoming smaller within the portrait, creating the illusion of fading into the distance. Emperor Dehartra's steady gaze pierced through those who stood before him, demanding all bow before his glory.

"They were all magnificent men, but none were ever quite what Dehartra was; not even in paintings," Kavra echoed my thoughts.

"Why?"

"I'm not sure if the perception of his power is real, or a figment of our imagination, because we are taught to revere him above all others. To put it in Earth terms, Emperor Dehartra was our…George Washington, or Elizabeth I, or in some circles our Jesus Christ. His is the name we call upon, both before the brink of battle, and in our highest moments of glory."

Tour completed, we returned to Kasar's castle. After dinner, I retired to my room and continued my studies on ancient torture tactics. The next two days were spent preparing for my first session with my patient.

Inquisitor Verayt has chosen a Potek to be my creative subject because of his physical resilience. Bald, with wide eyes and lips, the red-skinned creature provided a challenge in both torture tactics, and learning the alien anatomy. For the first meeting, I decided to start with a simple form of a rack torture, which would become progressively more complicated as the days progressed.

Verayt had written in his report that this particular prisoner was highly stubborn. Good news, as I hoped he would resist long enough to allow my training to progress to more difficult stages.

Kavra accompanied me from the home planet back to the interrogation center on the nearby moon. We were once again ushered into the upper floors, where a room had been prepared for my use.

The subject, Savrick, waited on a table. As I stepped farther into the room, Inquisitor Verayt moved to greet me and held out a rubbery black robe. "To keep blood from ruining your clothes."

I slipped it on and, with minimal assistance, used the adjustable snaps to close it snuggly around my body. "Thanks."

"Your report, on your planned treatment, thrilled me. It should be an interesting session."

Nodding at Verayt, and after an encouraging smile from Kavra, I approached my patient. Four others had gathered; assistants who would help to maneuver and monitor the subject.

"Hello, Savrick," I greeted amiably.

He opened his eyes at the sound of my voice.

"How are you feeling today?"

"Who are you?"

"My name is Chrissa."

"What are you doing here? You're a child."

"Yes, I'm young. This will be my first official session."

"What?"

"I'm here to talk with you," I clarified. "I have questions about your Sentile allies, and believe you possess the information I seek."

"They sent a child to break me?"

"You will find me very persuasive." I offered what I hoped was a charming smile despite my nervousness.

"I will not break."

"Yes, you will."

I turned to the men waiting on the left. "Administer four edt of *mori*, and move him to the rack. I want a clovis on both of his left hands; be careful to secure each finger."

The men quickly carried out my orders moving Savrick into position. His arms and legs were stretched tight to pulleys connected to the wall.

I took a seat in a chair beside the rack and asked the first question. "Name the Sentile's next target."

Predictably, Savrick did not answer.

"How about the name of your commander? Tell me that, and we can talk awhile. What do you say?"

More silence.

"Okay, Savrick, perhaps you'll be more talkative in a few hours."

I turned toward Inquisitor Verayt, who handed me a thin wand with a flat piece of rectangular metal at the end. Accepting the device, whose flattened end glowed red with searing heat, I moved carefully to where Savrick could see what I held.

"Take a look," I advised. "You really do not want this to touch you."

When he failed to respond, I lifted the device to his upper left hand. Aligning the heated metal with the first of his nine fingers, I slid under the nail, allowing the heat to sear the delicate skin beneath.

Savrick's scream pierced every corner of the room.

When his screams quieted, and the smell of burnt flesh singed the air, I eased the tool back out. "Are you sure you don't want to talk?"

Savrick addressed Verayt between ragged breaths. "You allow a child to do this?"

Verayt shrugged. "What can I say? The lady outranks me."

"Ready to talk?" I cut in.

No answer.

When the first tool was replaced by an assistant with a freshly-heated instrument, I slid the metal under another of Savrick's fingers, followed by another, offering no respite. "You have six more to go, unless you would rather talk? All I want is a few answers."

I moved to the other hand, and this time held the heat above the skin, but did not touch it. The flesh turned red and boiled. His scream was ear-splitting.

"Here." Verayt moved forward and handed me a set of ear plugs, which I inserted gratefully.

I put down the device and indicated a bottle of boiling water. After an assistant handed it to me, I slowly turned the vessel over, allowing three drops of the steaming liquid to drip onto Savrick's bare chest. He screamed again.

Moving from bare drops, to a small stream, his skin blistered everywhere the scorching water touched. Running out of chest space, in a burst of creative inspiration, I poured the water on his feet. Bad idea. The resulting smell was horrific, and I fought not to gag as I turned back to the screaming creature.

"Are you ready to talk to me yet? I want the name of the Sentile's next target, and I want it now!" I took a breath to control my unexpectedly raging emotions; the PTS had reiterated the critical nature of remaining calm and in control to bolster the patient's confidence.

"No," he whispered. "You can kill me, but I will not tell you."

"Kill you?" I repeated. "Trust me, Savrick, killing you is the last thing on my agenda. You and I are going to be spending lots of time together over the next few months. You might as well learn to talk to me."

When met with more silence I said, "When I nod to these men, they will tighten the ropes, stretching your arms. It won't stop until you either give me the information I seek, or your arms have been removed from their sockets. The choice is yours."

I nodded and my orders were carried out, one limb at a time. They started with one of Savrick's right arms, pulling slowly until a loud pop, and a gasp from my patient, confirmed its removal from the socket.

"Tell me the next target and I'll instruct them to stop."

He remained silent.

"Finish it."

The men complied.

"I am going to hand you over to our physicians now. They'll reset the bones and ensure you recover. In a few weeks, we'll meet again. For your sake, I hope the next session finds you in a more conversational mood."

Light-headed, I walked out of the room quickly and Kavra followed. When the door closed, I attempted to remove the stifling black robe, but my hands, steady only moments ago, did not seem to be working. "Hot," I complained. "It's too hot in here." My fingers failing to find the individual snaps, I attempted to tear the garment off.

"Here," Kavra moved forward, "let me help."

Freed of the robe, we walked quickly down the various stairwells and burst through the last door to blessedly fresh air. Evening had descended over the strange moon, bringing a cool breeze that caressed my hot skin. I drew deep breaths, gasps at first, which eased as my pulse slowed to a normal pace inside my chest. Looking at Kavra, I said, "I'm okay now," to ease his concerned expression.

"Don't worry, it will get easier. You should be very proud you made it through the entire first session; most don't."

I nodded, the crisp air refreshing me.

"Why don't we go back to the house and spend the evening playing cards, or watching a movie of your choice?"

"Sounds good."

"Tomorrow I have a surprise planned. Someone I think you will be interested to meet."

"Really? Who?"

"I'll tell you tomorrow."

Chapter XI

After sleeping as long as Aurora allowed, I spent the next day relaxing in the pool in a center courtyard of Kasar's castle. Four feet deep in the shallow end, and thirty in the deep, with several waterfalls, the pool featured multiple slides and several diving boards. It had been years since I had been able to play in the water, and I thoroughly enjoyed myself.

Late afternoon, Kavra informed me I should get ready for dinner out on the town. "We are going to an elegant restaurant. Perhaps wear your new dress."

"Okay," I replied excitedly before walking quickly to my room. After a quick shower, a maid dried my hair, and curled it into hundreds of tiny ringlets, which she pulled up around my face, but allowed to hang loosely in the back.

After cinching my corset, she held out the blue satin gown, which I stepped into carefully. Wrapped snuggly around my slim figure, the dress was perfection. Cut low in a v-neck, the sequins glistened in the room's firelight like the twinkle of a million stars dancing across a night sky. Sapphire earrings, and a diamond necklace completed my attire.

"It must be thirty carats," I said incredulously.

"Forty-five," Kavra corrected from behind me. "You look exquisite, my dear, absolutely exquisite." I blushed as I thanked him. A touch of rouge, blue eyeshadow, and a deep red lipstick finished the creation. My god, I looked at least sixteen!

Kavra was dressed equally splendid in a black tuxedo over a white dress shirt and bowtie. His shoulder-length blond hair had been pulled back with a golden band.

He offered me his arm. "Shall we go to dinner?"

I nodded happily and we walked outside.

With the suns setting, the sky washed in an array of colors; reds, yellows, and purples, which were beautiful to behold. At the end of the driveway, a white stretch limo waited. After another short ride to the city's center, the limo dropped us off in front of a gold building forty floors high. Kavra escorted me up a flight of stairs to glass doors that opened as we approached.

Standing inside an elevator, the operator asked, "What floor?"

THE INDOCTRINATION

"Seventeen," Kavra replied. "We have dinner reservations at the Dehartran." The man nodded and hit the appropriate button. The elevator raced upward. We exited onto a marble floor where two men waited behind a counter.

"Reservations for Kavra."

The man glanced down at the list and back to us. "Of course. The rest of your party arrived only a moment ago. Please, follow me this way."

Another set of glass doors opened to reveal a grand dining room beyond. Low lights winked off golden-edged plates and crystal wine glasses, which seemed to float against black linens. We wound our way to the far side of the room, to an intimate table for four. Two distinguished men, noting our approach, stood to greet us.

"Kavra," one man said with a smile. "How good of you to join us."

"It's been a while, Councilor," Kavra replied.

"Who is your beautiful companion?"

"Chrissalynn," Kavra addressed me, "it is my honor to introduce you to Councilor Revdran and Councilor Vektor, reigning members of the Setian Council. Councilors, this is Chrissalynn, daughter of Kasar, and my escort for the evening."

Startled at the realization I stood before two members of the council, it took me a heartbeat to drop into a curtsy. "It is an honor, Councilors."

"No, my lady," Councilor Vektor said, "the honor is ours." He moved forward and kissed my hand softly before moving back my chair and motioning for me to sit.

"Thank you," I said softly as he pushed my chair closer to the table and proceeded to once again take his own seat.

The waiter arrived and passed out menus. I made selections based on Kavra's recommendations. The first course was a salad, accented by thin strips of meat, covered with a light-blue dressing that had a sweet, buttery taste flavoring rather bland vegetables.

"Tell me, Chrissalynn, are you enjoying your visit to Setianta?" Vektor politely inquired. "Is it your first time on the home planet?"

I answered their various questions easily, excited to discuss all the beautiful things I had seen. The councilors listened quietly, seemingly charmed by my youthful enthusiasm.

"Tell me," Councilor Revdran asked, "have you been down to the actual land yet?"

"No," I replied, "but it looks absolutely beautiful! Especially the ocean."

"You like the beach?"

"Oh yes! Running my fingers through the waves' frothy tops, and the taste of the ocean breeze. There is nothing quite like it!"

Revdran laughed softly. "The only person I have ever heard speak so fondly of the ocean is Nicholas Kasar. You must indeed be his daughter."

"He likes the ocean?"

"Yes," Kavra responded. "He loves the beach. We used to go all the time when we were younger."

"My father used to take me…"

"Ocean water is the purest form of our Setian pools," Vektor explained, smoothly filling the awkward pause I had created. "It is considered sacred."

Conversation was interrupted when the second course arrived. Spark was a type of Setian fish. With a taste similar to swordfish, its bright blue color, with swirls of yellow and orange, made it unique.

The three men shifted topics to recent news from various battlefronts. I listened without interrupting as I focused on my meal.

"The Trests are giving us some trouble," Vektor informed. "Their planet is protected by some of the best shielding technology ever encountered, and they are hiding behind it. We can get some traders through, but only for a limited amount of time. Despite our best efforts, we cannot seem to get spies into the secure areas. Two of our most senior agents were caught last month attempting to break into the shielding facility. We recalled the rest of our troops until a better strategy is devised."

"How did they catch our spies?" Kavra asked.

"Reports indicate the Trests have devised a type of Setian detection device, which all visitors must pass through in order to reach sensitive military or political buildings. So far we have been unable to devise a practical way to fool these sensors." Vektor shook his head in frustration.

A thought occurred to me. "Don't the Trests live near Palta?"

"What?" Kavra moved his gaze to me.

"The Trests," I said again, "they are from the Eurken system, near Palta, right?"

Vektor nodded.

"Don't they have lots of pets?"

The two councilors exchanged a glance before nodding.

"Infest their semnas." Everyone stared at me. "Their pets! We could infest their pets. They go to all kinds of places, and I bet they don't have to go through the scans." I shrugged. "Father lets me take mine everywhere. Aurora can even get into the kitchen without the cook protesting."

The men managed to suppress their laughter to a soft chuckle. "Ah, how I have missed children," Revdran mused softly.

"Such creative minds," Vektor added with equal amusement.

I stared hard at my plate, embarrassed by their laughter.

Kavra pulled me to him in a light embrace. "We aren't laughing at you, Chrissa. We simply aren't used to having such a fresh point of view. Come on, smile for me." I looked up into his face as he ran a hand through my ebony curls. "What do you say about ordering some dessert? It is my understanding they have a few selections from Jereitinal."

"Jereitinal!" I exclaimed.

"Yes!" Vektor piped in. "Directly from the sweets capital itself."

"Do they have the pudding thing?" I asked, naming Kavra's favorite.

"But of course," said the waiter, who had walked up behind me. Dessert was served promptly, and we laughed easily through the remainder of the evening.

As we were about to leave, Vektor addressed me, "Chrissalynn?"

"Yes, Councilor?"

"I've had a pleasurable evening, and enjoyed your company. During your stay, I would like to grant you a request of your choice. Is there anything you desire within our," he motioned to his fellow councilor, "power to give?"

I looked at the councilors, considering. Finally, I nodded. "I would like to walk the beach, and collect a vial of ocean water, so that in a way, this place shall always be with me."

The councilors looked at each other and smiled. "Of course. You have our permission to take a vial of water from our beautiful oceans. It would be an honor."

"Thank you, Councilor Vektor, Councilor Revdran," I said softly, before we turned and walked from the dining room, back down the elevator, and into the waiting limousine.

"You did wonderful tonight, Chrissa," Kavra praised. "Did you enjoy yourself?"

"Very much. The councilors are amazing."

Kavra nodded. "They certainly are."

When we arrived back at Kasar's castle, Kavra escorted me inside and led me down a series of hallways. Soft music played in the background, growing louder.

When I hesitated, he encouraged, "Come."

I followed Kavra through several more halls until we entered a grand ballroom. Painted angels adorned the domed ceiling, their golden wings forever frozen as they rose toward the heavens. Some stared intently at the glory above, while others looked down upon the room's inhabitants, as though they could see straight to our souls.

"May I have this dance?" Kavra asked.

I accepted and he whisked me onto the dance floor. We swayed slowly to the music.

"The angels are so beautiful," I whispered.

"Not nearly as lovely as you."

The chandeliers sparkled across the sequins on my gown, surrounding us with an array of colors. We danced across rainbows under the watchful gaze of angels.

"This is a dream," I whispered through the soft music.

"No, Chrissalynn, this is your dream come true."

Resting my head against Kavra's shoulder, I closed my eyes and let the music take me to a place where nothing else existed.

Chapter XII

I spent the next few days deep in my studies, and playing. Somewhere between the torture studies, flurry of parties, dinners, and explorations, I even managed, begrudgingly, to complete a few interstellar math assignments. The weeks flew by until the day I received a call from the high inquisitor informing me my *patient* was once again ready to receive company.

Kavra and I left the residence around three o'clock, taking a small ship to the nearby moon. Anticipating my treatment, Savrick was already tied onto the rack, the ropes pulling on his freshly healed limbs.

"Hello, Savrick. How are you feeling today? Better I hope."

No reply from my subject.

Snapping a clean black robe into place, I pulled on white gloves and reached for something out of Savrick's line of vision.

"Derit," Savrick said. "My commander's name is Derit. I'm second *lekit* of my command."

I smiled, moving both of my empty hands back into his sight. "I'm relieved you're doing better."

"Better than when you left me."

"How many were in your command?"

"Forty-seven."

"How many commands?"

"I'm not saying any more."

"But I only require one more answer. Consider carefully, Savrick. One simple answer and we'll be done.

"You have a family, correct? We can send you back to them." I leaned closer. "Tell me the name of the Sentile's next target, and I'll send you on the next ship home."

He only glared.

"Savrick, please, I don't want to hurt you anymore. Keep conversing so we don't have to do this.

"Do you have children? What are your children's names?"

My sweet inquiries were met with stony silence.

I looked up at Inquisitor Verayt and he nodded an encouragement.

"Okay." I sighed, and picked up a device from the table behind me. Circular, it would expand once in place. "Open your mouth."

He did not.

"Open your mouth, or these men shall force you."

"Let them try."

I nodded to the men standing on my left. Two stepped forward. The first grabbed Savrick's thin lips and pulled them open, while the second inserted the device. With the press of a button, it expanded, forcing his mouth to remain open. A rubbery cloth was pinched over his nasal passage to prevent breathing.

"In ancient times," I stated, "prisoners used to be tied underneath a giant wheel. From this wheel, water was poured down the subject's throat, preventing breathing. As you can see," I waved my hand in a circular motion, "we sadly have no wheel. However, with improvisation, we are able to implement the basic concepts."

I was handed a plastic tube and rag.

"This," I held up the cloth, "you will find to be extremely absorbent." Under Verayt's watchful eye, I inserted the wad of fabric halfway down Savrick's throat.

Holding the tube where he could see it, I explained, "This contains an endless supply of water, our modern day version of the ancient wheel, if you will." I looked directly into Savrick's eyes. "Once the water starts running, the cloth in your throat will expand, causing you to drown and suffocate at the same time.

"Unlike our last meeting, once this begins, it will be several days before you are able to speak again. This is your last chance to tell me what I want to know. I will walk out of this room and give you exactly two minutes to think about your options. When I return, nod yes if you have changed your mind."

I stepped out of the room.

Kavra joined me on the other side of the door. "You're doing well."

"Thanks. Do you think he will talk?"

"It is learning that's important," Kavra reminded me.

I glanced at the clock and waited for two minutes to pass.

Returning to the room, Kavra following, I approached my patient. "Are we ready to talk? Nod if you are."

Frustrated, but unsurprised by his lack of response, I sighed. "Okay, Savrick. You brought this on yourself." I grabbed a tube connected to vat of water and took a seat near Savrick's upper body. "Last chance."

No response.

I turned on the water. He gasped as the first ice cold drop touched his throat.

Two minutes passed. The cloth in his throat engorged and he gagged. His arms fought against the bonds, ropes digging into his wrists, drawing blood. I kept pouring.

His chest rose and fell in a panic as his lungs screamed for air.

Allowing a brief reprieve, I turned off the tap and water drained as his throat convulsed, allowing him to take a shallow breath. "Have you had enough?"

When he didn't respond, I turned the water back on full, cutting off his air supply. His body jerked against the ropes again, cutting deeper into each of his wrists. Detached from the experience, I watched him as though from a distance, and came to the realization I was not horrified by the writhing, drowning creature. In fact, I pitied the stubbornness that forced such measures.

I turned off the water and reached for the cloth in his throat with my gloved hand. Gripping it firmly between two of my fingers, I jerked hard. The cloth was ripped from his throat, bringing with it tissue and blood.

He gasped great gulps of air, then moaned because the cool air hurt his raw throat. Turning his head, he coughed up water and blood.

When he'd regained air enough to be cognizant of what took place around him, I gently dabbed at his mouth with a clean cloth, like a doting nurse might. "Savrick, are we ready to talk?"

He nodded, but grimaced as he tried to speak.

"Regretfully, you won't be able to use your voice for several days. These men are going to take you to get some rest, and clean you up. Perhaps even some soothing tea. I will return in a few days, at which time I expect you to tell me everything I require. Do you understand?"

He nodded again.

"Good," I replied, motioning for the men to release him. "Tend to his injuries."

"You are handling this well," Kavra admired as I calmly removed my robe and hung it back on the hook.

"Thank you."

"I've never seen anyone employ that particular form of encouragement. If he does talk next week, other inquisitors might implement your chosen tactics."

"Thank you, Kavra."

"Shall we return home?"

A private shuttle returned us to the resort, where I lingered in a hot shower until I heard voices. Quickly dressing, I dried my hair with a towel as I peeked into the living room. Seeing who the visitor was, I dropped the towel and ran eagerly into Kasar's waiting arms.

"Hello, Chrissa," my adoptive father greeted. "I have some recent battle reports to give the council, and it's good news for a change, so I decided to deliver the update personally."

Grinning, I settled into the couch beside him.

"Have you been enjoying your stay on Setianta?"

"Oh yes! I saw the museum, and the Hall of Emperors, and even met two council members!" I spent the rest of the evening animatedly describing my recent adventures, and explaining my choice of gathering tactics. Dinner was eventually served, and when he could get a word in, Kasar told of his conquests and battles. Kavra complained about Kasar's old fashioned décor, to which Kasar only laughed.

The next morning we enjoyed a relaxed breakfast in one of the casual dining rooms.

Kasar sat back in his chair, to savor his hot beverage. "Chrissa, I would like for you to accompany me to give my reports today."

I nearly choked on the piece of toast I was eating. "You mean, to the council?"

He nodded. "It will give you a chance to actually see the council chambers, and meet the rest of the councilors as well. I thought you might enjoy it."

"Oh, yes! I would love to!" I glanced toward Kavra, who sat on my left. "Are you coming too?"

"No, but I'll meet you both for dinner, and look forward to hearing *all* about the session." He winked.

Excited by the prospect of being allowed to watch an actual session of council, I wanted my outfit to reflect the seriousness of the council's business. Rejecting my usual feminine attire, I chose a pair of tailored black slacks with a simple matching blouse. Leaving my hair straight, I pulled the front sections back into a partial ponytail, allowing the rest to lay sleek down my back.

Considering the mirror, my reflected image was too plain. Rummaging through my cosmetics, I placed a drop of dye in each eye, changing the color from my usual muddy green to a bold blue. Adding a simple gold chain, and a pair of thin hoop earrings, provided just the right touch of formality.

Kasar had also changed, and waited for me in the foyer. He looked sharp in a classic black and white suit. Taking my arm with an approving smile, he escorted me to the limousine, which delivered us to the council chamber's front stairs.

Standing beneath the building, with its tall spiral pillars and domed ceiling, filled me with awe. Climbing the golden steps, I read the immortal words, once spoken by Emperor Dehartra, engraved over the building's threshold: "Long live those who die in service. Long live the Setian Empire."

Two guards waited at the top of the stairs. "Please state your name, and business," one asked formally, though his voice rattled with nerves. Must have been a new guy.

"Nicholas Kasar," said the other guard, before father could respond. "I served under you for a time." He looked to me. "Who are you?"

"Chrissa," I answered shyly.

"My daughter," Kasar added. "I'm here to give reports to the councilors. They're expecting me."

"Yes, we were informed you would be arriving today. Please, come this way."

The doors swung open and we entered a brilliant corridor. My heels echoed down the white marble hallway no matter how carefully I stepped. Light cream walls speckled with gold played with light coming from large overhead windows.

After a silent walk, we stopped outside a door protected by four men. Two were dressed in red cloaks, the color of the council, while two were dressed in gold, the color of the emperor, which meant the emperor was in the session.

With a brief nod to us, one of the red guards stepped into the room to announce our presence, and less than a minute later, the doors opened. A human-looking gold-attired guard stepped forward and offered me his arm. "May I escort you to a seat?"

With a nod from my father, I accepted the man's arm, and allowed him to lead me through the tall black doors.

The room was massive, oval in shape, with a high, vaulted ceiling. On the far side of the room were thirteen chairs where the councilors were seated, and to the left additional bench seats for an audience. A raised platform in the center of the room ensured everyone had a decent view.

I was first escorted to the center, where I gave a formal bow before the councilors.

"Greetings, Chrissalynn," Councilor Vektor said. "You're most welcome."

As I was whisked off the floor to a seat, Kasar followed with a bow, and took his place on the center podium.

Bowing to each in turn, he began, "Good afternoon, Councilors, Emperor. I'm grateful for this opportunity to report to you personally."

"Greetings, Lord Kasar," Councilor Vektor welcomed him. "We are eager to hear your reports."

"As you know," Kasar began, "we've had particular trouble with the Trests for the past few months. Several of our spies were captured the Setian scans, which have been implemented throughout the planet. I am here today to inform you of some recent developments, which I believe you will find satisfactory."

Several councilors gave him a quizzical look as they waited.

"Harars 9 decided to try out a new plan, approved by Redim." Kasar cleared his throat. "They introduced Setians into the primitive minds of several *tenns* and semnas. These pets were allowed to enter sensitive locations unsuspected."

"What?" The question came from a councilor I did not recognize.

"Yes," Kasar acknowledged his incredulous challenge with a nod. "Truly ingenious."

"What happened?" asked another councilor.

"Our pet spies infiltrated the Trests' home world's major control rooms. Using the information they obtained, we coordinated a simultaneous attack involving Redim's spies and my troops. I positioned commanders around the planet, while Redim's teams neutralized the outer defenses. Once the shields were down, our troops had an easy victory. Because they relied so heavily on their superior technology, it seems they had no alternative defense plan."

"Are you saying..." Councilor Vektor asked.

Kasar nodded. "We have taken the Trests' planet. Eighty-five percent of their population is in a holding area awaiting infestation pools to arrive. A surprising and, of all things, easy victory."

Councilor Revdran balked, "Wait! You're saying we...infested their pets?"

"Yes," Kasar confirmed.

"You mean it actually worked?"

"The plan was your idea?" Kasar asked.

"Of course not!" the councilor replied.

A knowing, radiant smile bloomed across my face, anticipating the coming revelation.

Revdran exchanged a glance with Vektor. "Did you tell?"

"I told Councilor Kylen."

Kylen, a Horde, looked up from his seat. "I told Harars 3."

"You mean...it worked? I told Harars 2, but only as a joke."

A human man revealed, "I told a few people, and I think Harars 9 was among them, but I never thought anyone would take the crazy plan seriously."

Kasar looked at the confused faces around him. "Then whose idea was it?"

While most maintained baffled expressions, two councilors smiled.

"This brilliant idea, which won the battle of Trests," Councilor Revdran said, "was presented to us at dinner, a few weeks ago, by Chrissalynn Kasar."

All eyes turned toward me.

"His daughter?" one of the others said in disbelief.

"My Chrissa?" Kasar echoed his question. "My girl?"

"Yes," Vektor confirmed. The two councilors took turns enlightening the rest of the room regarding the initial conversation.

"Congratulations, Chrissalynn." Revdran stood, offering a bow. "I understand you have not yet had your promised day on the beach?"

"No, Councilor."

"You shall do so, in three days hence. We will make arrangements to have you taken to the Dehartra beach."

"Thank you, Councilor Revdran."

A mixture of ecstatic joy and shock stayed with me as my father escorted me from the chambers.

"That little girl may be one to watch," I heard a voice say as the black doors closed behind us.

Once in the hallway, Kasar stared down at me in amazement before lifting me in his arms in a joyous embrace. "Congratulations, my daughter. You have made me so proud today!"

I smiled; his joy meant more than the appreciation of all the councilors combined.

At a celebratory dinner out, we informed Kavra of our story. The look on his face was as stunned as mine had been at the news. We treated ourselves with some grand desserts, and when we returned home, a mean game of cards.

Chapter XIII

THE NEXT DAY I RETURNED to the nearby moon for another session with Savrick. Accompanied by Kasar and Kavra, I entered the room to find him secured to a chair that was bolted to the floor. A table and second chair sat beside him.

"Hello, Savrick. I understand you are ready to speak with me."

"Yes." While audible, his voice was soft; he was still in some discomfort.

"Give me a good faith answer," I instructed, sitting at the table and lacing my fingers together. "What is the next target?"

Silence once again fell between us. I allowed it to linger, waiting.

He finally revealed, "Palta."

"What priority level will the attack be?"

"One."

"When will preparations begin?"

"They already have."

I glanced behind me. Kavra appeared to be cursing with a shocked look on his face. He turned to one of their guards, who promptly ran out the door, presumably to warn the council.

"Palta?" I continued. "They are a peaceful and non-interfering species. Why would anyone wish to harm Palta?"

I recalled my last visit to the planet fondly. Kavra had been visiting with the leader. Their five-year-old son, a cutie with blue fur and a bright smile, had proudly displayed a picture he had drawn of his family.

"Why are they attacking Palta?"

"Because it is under your protection," came the reply. "It will strike a blow to the heart of the empire, and shake the confidence of your allies."

"So you would imprison the Paltas?"

He gave a rough laugh. "Who said anything about imprison?"

"You mean...you plan to kill them?"

"Every last one."

"When will this attack take place?"

"It is in the beginning planning stages. Possibly two *grets* to formalize the attack and gather our troops into the system. But do not be mistaken, the attack will come."

"And we," Kasar said, stepping into Savrick's line of vision, "will be ready, thanks to you."

"You will be defeated."

"Everyone falls eventually. However, you will not live to see our demise." Kasar turned to me. "You have done well, Chrissa. Time to finish."

"Finish?"

"This man is our enemy, and uninfestible. We cannot possibly allow him to live, and potentially warn his allies their plans have been compromised."

I stood from my chair and took a few steps back. "You…want me to kill him?"

Inquisitor Verayt stepped forward and handed a blade to Kasar, who proceeded to offer it to me.

"No."

"It's the last step, Chrissa. You've tortured and broken him. He's given you the necessary information. Now is time to end it." He took a step toward me, which I answered with a step back.

Pressed against the small room's wall, my eyes searched for Kavra, who held a grave look.

Kasar stepped between us, cutting Kavra from my view.

"Chrissalynn," he spoke my name in a commanding voice few ever refused. "Take the knife."

I wrapped my hand around the blade's hilt, and found it heavier than I'd imagined. Kasar stepped to my right, and motioned for me to move forward, which I did until I was about five feet from Savrick. I ran a finger lightly over the sharp end of the blade, hissing as the cold metal sliced my skin.

"That creature," Kasar said, "would annihilate every last person on the planet of Palta. Every father, mother, and child. Every friend, every animal, and pet. A genocide, he would kill them all.

"He's the monster, Chrissa, not us. We stand for improvement, and advancement in other societies. We protect others from creatures such as this. From your studies, you know I am telling the truth."

I gazed across the room, not at Savrick or Kasar, but at Kavra, my heart torn.

He met my gaze, unflinching.

We stared at each other, uninterrupted. Using glassy eyes, I pleaded with Kavra for help, silently begging him to tell me this was wrong. There had to be another way. A better way. He did not want me to become a killer.

He met my plea with silence.

Looking briefly at the blade in my hand, I closed my eyes and pictured that five-year-old boy, playing with his semnas, and accepted this creature would kill him if given the chance. Would brutally murder the family he loved, and the friends he played with in the fields. If this creature were allowed to live, he would kill them all. If he were allowed to live, he would find a way to warn his commander. Silencing him was the only way to save the gold and green-eyed child.

With a stroke of my blade, I could save a billion innocent lives. With a stroke of my blade, I would stop the holocaust of Palta.

Aligning the blade with Savrick's throat, I sliced deeply to the right.

A warm, wet liquid gushed over my hand, splattering my clothes. Belatedly realizing I should have donned the black robe, I stared numbly down as the monster's body gave its last convulsion, and his eyes faded to a blank, eternal stare.

Chapter XIV

Two days later, Kavra woke me from a sound sleep with a gentle shake. I opened my eyes groggily and glanced at the clock against the far wall. "It's too early," I complained in a rough voice.

"We're going to the beach!" Kavra reminded me, with far too perky of a smile.

I rolled over, putting my back to him with an insistent tug of my covers.

He laughed. Heavy footsteps preceded bright light pouring into the room.

When I pulled the covers over my head, Kavra jerked them away and threw them to the floor.

"Go away," I groaned, burying my head under a pillow.

"Rise and shine," he insisted, snatching a second cushion and softly hitting my upturned rump.

Laughing, I used my pillow to hit him back.

"Okay, okay," I finally said. "I'll get up, I'll get up."

With Kavra's exit, I pulled myself out of bed and asked my maid if I had a bathing suit. She promptly opened a dresser drawer with a rainbow's array of choices. When I selected a deep, emerald green two-piece suit, she handed me a matching pair of silky pants and shirt. After I'd pulled those on, and she'd styled my hair in a coiled braid, the maid offered an emerald wrap, which I draped over my shoulders like a scarf.

I found an impatient Kavra in the foyer, wearing a faded blue t-shirt and matching shorts. Kasar, also relaxed but more conservatively, wore blue jeans and a red short-sleeved shirt.

"Shall we go?" Kavra asked eagerly.

Indulging in an exaggerated sigh, I nodded and followed the men to a limousine, then into a private shuttle, which took us from the floating city to the ground below.

The shuttle landed on a concrete platform. Stepping off the ship, my eyes immediately jumped to the walkway's end, where the sand beckoned. The sight took my breath away; it had been years since I had seen a beach.

I ran forward, kicking off my shoes in the process. Pausing briefly as my bare feet touched the warm sand, enjoying the gritty sensation between my toes, I took off again for the water, Kavra laughing behind me.

Memories flooded my mind as I sunk into the cool, wet beach. I closed my eyes against the sun's brightness and imagined my *real* father watching. Recalled the sound of his voice.

"*Chrissa.*"

I turned.

"Chrissa," Kasar said again. "Beautiful, is it not?"

Turning back to the water as Kasar walked up behind me, I took a breath of salty air. "Beautiful," I agreed. Helped, or not, by the gusting winds, I removed my bathing suit covers and approached the gently lapping water.

Memories of my last time on the beach, with my father, flooded me. What would he think of what I had done? Would I still be his princess, after what I'd become?

"Chrissa." Kasar took my hand, breaking my melancholy, and led me forward until the cold water bubbled my toes. I reached down, putting my hand in the white foam—

"Home," Kasar spoke my thoughts aloud. "The ocean is home."

"Yes," I whispered back before wading deeper, inviting the ocean to cover my skin and hair with salt and sand. I ducked under the next wave, allowing it to wash away the memories that no longer had a place.

The morning and early afternoon were spent alternately playing in the waves, or lounging on a beach towel between the two men.

After lunch, Kasar produced a crystal vial in the shape of a spark—the thin, colorful fish native to Setianta.

"For your water from the sea. You can wear it," he reached deeper into his pocket, "on this golden chain."

He held out a thin rope chain, simplistic yet perfect. Pulling the stopper, I took the crystal spark gently in my hand and walked back to the waves a final time that day. Kneeling down, I held it in front of my chest, allowing the water to wash over and into the vial, taking only what the ocean chose to give me.

Eventually I stood and replaced the crystal top, sealing the contents. I then turned toward the afternoon sun, lifting the vial, to watch it sparkle with a rainbow of colors.

When I returned to the towels, I slipped the crystal spark on the chain and fastened it securely around my neck.

I lay back on the blanket and watched the sunset, wanting to savor the day. The sky painted a brilliant array of colors, from orange to red to pink, and finally, black night filled with a thousand twinkling stars and moonlight.

The next few days were almost as wonderful, relaxing by the pool and enjoying elegant dinners.

"Come in," I called to a knock on my door late one evening.

Both Kasar and Kavra entered my room. Kavra sat on the corner of my bed while Kasar stood beside it.

"We will be returning to the main ships tomorrow," Kasar explained without preamble. "It is sadly time to get back to work."

"Will Kavra be coming too?"

"Alas," he replied, "I must also be on my way. The council has assigned me to the Zauros system. I'm scheduled to leave early in the morning, probably before you wake."

"Oh," I said sadly. "You'll be careful, won't you? And you won't stay away too long?"

"I will be careful, Chrissa, I promise."

I rose to wrap my arms around his neck. Aurora protested the disturbance briefly, before curling against my pillow with one bleary eye open.

"Anytime you can't stand missing me, or simply wish to get away from this old man," he winked at Kasar, "call me and I'll send someone to fetch you. Or if you need to talk, we can initiate a holo-conference, okay?"

"Okay."

"I'll leave you two—err three," he amended, noting the kitty's persistence, "—alone." Kasar patted Kavra briefly on the shoulder, and left the room.

When the door closed, I turned back to Kavra. "I'll miss you."

"I'll miss you too, Chrissa. You keep up those studies, and I'll be back before you know it."

I made a face. "Not interstellar math again!"

He laughed, and to my surprise, kissed me lightly. "I'll see you in a few weeks, if not sooner. I can sit here until you fall asleep, if you'd like."

"Yes, I would." Holding hands, we talked until my eyes drifted closed.

"Goodnight, Kavra."

"Goodnight, Chrissalynn."

Chapter XV

Once we returned to Kasar's ship, my training was extended to new subjects, ones far different than those requiring simple memorization of battles and history. My first lesson was on the importance of appearing neutral at all times during public engagements, showing no emotions to anyone. Emotions are weaknesses, which can be used against us. Certain emotions cause people to make mistakes, which could prevent one from getting what they want and deserve. Without emotions, a person is able and better prepared to do whatever is necessary.

Emotional control came hand-in-hand with learning the importance, and acceptance of, sacrifice. All creatures, from the least powerful to the emperor himself, live their lives in service to the empire. Nothing is more important than living, and eventually dying, in that service. In such context, everyone of lower rank than I was expendable. I learned this the hard way one night when an unexpected problem occurred on the planet of Beckensailt, conquered only three weeks prior to our arrival.

Standing near Kasar by a Setian pool, we oversaw the last of the planet's inhabitants being rounded up and forced toward their inevitable fate. Beckens were pale creatures resulting from the fact their sun only lit the sky for two hours before being followed by thirty-seven hours of night.

Bright lights surrounded the pool though, making the night appear as light as day. Beckens squinted against the harshness as they were dragged forward, their four arms shackled behind them. Some struggled fiercely, requiring two, or in some cases three, of Kasar's guards, while others came quietly, accepting their fate.

A guard shouted in alarm. Looking in the direction of his call, we saw Beckens pouring into the area from all sides. Taking the guards closest by surprise, the Beckens knocked them to the ground, releasing the prisoners they had been holding.

Shouts, and conflicting commands, echoed as about forty Beckens surrounded us. Six personal guards took positions to shelter Kasar and me, blocking my view of the unexpected battle.

As we stood buffered in the chaos, a loud whistling sound resulted in two guards on my left falling to the ground, never to rise again. One of the remaining four grabbed me—a large Horde who practically tossed my fifteen-year-old frame over his shoulder—and the entire company ran back to the ship.

People shouted. Screams shattered the air. The men ran on, shooting their weapons blindly behind them, hopefully at the attacking Beckens. From my improved perspective, I finally obtained a clear view of the battle.

Bodies from both sides littered the field. Blue, red, and green blood soaked into the yellow grass creating a horrific swirled painting. In a fresh wave of fear, I clung to the Horde's neck, afraid of not getting out alive.

Grass turned to black metal, and four walls enclosed me, as I was taken safely aboard Kasar's ship. The guard, only slightly winded, put me down on unsteady legs and immediately turned away. I sat, or fell depending on your perspective, to the hard deck.

"Are you all right?" father asked.

The ship lifted into the air. I took a deep breath before nodding. "Yes. The guard saved me." I tried to give him an appreciative smile, but the burly man was nowhere to be seen.

"Come with me, child. Watch what happens to those who rise up. It will be a lesson for you to remember."

Clambering to my feet, I silently followed him through the dimly lit corridor until we reached the front deck. A break from the solid black walls, directly in front of us was a window offering a clear view of events outside the ship. We now hovered over the pool where the fight had begun.

Before I could ask what he had planned, Kasar ordered, "Fire."

A streak of yellow light originated from below us to completely incinerate the area. Where the pool had once been, nothing but a black scorch remained. No one survived. Not the Beckens who had rebelled against the empire, not the men who had been faithfully fighting to protect us, not even the Setians waiting in the pool for a host. Everyone was dead.

I looked at Kasar with utter disbelief. "The troops?"

Kasar stared in silence.

My eyes wandered the room searching for hidden answers, for the reasoning behind such indiscriminate brutality. "They were fighting. They were protecting us." My eyes finally returned to his. "Why, Father?"

"Several reasons," came his stony reply. "First, those men had a simple job. They were supposed to protect the pool. They failed, proving themselves weak. We do not tolerate weakness in this empire."

I fought tears. "The attack was a surprise. There was no way they could have known."

"Surprise or not, they were ill-prepared," Kasar explained. "You see, Chrissa, if those men had done their job, fear of our empire would have kept any remaining rebels far away. If those men had done their jobs, none would have dared to attack us."

"Also, rebellion must be crushed at all cost. A single spark can start a raging fire, so any hint of resistance must be completely destroyed in a manner that serves as a lesson to others. Destroying the pool, including our own citizens, will shatter any hope our enemies might harbor. Those who gave their lives today saved countless others from dying in later resistances this rebellion might have created.

"There is also the fact that the only way to be forgiven for failure is to give one's life to the empire. Those who died have regained their honor, and shall find themselves gloriously rewarded on the other side of existence."

With no words to breach his stern demeanor, I left the room in silence, lost in a million contradicting and confusing thoughts.

Several hours later, I knocked lightly on the door to the private quarters of Kasar's guard commander. Karagteon 27, a creature covered in brown fur with emerald eyes, answered.

Staring awkwardly up at the seven-foot-tall captain, I told him one of his guards had saved my life. That I wanted to thank him, but did not know who or where he was.

The captain informed me, "His name is Neilsv 247, but he went back down to fight. He refused to quit so easily."

"I'm sorry," I stammered. "I…"

"My lady," he answered, "he was proud to die in service. There is no higher glory than to give one's life for the empire. In fact, not only was he allowed to do so, he also had the privilege of giving his life for the daughter of Lord Kasar. His death is every Setian's dream."

"Their dream is to die?"

"To give their life for a higher cause, yes."

The fact others died for me kept me lying awake many a nights, alternately stroking Aurora's soft fur, and wetting it with tears.

Kasar, noting my extended discomfort, reminded me, "Their deaths should be honored, not mourned." A philosophy taught continuously throughout my training.

Over time, the constant death caused me to become withdrawn. With the exception of my already established friendship with Kavra, I stopped connecting with people for fear of losing them. Loss, all the way back to my first father, had become a far too-familiar theme in my life. With my detachment from outside relationships, my emotions dimmed, along with my guilt.

One day, I don't remember exactly when, I found myself believing, truly believing, they had died so one better than them could live.

A few months later, in the battle of Mesta, a knock sounded at my door. The battle had been won two days before, and Kasar had flown down to the planet, leaving me in charge of the ship.

"Come in," I called from the black chair in front of my desk. Karagteon 27 entered the room and gave a low bow.

"What is it?"

"During the recent battle, Septa 234 disappeared. He was listed among the dead, and would have received honors in tomorrow's ceremony."

"I detect a 'however,' coming."

He nodded. "He was found today by one of our commanders on the planet. After questioning, I believe..." He cleared his throat. "He abandoned the battle."

I straightened in my chair, surprised. "You mean he is a deserter?"

"Yes. I am seeking your instructions on how to proceed, or I can address the issue if you wish."

I shook my head. "No, I will deal it. Is Septa 234 on this ship?"

"He is being transported here now."

"Good. Have everyone who is not currently assigned to an essential duty assemble in the main interrogation room. Have Septa 234 escorted there as well."

My orders were carried out, and a half-hour later, everyone awaited my arrival. After exchanging a brief message with Kasar for approval, which was readily given, I left my room to enter the interrogation chamber.

Septa 234 occupied a Horde form, standing between Karagteon and another guard, with his arms chained behind his back. At eight feet tall, he towered above me as I stepped in front of the waiting crowd. Not from Kasar's personal ship, I had never seen this soldier before.

"Septa 234, do you know who I am?"

He glanced around the room and back to me. "The one in charge."

"Correct," I answered. "But do you know my name?"

He shook his head.

I motioned to Karagteon and asked Septa, "Do you know who he is?"

"Yes," Septa replied, "he is Kasar's captain."

"Tell me, Septa 234, did you desert the battle? A simple yes or no."

Silence fell before Septa hung his head and admitted, "Yes."

I turned to the men standing behind me, arms at their sides, backs straight at perfect attention. "You all heard the confession. I want to make it clear to everyone standing here today, cowardliness and desertion shall not be tolerated by this empire under any circumstances."

Two guards pushed Septa to his knees. Without a word, I leaned forward, unclipped, and removed the gun from the captain's side. "The penalty," I said, aiming the weapon, "is death." I pulled the trigger. As it had in the bazaar, the weapon obliterated all traces of the coward. "May your sins haunt you for all eternity."

I offered Karagteon his weapon back, before turning to the crowd of witnesses. "The next person to abandon a battle will not only die, but face inquisition as well. Are there any questions?"

The room remained silent.

Chapter XVI

During this time I began training in military strategy. Using holographic technology, battles in our history were reviewed. Supplementing lectures and quizzes, I completed countless simulations testing different strategies with the goal of improving outcomes. I learned the best way to attack any type of situation, commonly made mistakes, and how to readjust battle strategies in a limited amount of time to obtain a given objective. My tutors drilled me until I could recite the rules of war in my sleep, and celebrated the day Kasar began allowing me to plan some missions on my own.

At the age of sixteen, Kasar put me through the last, and what he considered to be the most important, part of my training.

We arrived at a planet I did not recognize. The sky was a shade of sickly green, and the ground was covered with coarse sand. As I stepped off the ship, a wave of intense heat, produced from three scorching suns high in the sky, hit me as it torched the arid land.

A guard escorted us to one of the clear Setian pools already located on the planet's surface. I watched as the helpless creatures native to this miserable world were dragged to the pool and infested. As I observed, and overcame my shock, I made a startling realization. Although what was being done was horrible to witness, it also represented an act of mercy. These poor creatures lost their minds so a superior race could live, and hopefully improve their conditions.

A native was brought before me. "This prisoner would like to speak with you." I looked at the gray-furred creature between the guards.

He spoke in an unfamiliar language.

"What did he say?"

"He asks for death."

I blinked. "Would you please repeat yourself?"

He did.

I looked at Kasar. He simply stared, waiting.

Slumped between the guards, his matted fur was soaked with blood from a wound on his front leg. But his eyes, laced with the sadness of utter defeat, were what held my attention.

The man said something else and I looked at the guard holding him.

"He is begging," the guard translated.

I once again glanced at Kasar, and back to the guards holding him. "Take him to the pool."

When they moved him back into the line of men waiting to be infested, he screamed and tried to run, but the guards held him tightly. I watched with empathy for his misplaced fear while he was moved to the end of the pier, forced to his knees, and enslaved.

Kasar and I stared into each other's eyes, both realizing my indoctrination was complete.

That night, I was surprised to find a dazzling gown laid out across my bed. A red rose lay across the black silk with a note written in bold calligraphy. *I would be honored if you would join me for dinner tonight at seven in my private chambers*, signed with an elegant 'K.'

I picked up the delicate rose and breathed in the sweet fragrance, closing my eyes to imagine they were all around. Gently placing the rose aside, I lifted the dress to more closely inspect it. A unique design, the sleeves were cut at sharp angles, leaving the top of my wrists only partially covered. The front was adorned in spirals of sequins that must have taken hours to apply.

Calling my maid, after a quick shower, she helped me into the gown, and pulled my hair into a simple updo, incorporating the fragrant flower. Finally she set a string of rubies around my neck, from which a single strand trailed down to touch my neckline suggestively.

At precisely seven o'clock, I entered Kasar's room. He was also formally dressed, and the table had been set for two. The glass rocks behind him glowed brightly, offering warmth, and the room's only light.

After seating me at the square table, Kasar opened a bottle of champagne. "A toast, to you and to the Setian Empire." I touched my glass to his before taking a sip. "It is only a matter of time before the council declares you a leader on your own."

"I would be honored to have such a title bestowed, Kasar."

"And the council will be proud to bestow it."

Dinner was brought into the room, and accompanied with more champagne. I have little recollection of what we spoke about, as I could not seem to keep my mind from wandering.

"Chrissa," Kasar asked, "what is the saying? A penny for your thoughts?"

I flashed a smile. "Kavra offers diamonds."

"Oh, does he? How about an empire?"

I laughed. "I wish he were here."

Kasar nodded. "You have much love for him, don't you?"

"I do."

Kasar nodded again, studying me in silence.

At some unseen signal, soft music filtered into the room. Kasar stood from his chair and offered his arm. "Dance with me, Chrissalynn."

I stood and placed my hand in his, allowing him to lead me to the center of his marble floor. He pulled me close and placed a gentle kiss upon my lips.

Startled by the unusual contact, I stood watching him, unsure.

"Do you know you are mine?" he asked softly.

"Of course."

"No." He shook his head and bored his sapphire eyes directly into my emerald ones. "I don't think you do."

I held his gaze in unspoken question.

"I love you as I love nothing else."

He leaned down and kissed me again. Not the brief caress of his last gesture, but with a deep, firm touch.

"I will protect all you love, Chrissalynn, including those you speak so fondly of, as long as you understand that you are mine."

Unease crept along my skin.

"Kavra will be safe, as long as you belong to me."

My breath caught as his meaning became clear. "Kasar," I answered carefully, fear increasing at the thought of Kavra without the empire's protection, "I hope to never give you reason to doubt my loyalty."

Without answering, he took my hand and guided me to the next room. My heart pounded at the sight of the bed, draped with deep burgundy blankets.

He directed me to the bed, and sat down beside me.

"Kasar—"

"Nicholas," he corrected. "Within these chambers."

"Nicholas," I echoed.

An extended kiss was a prelude for wrapping his arms around my thin frame. He unzipped my gown slowly before leaning back to pull the sleeves from my shoulders down my arms. Standing, he lifted me to my feet, causing my dress to pool on the floor.

"You are truly beautiful." His voice sounded haunted as he moved his hand to touch my cheek, slowly raising my gaze to meet his own. "The most beautiful thing I have ever seen."

Chapter XVII

THE PLANET OF PALTA WAS under Kasar's jurisdiction. Shortly after my seventeenth birthday, Kasar and I were in the Cultra galaxy when a report came in that Sentile scouts had been seen on the planet's east side. Ultimately, we discovered the entire Sentile army was hidden only two respecta away. The battle Savrick had foretold with his final words was about to take place.

Kasar summoned additional Setian commanders to his side. He split the resulting army between the other commanders and himself. I was sent down to the planet to lead a ground-based group in order to protect the natives from any enemy ships that might slip through the outer defenses.

As you know, the Paltas are a peaceful species who, despite having a high-level of intelligence, have little use for technology. What they lacked in stature they made up for in creative tales and relaxed minds, attributes we valued. After hard battles, top commanders are often sent to their planet as a reward for their services.

A beautiful destination, the planet is among the most colorful of any within the empire; no cities clutter its surface. Paltas spend their days tending flowers, playing in the sunshine, and telling stories on starlit nights. One of my favorite allies, the very idea the Sentiles would ever want to harm such a wonderful species baffled me.

I fortified our inner defenses. Working by night, in an attempt to avoid detection, I relocated the Paltas from open fields to trees deep in the forests. We installed high-powered force-fields, and placed armed guards in each of the thirty camps.

When the Sentiles arrived, we were as ready for them as we could be. Their initial reaction was to pull back and regroup. They had not expected such a force to be mobilized to protect a species they considered so far beneath them.

Though the sound did not carry, gaseous explosions from the battle above lit up the night sky, and lasers streaked like shooting stars. I spent much of my time in the communications room anxiously awaiting hourly updates.

Setian troops fought fiercely to prevent the Sentiles from bringing the battle to the planet's surface, but on the second night, a force broke through.

Enemy ships flew over the open fields where the Paltas had built their homes, burning the currently uninhabited structures to the ground. I had placed scouts near each of these major fields, who were quick to report, "Sentile ships firing on planet!"

Another reported over the planetary communications system, "I count twenty-two on the north side."

"More on the west!" another voice called, screeching lasers in the background.

"All scouts, return to the nearest camp immediately!" I ordered. "You have exactly four minutes to get behind those force-fields before they go up. Four minutes, do you hear me?

"All troops, prepare for battle. Commanders, I want outer perimeter sweeps every three minutes. Remember, the Sentiles don't know there are ground forces. We have the advantage. Take a few ships down before they figure it out."

"The houses!" someone cried.

"Can be rebuilt," I answered. "I want everyone back here, now!"

I turned to my communications commander. "Contact the main fleet, let Kasar know what's going on."

"Yes, my lady."

I ran outside to where the Paltas had gathered, many reading books, attempting to sleep, or calming younger children. After advising them of the current situation, I ordered everyone to stay by the command center for further instructions. Four minutes later, everyone was inside and the force-fields were up.

Returning to the communications room, the situation was tenuous. "More reports have come in. A total of eighty ships have been sighted, and I'm sure more have made it through."

I took a deep breath and exhaled slowly. We had recently installed a new satellite-based system for this purpose. "Turn on planetary radar and uplink to the main system so we can track exactly where these ships are."

"Already done," someone said. A three-dimensional hologram of the planet appeared in front of me. As I watched, red dots appeared on the screen representing all unidentified ships within the atmosphere; the software marked known ally ships in bright blue.

I studied the resulting map for several minutes. We had sixty-five ships safely hidden behind force-fields. According to our data, perhaps ninety ships had managed to break through battle lines and enter the planet's atmosphere. "Contact high command," I ordered.

Kasar answered the transmission himself. "Report," he demanded.

"Ninety enemy ships in planet atmosphere. What are your orders?"

"Protect the natives. I give you permission to do whatever is necessary."

"Kasar."

"Make sure to—" The hologram vanished.

"What happened?"

"We have lost communication."

"Have they blocked communication within the planet?"

"No," he replied, frantically fiddling with various controls. "Our signal with the fleet is a direct contact. There should be no way to jam communications between us."

"So what happened?"

He shook his head. "The only way for us to lose communication is if the failure impacts the entire fleet."

"Meaning?"

"No ship in our fleet can communicate with another."

"What?"

"The only way this could have happened is if the device being used to jam communications is on this planet. It'd have to be a substantial piece of equipment, requiring a large power source. Weeks to put it together, and even longer to set the right frequencies. Not to mention they would require those frequencies in the first place."

"But the only people who know the frequency numbers for upcoming battles are the top commanders."

"Well, someone must have given it to them, because our communications are effectively blocked. If our troops can't communicate with each other…"

My mind raced with questions, but none of those answers would help. I had to think. "Do our planetary communications work?"

"Yes, they are on a different frequency."

"What about our satellite uplink?"

"Functional as well."

I turned to the blank white wall on my left, staring at nothing as I tried to gather my thoughts. "Are the enemy ships in the air, or have they landed?"

My commander pushed buttons. An electronic voice stated, "Seventy-one ships on ground at centralized location. Twenty-two ships in air."

"Only twenty?" my commander stated. "There's no way they know we are here."

"No, not yet," I replied. "We were very discrete in how we set up these camps. If a smaller party set up this jamming device in a remote location, they probably wouldn't have noticed us. Is the signal also coming from this centralized location? Obviously, that's where it should be, but I wouldn't put it past them to have set up a decoy."

"Shall I send out some scouts?"

I nodded. "Meanwhile, send up fifteen ships from the farthest three lots as a distraction. Make sure they fly very high before they engage. Hopefully the Sentiles will believe they came from the main fleet. It may buy us more time before they discover our presence here.

"Keep communication to a minimum. Give whichever scouts you send direct communication access with this command center. If they need help, I want to know about it."

"Understood." Harars 8 left the room to choose scouts.

My commander contacted the camp farthest from the enemy location and ordered our own ships to engage, hopefully keeping our enemies' attention focused on them, allowing our scouts on foot to enter unseen.

Within ten minutes, our ships were in the air. Every second counted.

"The ships are approaching range of the enemy targets," one of my commanders said, drawing my attention. "Shall they engage?"

"Yes. Do it now, destroy as many as possible before they realize we're there. Also, open full communications between the ships and this room. I want to hear everything."

Communications were open and I listened intently. "Targets in sight. Firing!" A high-pitched sound filled the room. "Missed!"

"Direct hit!" yelled several others. Nine of the twenty-two airborne enemy ships were taken out of commission before the Sentiles even realized we posed a threat.

More screeches filled the room as the enemy ships turned and engaged. From the satellite uplink, I watched as several grounded ships rose, red dots rushing to help their fellow comrades. "Be advised, ten more ships headed your way."

Shouting followed as a full aerial battle began. Meanwhile, our scouts quickly made their way toward the remaining land-based ships, in a deep valley on the south side of the planet, searching for the source of the jamming signal. Over the next half-hour, ten of our ships went down with fifteen of the enemies.

As the Sentiles deployed another twenty ships, I made a judgment call and ordered fifteen more of our own into the air. Our ships were all called by various numbers, identified on the virtual map in front of me.

I saw two red dots teaming up behind one of our pilots. "Number 16, pull up!" I ordered. He complied and managed to scarcely avoid the shot in his direction.

"One of the Paltas who volunteered to scout for us has returned."

"Bring him, or her, here immediately."

Two minutes later, Tanya stood before me.

"Kasar's daughter, the device is there." She pointed with an emerald fur-covered finger.

I turned to my second in command. "We *must* destroy the device."

"Shall I send the ships?" Harars asked.

I shook my head. "They won't break through the force-field. They have to be knocked out by hand. Ask for volunteers. I'll lead the team myself."

"You?"

"Yes, me."

"You're in charge. We need you here."

I hesitated.

"I'll do it," he said. "You will know that someone competent is in charge of the mission, and can stay where you're needed. I'm a better soldier than leader."

"Harars, do you understand what's at stake? If those force-fields aren't destroyed, we won't have anything left to defend."

"I swear those fields will go down."

"Failure's not an option."

"I understand, implicitly." He left to assemble his team.

I turned my attention back to the ongoing battle. "Number twenty, turn left!" I yelled, saving his life. More shots were fired. Ships went down, and more rose to meet those in the air.

A call came over the communications system. "The ground force you sent is behind enemy force-fields."

"How many did he take?"

"Two groups of ten," the man by my side answered.

A pilot called, "I think our secret is out. They are disengaging, and must realize we have soldiers on the ground."

"Send ten ships up from camps fifteen, eighteen, and five," I ordered. "If they know we are here, we might as well let them know we're present in force."

"Should we send up ships as well?"

"No. Conceal this command base for as long as possible.

"Number Eight, hard left!" I turned back to my fellow commanders. "Someone go outside, inform the Paltas what is going on. Assure them we are doing everything we can."

Someone nodded and ran outside.

"Do we have communication with the force-field team?"

"Yes."

I reached over the control panel in front of me. "Harars?"

"Here."

"Status?"

"We've found the generators. There are eight guards surrounding them. Our other team is approaching from the opposite side. They should be here in a few seconds."

I took a step out the door and looked up. The sky was streaked with unnatural lights as confused and fierce fighting took place above. Returning back inside, "Harars, please hurry."

I glanced back at the ongoing atmospheric battle. "Ten and Twelve, watch your back!"

"Going in," Harars advised. Screams drifted into the room from his open mic. I closed my eyes and could picture the lasers firing, bodies disappearing, air singed from the heat of the blast. Leaning toward the speakers, I strained to hear every last sound.

"They're everywhere!" I had no idea who said it.

Harars reported, "We've reached the generator, but we are surrounded. I have no idea where the extra troops came from, but there is no way to plant these bombs and get away. Your orders?"

"Destroy them!"

From Harars, but muffled, as though he'd turned his head, "Everyone out! Use whatever means you can to defend yourself. Get back to camp!"

"But, sir?" someone else asked.

"Go now!" More screaming followed.

"What's happening?" I demanded.

Harars answered, clear despite being a whisper, "I'll take care of the force-field. Tell Kasar, of all the commanders I served, he was the best."

The line went dead.

A different voice came across the line. "Lukare 72 speaking. The generators have been disabled."

"Destroy the camp!" I ordered.

"All ships," one of my commanders yelled, "launch full aerial attack. Target the communications device!"

Our ships raced toward the enemy camp.

"Communications are back up!"

"Give me high command!"

"Chrissa!" A hologram of Kasar appeared before me.

"I'm here."

"Are you?"

"Fine," I assured him.

"Communications are working. Your doing?"

"Yes."

"Kasar," one of my sub-commanders called, "all enemy ships have been destroyed."

"We have things under control here. Go fight your war."

"Our war," he corrected, cutting communications.

Reports poured in. Our forces had sustained some losses, though not as many as I had imagined. Most of our captains defensively pulled back their ships until communications were re-established. Thanks to the efforts of my troops, the system had been down less than two hours.

Kasar's forces surged forward. Setian ships patrolled the skies around the camps, destroying enemy vessels that managed to reach the planet's atmosphere. I oversaw the battle from the control room, giving the Paltas frequent updates.

"A message is coming in from a secure channel. The signature reads from Kavra's ship."

"Kavra?" He was supposed to be in the Seltas galaxy. "Put it through."

A new hologram appeared, but the person on the other side was not Kavra.

Instead I faced a woman with short red hair. Her green eyes studied me from her side of the hologram as I waited expectantly for an explanation.

"Chrissalynn Kasar?" she asked.

"Yes, and you are?"

"I am Sub-Harars 3. Kavra came to join the battle when we lost communication with his fleet. In the fighting, Kavra's ship crashed on the surface. We have been trying to get down to the planet, but have been unable to do so. I..." She looked lost. "I don't know what to do."

"I'll find him."

"The chances he is alive are..."

"I said, I'll find him."

Chapter XVIII

I HAD NOT SEEN KAVRA since the eve of my sixteenth birthday, when Kasar had escorted me to Setianta for what would become the event of the season. Other leaders had travelled from the farthest reaches of the empire to line the walls of Kasar's elegant ballroom. Together they exchanged stories, drank, and danced old, formal dances, which incorporated various cultures and traditions from the different corners of the empire.

I forewent the usual full flair gown for a simple floor-length red satin dress that clung to my blooming curves. The gown had an open back with thin straps, which buckled on both shoulders with a single diamond.

Kavra had arrived several hours into the affair, gliding across the room in a traditional black tuxedo. His blond hair had been pulled back into a thin silver band and his eyes were the palest of blues. From my peripheral vision, I'd watched him approach as Councilor Vektor spoke of the latest problems in the Seltas galaxy.

When he finally reached us, Vektor had turned with a smile. "Hello, Kavra."

"Hello, Councilor." His eyes slid over my slim form as he bowed and my cheeks flushed.

"I worried you wouldn't make it," I had addressed him with a relieved smile.

"And miss you in that dress? Not for the empire." He turned back to the councilor. "Do you mind if I borrow this young enchantress? I believe I owe her a dance."

"By all means." Vektor had smiled at Kavra. "Though I expect one as well, before the night's over."

"Of course, Councilor," I had managed to say before being whisked off to the dance floor and into Kavra's arms.

"Four months," I had complained, once we'd claimed a spot on the marble floor. I shook my head before resting it against his shoulder.

"I'm sorry."

"I missed you."

"And I you, Chrissa."

A comfortable silence fell between us as we danced through the first, second, and third song. On the last refrain, he spun me in an elegant twirl across the floor. When I turned back to face him, Kavra leaned forward and pressed his lips to mine. The kiss deepened as I responded in kind. When the song came to an end he pulled back. "Happy Birthday."

"You've never kissed me like that," I had said breathlessly.

"I've never felt like this before." He drew me further into his arms.

"Kavra, I want to tell you—"

"May I cut in?" a voice interrupted.

We turned to see Kasar standing beside us.

"I have not yet danced with our guest of honor."

"Of course, Kasar." Kavra placed my hand into his. "I will see you later tonight," he had promised before walking off the dance floor.

That was the last time I had stood in the same room with Kavra. When I had tried to find him later that evening, Kasar informed me an emergency had arisen in the Seltas galaxy. Kavra had departed immediately.

My heart sank. Without thinking I had asked, "May I go with him, Kasar? I haven't seen him in months."

"You know you can't. You have training, and Kavra has a job to do as well."

"He didn't say goodbye."

At my hurt expression, Kasar had softened his tone. "He wanted to, but knew his abrupt departure would ruin the party for you. He left a note in your chambers." Kasar reached his hand to my cheek. "He'll be fine, Chrissa. You'll see."

I had nodded and turned toward the door before racing back to my room. As promised, a letter waited atop the deep-red blankets beside a single red rose. I picked up the thin paper with Kavra's elegant handwriting.

Dear Chrissa,

I'm sorry to have left without saying goodbye, but could not bear to ruin your birthday with this news. If I did not adequately tell you before, you looked exquisite tonight, and I wouldn't have missed our dance for all the galaxy. Please forgive my unexpected departure and know, as always, my heart remains with you. Happy Birthday.

Forever yours,

William Kavra

I had traced my fingers over the signature, which was indented into the paper, when a knock at the door drew my attention.

"Chrissa," Kasar had called, "you must return to the party. It will not do to have you disappearing."

Taking a deep breath, I had walked to the door, allowing Kasar to escort me back with a heavy heart. No one saw through my carefully placed smile, until Vektor claimed his dance.

It had taken him but a single glance.

"What troubles you, Chrissalynn?"

"Nothing, Councilor."

He took a step back to better see my face. "You are close to tears." His gray eyes had showed genuine concern. "What is it?"

In a rare burst of defiance, I had asked, "Call him back."

The councilor drew a slow breath before he spoke what weighed on my heart. "Kavra returned to Seltas."

He had eyed me as I nodded, struggled to control brimming tears.

"Chrissa, standing here, there is almost nothing I would not give you. However," he had leaned forward so to not be overheard, "you must consider what it is you ask. There are consequences to every choice. Nicholas ordered Kavra away, and to bring him back would be a direct challenge."

Vektor drew a breath. "If, in the light of the Setian suns, you ask it of me, I'll return him to you. But be prepared for consequences." He had leaned back and brushed a stray piece of hair from my cheek. "Consider carefully."

I did not call the councilor, the following morning or any other, and Kavra had never returned from the Seltas galaxy. Nor had he allowed me to come to him.

"I'm sorry, my dear," he would always say. "This system is too unstable. I will not risk your safety."

A year later, not long after my night with Kasar, I had begged.

"Chrissa." His voice had sounded strained. "You cannot come here, it's not safe."

"That is such bullshit!" I had exclaimed. "It's no more dangerous than any other empire outskirt."

"Chrissa, don't you think I want you with me?"

I had shaken my head, tears falling freely for him to see through the hologram connection. "Do you? I don't know anymore."

His expression had said my words stung, but in my anger, I could not take them back.

"Why are you doing this, Kavra?"

"I wish I could tell you yes," he had said gently.

"You don't understand."

"What is it, Chrissa? What's wrong?"

Multiple answers rose, but the one uttered was simply, "I need you."

"Chrissa." He had spoken my name as though wrenched from him. His hologram stepped closer as I stared into his blue eyes, a part of me expecting to feel the touch of his warm skin. "I would give anything in my power to be with you. To wipe the sorrow from your eyes." He paused long enough to let his words settle over me. "Please don't cry."

So close. I had reached my hand toward him, but it passed through his left arm, causing the hologram to shimmer in the disrupted light. My tears fell faster as I had looked up into his ghost-like form. "I'm afraid, Kavra."

"Of what?"

I forced a harsh breath. "What I've done."

"Chrissa," he had answered firmly, "there is nothing you could do that would change how I feel about you. Nothing."

Tears still fell as I confessed, "I miss you."

"And I you, Chrissa. Every day."

"Promise you'll come back. Please, Kavra."

"I will," he had promised. "I swear."

LATER COUNCILOR VEKTOR HAD COME to speak with me.

"A little bird thought you might need a friend tonight," he had said as he walked through the door to my private chambers.

"He shouldn't have called you." Even to me, my voice had sounded bitter.

"Chrissa, do you remember when I spoke to you of choices and consequences?"

I nodded.

"A day will come when you will be asked to make a choice."

"Between what? Two who love me?"

"No." Vektor had shaken his head. "It's far greater."

"You speak of choices," I had replied with venom. "What choices have I ever had?"

"The choice to be human."

"I don't understand."

"To be Setian is not to love, Chrissa. Yet, Kavra loves you. Not in a way of possession, or power, but a pure and simplistic love. You humanize those around you." He sat on the couch beside me. "Kavra was not always like this. Before you, he never would have called and asked me to bring him back, in spite of Kasar's wishes."

"He what?"

"It's as though the human soul you are slowly losing has found its way into his heart."

"I'm not human."

"No, but you are not Setian either. Not yet." He had paused for breath. "A human heart with a Setian soul. It is the heart they covet. A frail piece of humanity that, despite your thorough indoctrination, lingers in you still. One day you will be forced to make a choice between the humanity *he* loves, and the empire to which you are eternally bound. You are unique within our empire, for no human has ever before been admitted to our ranks."

I had looked into his gray eyes and asked, "What would you choose?"

Sadness filled his warm eyes. "If you decided to fight your fate, it would be a sight to behold." Then, in a dead gaze he added, "But you won't."

His words sank over me as I swallowed back the threatening tears. I struggled to school my voice before I had stated, "I shall pray to the emperors of the past for Kavra's safe return, when the council and Nicholas deem such an event appropriate. You shall not be troubled by this issue again."

"Thank you, Chrissalynn."

I had never again asked to see Kavra.

What if he's?

The fear-laced thought was interrupted by Harars 15's voice as I turned to leave the command room, "You can't leave…"

"Yes, I can." I turned to face the Horde, who towered above me in his alien form. "Communications have been restored. The Sentile command base has been destroyed." I drew a breath. "A leader of this empire has crash-landed. I'm going to find him."

"Let me take the search team instead," he offered.

"No."

"Please—"

"A Paltian child could oversee what's left of this battle." My voice held a calm I did not feel. "Are you going to watch those monitors, or do I need to find someone who will, give them your rank, and have them clean up your residue?"

The Horde stumbled over his response, "I shall take command."

"If the battle's status changes, contact me immediately."

I did not wait for his acknowledgement, but instead turned and walked toward the center of camp. After providing the Paltas a brief update, I turned to Fillas, the elected leader while the emergency camps were up. "I need your help," I said, and proceeded to tell him about the missing commander. "I require someone to be my guide."

One of the natives who had been standing near us, Figus, immediately offered, "I will." He looked at me solemnly. "My wife and child are alive because of you. I would be honored to help you find your missing ship."

I nodded. "I would appreciate it."

Thus began our search for Kavra's crash. The satellite uplink indicated fifteen fallen ships at various locations around the planet. Eight of those were from our fleet and specifically identified as belonging to a particular commander. Of the remaining ships, four we were able to reach by air and quickly determined they were not Kavra's.

The last three proved more of a challenge. They had each fallen in the middle of deep forest. We landed in a central location, and proceeded to search for the ships on foot.

The first, found after hours of rough terrain hiking, was thankfully not Kavra's vessel; everyone had died from the crash's impact.

The next ship we went in search of was located in the densest part of the forest. We hacked through thick underbrush, and climbed over huge fallen trees, seeking signs of life.

Ahead, two Hordes stood outside the fallen silver ship.

I motioned to my sub-commanders, who nodded in acknowledgment.

We moved forward with more caution; I cringed every time a leaf crunched beneath my feet. The guards stood to the right side of the ship, unfortunately for them, staring in the wrong direction. I slid behind them, using the ship to cover my approach. The laser gun was warm with readiness beneath my fingers.

The two were whispering, and must have been distracted, as I managed to reach them before they realized I was there.

I put the gun against the back of the closest Horde's head. "Don't move!"

The man beside him spun around, but the Slith behind me was ready, and knocked the second Horde's weapon to the ground.

"Turn around, slowly." I took one step back so he could comply.

Situation tense, the Horde did as I had ordered, raising his hands and turning around.

When we made eye-contact, he burst out in relief, "Chrissalynn, thank the gods!"

"Name and rank?"

"Septa 15. I served on your guard detail the last time you visited Kavra."

Uncertain, I asked, "What planet did we stop by on our way home from the trip?"

"Jereitinal. Famous for desserts."

Satisfied, but not yet relieved, I lowered the gun. "Where's Kavra? Is he alive?"

Beside me the Slith and second Horde also relaxed.

"Yes, but he was injured in the crash. The ship's power has been completely knocked out. We don't know how the battle is going, so could not risk walking into enemy lines."

I turned back to take a more thorough look at my surroundings. Black scorched one side of the otherwise silver ship. Trees destroyed by the crash lay on their side, shattered and burnt.

The Indoctrination

"The battle has turned in our favor," I informed Septa 15. "I was sent to find Kavra."

Septa led me into the ship. After only a few turns, I stood in front of the man himself. Kavra sat against an interior wall, a blanket thrown over him for warmth. His eyes were closed as I approached and his blond hair was matted against his forehead.

"Kavra."

He opened his light-blue eyes and blinked, attempting to focus. "Chrissa?"

"Hello, Kavra."

"Am I dead?"

I shook my head.

"You came."

"Of course I did."

"You came yourself?"

"You know me," I replied. "An adventure with certain death assured? I wouldn't miss it."

I knelt down beside him and watched as he tried to straighten. In doing so, the blanket slipped from his shoulders revealing a gash across his upper chest. It appeared a piece of glass had attempted to slice him in two, but failed half-way.

"Kavra…"

"Came for nothing, huh?" How he managed to smile, I did not understand.

"Listen to me. If I came all this way, the least you can do is not die on me. I am going to call a medical transport, have this area cleared, and get you back to the fleet. Do you hear me, Kavra? Don't you dare die on me!"

He coughed. "I thought I was the higher commander here."

"You may be the sixth-in-command of the military, but I'm a spoiled brat who always gets her way. You wouldn't want to ruin my perfect record, would you?"

"Oh no, I wouldn't want to do that." He laughed, then grimaced because laughing hurt.

"Hold on, we'll have you out of here in a few minutes."

I picked up the communication device from my belt and called the main fleet. "Requesting immediate medical support. Priority silver." The code for an injured commander.

"Acknowledged," a voice came through. "I'm sorry, but based on your beacon, it will be at least an hour before we can get to your remote location."

The answer surprised me. "Did you not hear me correctly? Get a fucking transport down here now!"

"We will be there as quickly as we can." The device gave a sharp beep as communications were cut.

After instructing Septa to engage all able-bodied guards in preparing a landing spot, I turned back to Kavra. "They will get here soon. Don't worry."

Silence filled the air, the surrounding forest swallowed every sound, as we waited to hear the engine whine of the rescue ship. I slowly reached my hand toward his, but stopped involuntarily, inches above his skin.

"Chrissa." Kavra drew a labored breath and grasped my hand in his own.

Sitting beside him, I pulled Kavra against my chest. "I'm here. Please, hold on."

Time moved slower than it ever had before. Every minute a horrifying eternity as Kavra's breathing became increasingly ragged.

"I'm sorry, my dear. I don't think I'm going to make it out of this one."

"Don't say that," I protested fiercely.

He coughed, blood splattering my sweater. Kavra jerked back.

"It's okay." I pulled off my outer clothing to reveal the clean black shirt beneath.

He leaned his head back against me. "I'm sorry."

"It's fine. Don't talk." I used my sweater to dab some of the blood from his lips, and then held it tightly against the main wound as a crude compress.

"Chrissa, you need to know how sorry I am. I never should have stayed away..."

"You can apologize later. Preferably with roses, diamonds, and groveling."

The words brought a smile to his pained features.

I turned back to the guard on my left. "Call the fleet again. Tell them it's Kavra."

"They're in the middle of the battle," Kavra chided. "You know the rules, Chrissa. They won't come until it's safe to do so."

I kept my eyes on the guard. "Tell Kasar it's Kavra. Protocol be damned."

He nodded and left to make the call.

"Chrissa—" He fell into another fit of coughing.

Fear clamped my throat making breathing difficult. He was dying in my arms. I closed my eyes, trying to clear my head.

After forcing air down my constricted throat, I said, "Take me."

"What?"

"Take me," I repeated. "I'm un-infested. You can transfer to me, and even if your host dies, you will survive."

Kavra looked at me with a mixture of disbelief and sadness. "Even if I wanted to accept your offer, Chrissa, it's not possible. A Setian cannot transfer from one host to another directly. You know this."

I did know. I wasn't thinking. My left hand flew to the golden chain around my throat in a nervous gesture. As I ran the thin links back and forth between my fingers, my hand touched the glass cylinder, a gift from Councilor Vektor.

"Of course!"

Kavra looked up with tired eyes.

"You have to absorb the water of Setianta before transferring, correct?"

He nodded.

I jerked the chain from my neck, breaking it cleanly in half. "I have some, right here. A gift from the councilors. Use this water and transfer yourself to me."

He glanced at the vial. "Normally I would say that's not enough. However, since the water comes directly from the Setianta Ocean, perhaps…"

"Let's do it."

"Chrissa," he said, wasting time we did not have, "do you know what you are offering?"

"Yes! Now please—"

"No!" He shook his head. "You don't understand. You will have no secrets from me, Chrissa. There will be nothing I will not know." He coughed more blood into his hand, painting his lips crimson. "No memories I will not see, and no thought I will not hear. You will not be able to speak, move, or even draw breath without me allowing it. This cannot be what you want, and I'd rather die than force myself upon you."

I let his argument roll through my mind. I'll be honest, it scared me. But when I glanced down into his light-blue eyes, and tried to imagine a life without him, the thought was unbearable. "I don't care. Please." Tears flowed down my cheeks. "Let me save you." My heart thumped rapidly, fear clutching my body as I waited for his response.

His gaze held mine, and prolonged into a silent battle of wills, both waiting for the other to speak. "Chrissa, I don't think—"

"You are a commander of this empire!" I yelled. "You will not give up your life. Not when I can save you! Let me, Kavra, please. Let me." I forced myself to lower my voice, moving my lips to his left ear. "I can't live without you. Please don't force me to. Kavra, please. I—"

"All right." His voice was hoarse and unsteady. "Okay, Chrissa, you win."

My tears ceased. "Tell me exactly what needs to be done."

"It's rather simple. I will remove myself from my host. When I am completely withdrawn, you will pour the water over my body slowly, so I can absorb it through my skin, covering as much as you can." He drew a deep breath, exhaled, and continued, "You will…"

"Insert you into the new host?" I finished for him.

"Yes."

"Let's do it."

One of Kavra's guards stepped forward "Septa 49. May I be of assistance?"

"Yes. Can you hold him while I pour the water? You will need to be as gentle as possible."

"Of course." The guard, a young man, knelt to the ground in front of me as we watched Kavra remove himself from his host. His thin, gel-like form slipped slowly out of the dying body's left ear.

"Easy now," I cautioned. Once Kavra's clear body was cradled in his hands, I took the vial off the broken chain. The blue water appeared softer in these woods than in the brilliance of the sunlight on the home planet.

Opening the flask, I hunched over the Septa's hands, where Kavra appeared tiny and vulnerable. The realization this creature was the same powerful man was unnerving. I carefully poured the water as evenly as I could, and it seemed to vanish as it touched him. His skin, if you could call it skin, transformed to match the blue of the liquid. When the vial was empty, I glanced at the watch around my wrist. Three minutes. Kavra's body now changed from blue to pink.

"What's happening?"

"Everything is fine," Septa 49 assured me. "He's expelling chemicals from his previous host. It's working."

With his assurance, I remembered Kavra's injured host. I ran inside the ship, searching the emergency medical supply room. Finally, I found what I was looking for, *vlosnof*, which would shut down brain function for a period of several hours, trapping the injected body into a type of stasis, preventing further deterioration. The problem with the chemical was, of course, if you stop all brain function, the Setian inside the host will not survive.

I grabbed two syringes, the chemical, and a bag of universal blood replacement. Returning outside, where Septa held Kavra, I hit my knees beside the host body. He shook violently, likely not only from the injuries, but also I assume the shock of regaining control of his body for the first time in years.

With practiced hands, I inserted the first needle into his vein and began transferring the clear blood replacement. Unable to do anything else to stabilize him, I filled the syringe with vlosnof. "This will put you to sleep," I told the shaking man. "It should give us enough time to save your life."

I moved to inject his right arm. As the needle approached, he jerked his hand from my grasp. "The medicine will help you." I reached for his hand, but he refused to comply. "Is it the needle you don't like?"

He shook his head.

"What?"

"No," he whispered.

"I don't understand."

"No, please."

"It won't hurt. You'll close your eyes, and when you wake up, you will be back on the ship."

I glanced back at Septa 49. Kavra's body was now a clear color, which meant the decontamination process had worked. However, he could only survive a limited amount of time outside of a pool or body.

"No," the host said again. "Please, no more."

"It will make the pain go away," I assured him as I grabbed his arm again.

"No!" His voice sounded panicked. "Let me die!"

Realization dawned. He was not attempting to escape the pain, but instead, the slavery.

"You're a good, sweet girl. Don't do this to me. Please, Chrissalynn, let me die."

I felt sick as I gazed down into Kavra's eyes… No wait! I had to correct myself, not Kavra—his host. Kavra waited for me in the hands of Septa 49. This man was merely the body he had used.

With this justification, I motioned to the Slith on my right. "Hold his arm."

The guard did as ordered and the host screamed. "No! Please, no! Chrissa, please. I am your friend, you love me. Please, Chrissa, stop this. Please, let me go. Please," he sobbed. "You love me."

"No," I said firmly. "I love Kavra, and you are not him." I lined up the needle to his upper arm, sinking it deeply into his flesh, and pressed down on the syringe. Before I'd completed the injection, his eyes closed and his protests ceased. I put the empty needle down and cupped his cheek in my left hand. "It's okay," I whispered. "When you awake, it won't hurt anymore."

I turned back to Septa 49. "How does this work?"

"The best way is for you to lie down. I will place Kavra by your left ear, and he will…"

"Enter me."

Septa nodded.

"Should someone hold me down?"

"I will," one of my personal guards, Sub-Harars 18, volunteered.

Nodding to the Horde, I lay down, moving my hair to the side. "I'm ready."

Septa moved to my side, and I closed my eyes as something cold touched my left ear. I fought to remain still, but struggled to do so as the slimy body slid into my ear canal.

A sharp, stinging pain caused me to cry out, followed by a burning sensation that grew steadily worse as the Setian slid deeper. Another jabbing pain and I jerked, trying to escape the torment. More hands grabbed me.

"Chrissalynn," a voice cut through my panic, "you're saving Kavra's life, remember? Hold on—it's nearly done."

I fought to calm my body. The sensations faded.

My heart slowed and my breathing became more regular.

My eyes opened, but I did not open them.

Chapter XIX

I JERKED IN SURPRISE, BUT my body did not move. Panic set in, my mind not comprehending this new dynamic. I tried to move, but remained motionless on the floor.

"Chrissalynn." The voice was silky and deep, a voice I had never heard before.

I turned my head to the left, seeking the speaker, and this time it moved.

"Chrissa," the voice said again, "it's Kavra. The transfer worked."

"Kavra?" I asked, but the voice echoed only in my mind.

"It's okay, Chrissa. I'm sorry I scared you. I would never purposefully scare you."

"So, this is what it's like?"

"Yes." His voice seemed to hiss through my mind.

With my voice, Kavra announced, "The transfer worked."

The act of speaking without meaning to was startling, and sent a fresh wave of panic through me.

"Relax, Chrissa. It's me, Kavra."

My body stood. A strange sensation, moving without meaning to.

"Stop fighting me," Kavra cautioned.

"Sorry. I'm dizzy."

"It is natural." We walked into the ship and sat down on a chair.

"My lady," a guard said. My head snapped to the left. "Or rather, my lord? Or—"

"Yes," my voice interrupted, "what is it?"

"The fleet called, they should be here within the next few minutes."

"Thank you."

I sat in the chair, elbows on my spread knees, gazing through eyes beyond my control. "Is it really—"

"Yes."

"You don't even know what I was going to ask."

"Actually, I do. I see your thoughts as I see my own. The answer is, yes, it is true that no amount of resistance can give a host back control of their own body. And yes, you are free to try."

"You want me to try to stop you?"

"I want you to learn what it is you are a part of. Try, if you wish."

I attempted to stretch out my left arm. It did not move. I tried harder. "I can't," I admitted.

Kasar appeared before me. "*Congratulations, Harars 3.*"

What? I did not understand what was going on.

"*Your success in the battle of Getrad was worthy of the highest honors. You are aware that this achievement has earned you a reward?*"

"*Yes, Kasar,*" Kavra replied.

"What's happening?"

"You're seeing my memories." Similar to watching a film, only I was in the movie, seeing through Kavra's eyes.

"*In reward, Harars 3, you are hereby promoted to the rank of Setian lord, and placed ninth in command of the military. As is custom, you're allowed to choose a name to accompany your rank.*"

"*I would ask,*" I...no, Kavra, replied, "*for you to choose for me.*"

Kasar gave a nod of consent. "*I would be honored to do so. I bestow upon you the name Kavra of the Setian Empire.*"

"*Thank you, my fellow commanders, councilors, and emperor. I only hope to merit this great honor.*"

"*Live to serve,*" Kasar informed Kavra. "*Die for honor.*"

Kasar disappeared.

I stood aboard a ship's bridge, staring at a pool complex. Turning left, I faced two guards who held a young Horde between them. "*Kavra,*" the guard on the left said, "*this Horde would like to speak with you. I think you will find what he has to say interesting.*"

I took a few steps closer and nodded for the captive to speak.

"*I am from a group in hiding. Ones you will not find, because we'd rather die than submit to infestation.*"

"*Yes.*"

"*What if I told you that I could take you to their hidden location?*"

"*In exchange for what?*"

"*Freedom, for myself and my betrothed. Transport us to whatever planet you deem appropriate, away from the empire, and I will show you where hundreds are hiding.*"

"*For freedom?*"

"*Yes.*"

"*Computer,*" Kavra commanded, "*show us a map.*"

A three-dimensional map of the planet appeared in front of me. I studied the geography through Kavra's eyes and recognized it as the Horde home planet. I had never been there, but had learned much about it throughout my studies.

"*Here.*" The prisoner stepped forward, pointing to a specific place on the map, which was magnified by the touch.

"*Are you sure?*"

"*Yes,*" the Horde replied.

The scene once again faded, but this time instead of moving to a new memory, images flashed through my mind. Troops moving in on the location. Fires lit to drive out the rebels. Screams of those who died in the flames rather than face the Setians. Lasers flew past my body, deafening my hearing and warming my skin. The stench of burning flesh filled the air. Horrific and yet, I could not ignore the immense satisfaction which seemed to flow through my head.

I finally realized these were not my emotions.

"Mine," Kavra confirmed. "The feelings were mine."

"Wow," I whispered.

The images faded and a new landscape took their place.

A lost beach. My handsome father smiling as I built my castle.

"A real princess, daddy?"

Through my eyes, Kavra saw my beautiful sunset, and the tears that ran down my cheeks as I learned of his death a few weeks later.

"You loved him very much."

"Yes." Fresh tears ran down my cheeks as I gazed into my father's deep eyes.

The tears were Kavra's, crying because I could not. Would not. "I never knew."

"He died. Please don't make me relive it."

We skipped ahead to the night of my abduction.

"You had a brother?" Kavra asked, surprised. "What happened to him?"

"I don't know. I haven't seen him since that night."

A new image.

Kavra running around with two little girls close behind, playing in the waters of Setianta.

"My two sisters. Both younger than I."

"Where are they now?"

"Dead," came the short reply. "They died in a battle years ago, achieving the glory they deserved."

"Eternal glory," I whispered. "You must be proud."

"Yes," he lied. "The younger made it to the rank of Harars 5, and died in service to the empire."

I stood over a beautiful young lady, lying peacefully in death. She wore a deep blue gown, and her blond hair had been arranged in curls around her face. Kavra leaned down and kissed her cold, clasped hands. "With your death," Kavra breathed the ancient words, "we forgive you for your sins. Go to glory and to peace, my sister."

"She was beautiful."

"She was," Kavra replied bitterly, "and fearless, not unlike you."

"This is…"

"Amazing," he finished for me.

"Yes. I have never felt more connected to anyone than I do to you right now."

"It can be a beautiful thing, when the host and Setian come to an understanding. We like to encourage both to work toward such a relationship. Hosts born within the empire are taught from birth such a bond is the only way of life.

"Eventually, a species comes to believe Setian history is their own. We prefer to pair hosts who are raised this way with the youngest Setians, so they can hopefully form a binding partnership."

I could see it. Millions of hosts taken by force and bred in captivity. Children raised to believe their sole purpose was to serve the empire. Taught how perfect the symbiotic relationship would one day be between themselves and their Setian superiors. A world where their history had never been separate from that of the Setians. Seeing the potential through Kavra's eyes, I marveled at the simple perfection.

"Let me show you what it can be like," Kavra offered.

Before I could respond, I found myself back on the Earth beach, but this time, I was overwhelmed with a profound sense of pure happiness, the kind which I had not experienced since childhood.

I ran on yet another beach, his sisters close behind me. We splashed in the blue water, waves cooling our feet.

Lying in a pool on Setianta, laughing at whatever joke Kavra had thrown my way.

Memory after memory flashed before me, each filled with happiness and fleeting joy. Joy had become something physical that could be touched. A blanket wrapped around my mind, embracing me with happiness. I was warm, safe, and loved inside the power of Kavra's mind.

Chapter XX

I STOOD INSIDE KASAR'S MEDIEVAL mansion on Setianta, engaged in a conversation that I had never been a part of.

"*She was born human, and a part of her is human yet. Their ways are not ours. To do this to her...*" Kavra shook his head.

"*She will learn,*" Kasar informed him. "*You will help her to understand.*"

"*Nicholas, you can't do this to—*"

"*Careful, Kavra. I can, and I will.*"

"*I love her,*" Kavra's voice spoke with as much intensity as I had ever heard. "*I will not watch you do this to her.*"

"*Then don't!*" came Kasar's brisk response. "*I'll send you to the Seltas system.*"

"*Please, if you would hear me—*"

"*No,*" Kasar cut him off. "*You may hold her heart, Kavra, but never forget...she belongs to me.*" He paused and cleared his throat. "*Leave for Seltas immediately.*"

The scene changed.

We had finished dinner in Kasar's private chambers. His arms held me tightly as we swayed to soft music across the dance floor.

"*You are mine.*" His words echoed across my memories. "*Kavra will be safe, as long as you belong to me.*"

The implied threat unmistakable.

"*I'm sorry,*" Kavra whispered, "*I am so sorry, my love.*"

I OPENED MY EYES TO find myself lying on a bed between a set of clean white sheets. I sat up startled. My head spun with a sharp pain. I turned in time to find the silver basin and spewed vomit.

Kasar, who had been standing by the bed, moved forward and held back my hair. It took several minutes before I could once again lie back down. A maid appeared and placed a cool cloth on my forehead.

"Where's Kavra? Is this another memory?" I asked softly.

"No," Kasar replied.

I cleared my throat. "What's wrong with me?"

"It is a natural reaction. Many people find themselves sickened by infestation."

"Where's Kavra?"

"Kavra kept you in *rephta*, a Setian term for the memory wrap, while the rescue ships picked you up and brought you back to the main fleet. Kavra's original host survived, thanks to you, and Kavra has returned to his body. What you did was very brave, Chrissalynn. I'm proud of you."

"Where is he?"

"Here," a voice replied. I moved my head slowly to the left. Across the room was another bed on which Kavra lay. "I'm all right. Just tired."

"Trading hosts so quickly has left him exhausted, and the host is recovering. I tried to convince him to remain with you for a while, but he insisted on allowing you to return to freedom as quickly as possible."

"You should have forced him to stay."

"You know how Kavra is."

My head pounded painfully.

"Lie still," Kasar cautioned.

"She's really taking it badly," I heard Kavra say. "I'm sorry."

"Yes," Kasar replied. "Normally it is not this bad, but the rephta made it worse." He turned toward me and adjusted my pillows. "Lying down will help, and I'll dim the lights. You'll feel better after some rest."

The next few hours were miserable. At some point, doctors came in with Kasar to take my temperature.

"She's running a fever," the physician said, before giving me an injection. "To help you sleep."

KAVRA LAY AGAINST THE SIDE of the wrecked ship, blood gushing from his chest. I rushed forward, skidding to my knees, which sank into a pool of thick blood. I peeled off my sweater, pushing the material to his chest, yet the blood spread, coloring the fabric as I tried in vain to stop the outpour.

"Kavra!" I pleaded. "Please!"

My efforts had little effect. Blood seeped from the corner of his lips, and his chest rose and fell as his lungs refused to gather the breath required to live.

Tears wet my cheeks, falling uncontrollably. "Please, Kavra. Don't go. Stay with me!"

"Chrissa!" Kavra's voice cut through the nightmare. "Wake up!"

I opened my eyes, jerking to a seated position. An act I immediately regretted as the pounding grew worse.

Sluggish, with cold and clammy skin, I turned to Kavra, who stood beside my bed.

"A nightmare," he explained.

He sat down on the bed's edge and I wrapped my arms around him. He returned the embrace, hissing as I pressed against his injuries.

"Sorry," I said, but did not pull away, touching my cheek to the side of his neck. "I dreamed I had arrived too late. That you were—"

"I'm here," he soothed. "Thanks to you."

I trembled, earlier illness replaced by chills and fatigue. Kavra moved to lay me on the bed, but I struggled, clinging to him.

He pulled back the blankets and maneuvered me enough to climb in beside me. Once reclined, he tucked me against his chest, careful to avoid direct contact with the still-healing gash.

"Kavra," I said his name on a shivering breath as he secured the blankets around us. "I'm sorry."

"Don't apologize." He adjusted so I lay more comfortably, curling into his offered warmth.

When my shaking ceased, he traced his fingers through the locks of my hair. "Chrissa," he whispered, "it breaks my heart to have hurt you. I wish there had been another way."

"You didn't hurt—"

"I did," he insisted. "The last thing I wanted to do."

I twisted to meet his concerned blue eyes and confessed, "No pain I've endured would have been as horrid as waking to a world without you."

My words brought tears to the surface of his eyes, but they did not fall. Instead he offered a tight smile.

"Hold me, William. Please."

He nodded, leaning down to press his lips against my forehead when I closed my eyes.

As I drifted back to sleep, the words *I love you* echoed on an undrawn breath.

Chapter XXI

Days later, the Sentiles officially surrendered. Better, but not back to full-duty, I was reclined on a couch near Kavra's bed, glancing over recent battle reports, when Kasar's entrance caused me to set the papers aside.

"Chrissalynn," he said, "I thought you might want to know official numbers have arrived concerning native lives lost in the battle."

My heart beat faster, my mind racing with horrible potential.

"Zero. Not one single Palta native was killed during the battle."

"Oh my…"

"Congratulations, Chrissalynn."

"Thank you," I replied. *We had saved them all.*

"Tell me," he said, taking a seat beside me, "when communications went down, what was your first thought?"

"There wasn't much thinking involved. I turned to my commanders, issued orders, learned what needed to be done, and did it."

He leaned forward and kissed me. "When communications went down, I wasn't worried. I realized there was no one I trusted more than you. You have made me very proud, Chrissalynn, very proud."

"Thank you. I was—"

"Well, what do we have here?" a loud, rough voice interrupted.

We both turned as a Horde walked through the infirmary. With the usual pig-like nose, and an ugly, wide mouth, at eight feet tall, he towered above us.

Kavra's bed stood between us and the door, and the loud, unfamiliar voice brought him out of his sleep. He turned his head toward the new visitor.

"Jetreal," Kasar addressed him.

"Kasar," he replied curtly, before addressing me in a mocking tone, "*Lady Kasar.*"

Jetreal should not have been here. The council had stationed him in the Rementil quadrant, at least a three day journey, even at top speed. "What are you doing here?" I asked.

"He was found on planet," Kasar answered.

"I came to help." He made the word sound like something foul.

"He arrived when the communications were down." This from Nicholas, whose eyes were studying Jetreal intently.

"Yes, and I engaged in battle anyway, only to crash onto the planet. I spent three days down in that filthy place. Evidently, I'm not as important as *some* people."

"Had I been aware you were stranded, we would have sent scouts for you as well."

"Like you knew Kavra was stranded?" He walked to the bed.

I moved, placing myself between Kavra and Jetreal.

"You wouldn't dare."

He stopped within arm's reach.

"This is not your ship, and you are not the highest-ranking person in this room. You're not even the second-highest."

"And you are important? Ha!" he scoffed. "You hold no title; you are not even a member of this empire."

"Oh really? I would have sworn you called me, 'Lady Kasar.'"

We glared at each other.

"Tell me, Jetreal, on the planet, you didn't happen to see anyone else, did you?"

"What do you mean?"

I stepped to the side so I could see both Nicholas and Jetreal at the same time. "The communications disruption device had to be programmed to the exact frequency we use in order for it to work. My understanding is only commanders of high rank know the specific frequency."

"You dare!" Jetreal moved a step closer.

Kavra and Kasar both called, "Jetreal!" in a warning tone.

He froze and stepped back.

"Enough," Kasar said. "I'm sure Kavra is touched by your concern, but he really must rest now."

Kasar escorted Jetreal out of the room.

"Chrissa," Kavra called softly.

I turned around. "Don't worry about it. Rest now."

He nodded. "Thanks for getting me out of there."

"My pleasure."

The following day, Kavra was transferred to Setianta. Kasar put me in charge of the infestation of captured Sentile forces. I had nearly completed the job when I was summoned to appear before the Setian council.

Chapter XXII

WHEN WE LANDED BACK on Setianta, I was ordered directly to the council chambers. As I reached the door, I was sure the council members would be able to hear my heart pounding clear across the room.

Kasar walked me to the door, but would not be allowed to accompany me inside. "I will see you back at the mansion," he told me.

As I entered the chamber, I knelt and bowed my head low until a voice said, "Arise." I stood, but the movement was far from graceful.

In front of me sat the thirteen councilors, all dressed in black.

"Councilors," I said in a voice far too soft, "you sent for me?"

"Yes," a feminine voice replied from the left. I turned to see a tall woman with piercing emerald eyes. "Kasar tells us his recent victory over the Sentiles was, in large part, the result of your leadership. Would you agree?"

Startled, I paused before responding, "I was in charge of the ground forces. Kasar led the main fleet."

"Yes," Councilor Vektor cut in, "but you restored sabotaged communications, lost only twenty-four of sixty-five ships fighting a force greater than your own, saved Kavra's life, and somehow managed to not lose a single native in the process. Is this correct?"

"Your information is accurate, Councilor."

"Do you know why you are here?"

"No, Councilor, I do not."

"Allow me to enlighten you. We have summoned you here to inform you we are aware of the glorious job you have been doing, and the superior training you've received. Your quick thinking, and strategy, on Palta saved the entire fleet. Kasar believes you are ready to venture out on your own, despite your youth. What do you think of this evaluation?"

"I…" I took a breath in an attempt to keep from stuttering. "I am not sure what to say."

"This council has come to the same conclusion. We believe you are ready to lead, not only on your own, but with the rank and title deserved by one who has successfully given us not one, but two victories over major empire threats.

"Chrissalynn, we bestow upon you, in your own right, the rank of a Setian commander, along with the name of Dehartra. You are hereby granted the fifth-highest commission within Setian command. In addition, Nicholas shall also be promoted to the highest position available under the council, for his extraordinary work with you."

Silence followed this statement as I stood dumbfounded.

Vektor broke into a smile. "I knew you were one to watch since the crazy 'infest their pets' plan you came up with all those years ago."

"Thank you," I finally managed to say. "Thank you so much."

Vektor stepped down from the panel and approached me. "Come with me, Dehartra."

My mind in a daze, I focused on not stumbling as I walked down the corridor behind him. After a few turns, we stepped through a door and entered a vast lounge. Portraits of current and past council members lined the blue walls on both sides.

A bottle of champagne waited on a wooden table with crystal flutes. At his invitation, I took a seat beside the table while Vektor poured the golden liquid. Accepting the offered glass, I eyed the councilor.

"Congratulations, Chrissalynn." He leaned forward and touched the side of his flute to my own.

"Thank you, Councilor Vektor."

"I wanted to offer my personal congratulations for your success in battle, and of course, thanks for Kavra's life."

"Don't thank me, Councilor."

He nodded.

A third man I did not recognize appeared.

"Dehartra," Vektor addressed me, seeing my puzzlement, "this is Councilor Sorid."

"Oh, forgive me, Councilor. I did not recognize your new host."

"Quite all right. I'm getting used to it myself."

I turned to Vektor expectantly.

"Do you remember what I once told you, about choices and consequences?"

"Yes, Councilor."

"Well," Vektor replied, seeming to select his words carefully, "sometimes there are also rewards."

"Rewards?"

He nodded.

"For the victory you gave us," Councilor Sorid stated, "it is customary for you to name your reward."

I looked back to Vektor, who gave the slightest of nods.

Shifting from my chair, I knelt down to one knee before the councilors. "Prior to this promotion, which you have so graciously seen fit to bestow upon me, I was set to assist in the conquest of future Setian Colony 428. With your permission, Councilors, I would like to continue with these plans, and request Kavra be sent there as well."

This seemed to surprise Vektor. "428? Are you sure, Dehartra?"

I did not hesitate. "Yes, Councilor."

"As you wish," Sorid informed me, "so it shall be."

I stood from my kneeling position. "Thank you, Emperor."

He nodded and turned toward the doors. "We expect great things from you," he said over his shoulder before leaving the chambers.

"He is not one to grant such requests lightly," Vektor informed me.

"Thank you, Councilor."

"Chrissa," he broke formality, "do you remember what I said about having to make a choice?"

I looked up at him.

He leaned forward and pressed his lips to my left cheek. "You just made it."

Chapter XXIII

When I left the councilor's chambers, I was informed by a guard that Kavra had requested my presence at his estate on Setianta. A far cry from Kasar's Gothic castle, Kavra's manor was a modern marvel. Glass dome ceilings filtered the light of Setianta's three suns, flooding the room with brilliant color, from bright yellows, to dazzling blues, and neon greens. The only fireplace in the entire house was in my room, which Kavra had installed especially for the visits I had enjoyed as a young girl.

Arriving outside the glass doors, I was quickly ushered inside and into a bedroom. Kavra sat on the bed against the wall, reviewing paperwork.

When I called his name, he looked up from his reports and smiled. "Hello, Chrissa."

"You sound much better."

"Thanks to you. Though, I still resent you giving me orders when I clearly outrank you."

"You mean you *did* outrank me."

He stared, tilting his head. "You mean…they finally?"

I nodded.

"Well, it's about time!" He gave a mock bow from his seated position. "My esteemed Setian Lady…"

"Dehartra Kasar."

He straightened. "Dehartra?"

"Yes."

"Well." He cleared his throat. "I suppose a more serious level of congratulations is in order. No one has been given that name since the emperor himself. It's the highest of honors."

I smiled. "Thank you."

He motioned me forward. "I have a gift for you."

I walked toward him and sat down in a chair beside the bed.

"My sister, as you know, died." He held out his hand.

I leaned forward in the chair to get a better view of the golden ring held in his palm.

"This ring was hers, and very special. My sister wore it every day until she died. I have carried it with me ever since. I would like for you to have it."

"Kavra, I can't."

"Yes, you can. My sister received this ring as a gift for the life she had saved. During this battle, you did the same for me. It's only a simple gold circle, but to me it holds a world of meaning. It would be my honor if you would accept this token from me."

I stared into his pale blue eyes. "William," I used his first name, "what you're offering means more to me than you can imagine."

He reached for my left hand and slid the ring securely on my third finger. "A perfect fit."

"I want you to know..." But words failed me.

Kavra shook his head and leaned forward, offering a soft, chaste kiss. When he pulled back, he was unable to hide the sorrow in his eyes.

I slipped down to one knee beside the bed. Kavra touched my cheek, and I pressed his hand against my skin. Eyes closed, I drew a deep breath, and forced a smile to my lips before meeting his gaze. "Thank you, Kavra. I shall wear it always."

He pulled me close, pressing his cheek against my own. "I never should have left."

"You didn't have a choice."

"He used me to take you to his bed. To force..."

I pushed back, his broken words pulling at the heart I was not meant to have. "Kavra, please. That memory...it was not meant for you."

"But I saw. And worse..." His eyes moved to stare at the floor. "Chrissa, I knew. I knew what he planned to do and I let...I loved you, and I allowed him to..." He shook his head. "I'm sorry, Chrissa."

"Kavra," unshed tears seeped into my voice, "it doesn't matter."

"Chrissa—"

"You were in my head, William. You know what I've said is true. Please, you're alive, and you're here. I don't..." I pressed my chin to my chest, eyes squeezing shut of their own accord. "You're here," I said again. "You're alive. I thought...I was afraid, Kavra. So afraid I would never see you again. That you—"

"I'm more sorry for scaring you than I will ever be able to express." His fingers traced down my neck, raising my gaze back to his. Then he kissed me, an expression that contained words I knew could never be spoken. The kiss lingered, and deepened, before we both had to draw breath.

When he leaned in for a second kiss, I stopped him, pressing a hand to his lips as my first tear materialized.

"Chrissa," the word a painful sound.

"I can't," I told him. "My love almost cost me your life."

"That's not true."

"It is. My love is a threat to your life, William. If I stay with you, it's the price we shall both pay." My body trembled. "If I tell you I love you, if I show you how much I care, how I dream of being with you every night, it will cost me your life. And that is a price I am not willing to pay."

Leaning forward, I pressed my tears into his shirt as he wrapped his arms around me. "I want to stay. I want to fall asleep listening to the steady rhythm of your heart. I missed you, and was so angry when you left. I didn't understand. I'm sorry." I shook my head, pulling back. "Don't you see? I can't do this. Living without you—it's too painful."

Tears fell faster, my voice matching his sorrow. "Forgive me, William."

"Chrissa, please, stay."

"If I do, they'll send you away, and I can't let that happen. I'm sorry, my love. I can't live without you anymore." I stood and left the room without another word.

I left Kavra, but did not return directly to Kasar. Instead, I took a transport down to the Setian beach, my final request of Councilor Vektor.

Mid-afternoon, the first of Setianta's three suns eased from the sky. I removed my shoes and walked slowly to the water's edge. As the waves danced over my bare feet, I closed my eyes and allowed my mind to wander back.

"Will you make me a princess, Daddy?"

The next wave crashed upon the golden sand.

"A choice to make," Vektor whispered. *"A human heart with a Setian soul."*

"You are mine." Kasar's voice rose on the cold ocean wind.

"A real princess, Daddy?"

The wind blew harder, whistling the fleeting words in my ears.

I ran my fingers through my hair.

Kavra's turn. *"I'm sorry, my love."*

"Stop it," I said, tears gathering in the corners of my eyes.

"A human heart with a Setian soul. A choice to make."

"Stop!" I said again.

"A Setian soul."

"Stop!" I screamed, falling to my knees in the coarse sand. My voice carried across the empty beach, pulled by the powerful Setian winds.

I have no idea how long I knelt there, staring into the blue water as the wind saturated my skin.

I closed my eyes and could see my tall, handsome father; the light in his golden brown eyes.

"I'm sorry, Daddy. I can't be your princess anymore."

Chapter XXIV

THE YEAR I TURNED TWENTY-ONE, I was assigned to help Kasar in his conquest of future Setian Colony 428, known as Earth. As I saw what had once been my home planet, I expected emotions to build within me, but they did not. Strangely, this planet seemed no different from any other.

I met Kasar down by the secret Setian pool, deep beneath Earth's surface. There, he greeted me with a smile. "Greetings, Chrissalynn, and may I congratulate you on your recent promotion."

"Thank you. I find third-in-command has a much nicer ring than fifth."

He nodded. "Everything is going according to plan."

"Good to hear, though I never assumed it would be otherwise."

Developing smoothly, of course, because the people of Earth had no idea they were slowly, one-by-one, being dragged beneath their planet's surface and into the Setian pool. A quiet battle, which we were winning easily, because most humans did not know they were at war. Observing a new group of subjects being placed into cages, to wait their turns to be infested, I was pleased at how orderly things were progressing. As I watched, I felt pity, but not for humans being infested. Instead, my sad regret was based on the fact they were not good enough, not strong enough, to protect themselves.

My attention was drawn to a young girl standing alone in one of the left cages. Probably fourteen years old, and so scared she was shaking. The guard opened the door and grabbed her, paying no mind to her fear or youth.

"No," she screamed. "Please, no!"

Another guard, waiting at the pool, helped the first to bend her over the edge, pushing her head into the water. She struggled, but those holding her were too strong.

I stepped close enough to see her face, eyes wide with terror through the clear liquid, as a Setian swam toward her. Once infested, her head was jerked back, and she tried to escape with her last few moments of freedom before the Setian gained control.

Abruptly, she stopped screaming, stood, and calmly walked away.

As it happened, our invasion had been discovered by a select group, and an underground resistance had formed. While they achieved minimal lasting damage, they were a continual nuisance. Little problems tend to add up. As our invasion reached a climax, I realized this resistance had to be defeated before victory could be claimed.

One day, an opportunity arose. Lukare 15, who had infested a human host early-on in our attack, discovered the resistance's headquarters in an Arizona town. Remote, it had been the perfect place to remain undetected, until he stumbled upon one of their leaders.

Lukare's host was infested, but his family was not. To keep up appearances, he took them on the same vacation they took every year. Lukare drove from his home in Dallas to California, with his wife and daughter, stopping for the night at a motel in Arizona. At a local restaurant, he spotted a man he believed to be Ryan, one of the few known to our forces as a resistance coordinator. Lukare excused himself, stepped outside, and put in a call to Harars 18.

After midnight, Kasar had issued orders not to be disturbed. Jetreal, after a recent promotion, was second-in-command, with Nicholas a step above him. Jetreal tended to be surly, and guards avoided him, so news of this possible sighting came directly to me.

I was lying on my bed, plotting our next attack of the Lorid home world, when a knock sounded at my door. "Come in," I called.

"Dehartra," one of my guards stated, bowing low before me, "a report has come in from Earth. Lukare 15 believes he may have found Ryan Shore in a restaurant."

"Where?"

"Arizona."

"Where is Jetreal?"

"On his ship, I assume."

"Open a communication on the main deck, and request a virtual audience with him. I believe he will want to know this."

The guard bowed and left the room.

I followed a few minutes later, and as I stepped into the communications room, a 3D version of Jetreal filled the holospace. He had decided against taking a human body, instead maintaining the form of a Horde with their incredible strength, short fur, and pig-looking nose. His choice of host spoke volumes. This was a creature who had no use for finesse, and believed brute strength solved everything. How he was possibly ranked above me, I would never understand.

"This had better be important," he grumbled in strongly-accented Setian language. His eyes were blinking. Had he been sleeping on his night in charge?

"A report arrived: one of our men, Lukare 15, believes he has found Ryan Shore."

"Ryan who?"

I resisted the urge to shake my head as I answered, "Ryan Shore, third-in-command of the Earth resistance forces. Lukare believes he has found him in a town in Arizona."

"Where?"

"Southwestern United States."

"You're telling me some nobody randomly happened to find rebel forces, after they have eluded our best trackers for over a year? Rubbish!"

"I agree it is unlikely, but surely not impossible. Someone should investigate."

"A waste of resources and time."

"I'll do it myself."

"You think," he growled, "because Nicholas favors you, you can get away with whatever you wish."

"Kasar has nothing to do with this," I replied sharply. "A report has come in, and I think it should be investigated."

"Don't play dumb with me! I am perfectly aware why you hold the title you do. I wonder if you have ever been told *no* in your entire life? Well, it starts now! You're not to go down to the planet, do you understand? That's an order!"

I narrowed my eyes, anger heating my words, "For your information, people have told me 'no' before. They've just never lived long enough to tell about it."

"Are you threatening me?"

"I'm teaching you."

"Stay on your ship!" he said one more time as he cut the transmission.

Kavra appeared beside me. Assigned as one of my consultants for the upcoming attack on the Lorid home world, he was spending a few nights on my ship. "What you are thinking is dangerous, even for you."

I nodded.

"If you're wrong, you could lose everything. But if you're going to do this, I will go with you."

"I can't ask you to."

"You don't have to. An adventure with certain death assured? Sounds like fun."

I couldn't help but smile. "Captain," I called, "gather a task force with only human hosts."

"Right away."

A few minutes later, Kavra, I, and a small group of discretely dressed guards stepped out into the Arizona night.

I took a breath of the warm, dry air.

"Where's Lukare?" I asked.

"Local hotel," came the reply. "He's waiting on us."

We walked down the street lit by dim lamps until we came to the motel only a few blocks away. When we entered the lobby, a thin man with glasses came up to meet us.

"Lukare 15?" I asked.

He nodded. "It sounds crazy to say I ran into him like this, but I'm sure it's him. He has the same eyes, the same hair and," he paused, looking for the word, "mannerism."

"Do you know where he went after leaving the restaurant?"

"Yes. He has a home, two houses down from here. By the way, you responded awfully fast. Who are you?"

"I am Dehartra, servant to the empire, third-in-command." I smiled. "Any other questions?"

What little color Lukare's cheeks held seemed to disappear.

I turned to my guards. "Hand me a *casdael*." The Setian word for gun.

He complied.

"You," I motioned to Lukare, "are going to point out this house to me. Then return to these men while I go see for myself if this is the man we have been searching for."

"What about my host's family?"

"They'll be taken care of," I replied before addressing my guards. "Call in additional forces, and have Lukare's family infested immediately, but," I added hastily, "call those forces in from an Earth-based location. No outer planet communication whatsoever."

I turned to the informant. "As for you, Lukare 15, if you are right about who this man is, you shall be promoted immediately. On the other hand, if you are wrong..." I let my voice trail off. "Now, which house am I going to?"

He pointed to a one-story home with a blue front porch.

Kavra stepped up beside me. "So what's the plan? Should I surround the house and send a force to take down whoever is inside? Or do you want that job?"

"Actually," I replied, "I thought I'd go knock on the door."

His eyes shifted from the house to my face. "You're serious!"

I smiled. "We are not here to take anyone down tonight. We're merely verifying a report. All I want to know is if the man in the house is Ryan or not."

"And?"

"Taking down the third-in-command is not exactly what I have in mind."

"You never did like being second-best."

"Think about it, Kavra. If I capture Ryan Shore, I'll get a pat on the back. But if I were to take down Darin Hoyle?"

"The resistance would be over," Kavra finished.

"Jetreal would be demoted for ordering us not to come. Councilor Selorim will be executed for promoting Jetreal to a top position in the first place. And we will become first on the promotion list to the council itself."

Silence followed before Kavra said, "You're a special kind of crazy. Go knock on the door already."

After stuffing the gun down my pants, I pushed my hair back from my face, walked down the street, and up the steps to the front porch. Glancing over my shoulder, I ensured none of my team were visible before knocking on the door.

A woman answered. "May I help you?"

"Hi, is Ryan here?"

"No," she replied. My heart sank to the floor. "He's out for the evening."

"Do you know where he might be? I really need to speak with him."

"Sure," she replied. "Thursday nights are dance nights down at the local bar and grill. Only one in town, so it shouldn't be too hard to find."

I offered a smile and said, "Thanks!"

As I turned to walk back down the steps the door closed with a soft click behind me.

After walking at a steady pace for several blocks, until I was sure no one standing at the window of the house would be able to see me, I stopped, and Kavra was immediately at my side.

"What's the verdict?"

"The verdict," I answered, "is I need to change into boots."

"Excuse me?"

"I need boots. Black, high-heeled, snakeskin boots. Where are my captains?"

Two men stepped forward.

"I'm going out to a bar tonight, western style, but I'm not dressed appropriately. What I really need..." I paused to think.

"Forgive me, but you are going to a what?"

"A bar," I repeated. "I need some snakeskin boots, a western style shirt, a belt with a buckle, and a pair of Rockies."

"You want some rocks?" The guard beside him shrugged. "How many rocks would you like?"

"No, not rocks. Rockies, as in Rocky Mountain jeans. You do know what jeans are, don't you?"

"Yes, Dehartra," said the guard on the left.

"We have a disguise designer on staff. Have her bring me a pair, along with an appropriate shirt, and make them tight."

"How tight?" This from Kavra, of course.

I returned his teasing smile. "So tight I have to lie down to zip them up." I turned back to the guard. "I'll also need a western belt with an elaborate gold buckle. Oh, and some cash."

They bowed.

"Don't forget to mention the boots!" I called after them as they left to follow my orders.

I had made a point to always keep someone on ship who was up-to-date in the latest fashions on different worlds. I had brought Septa 19 with me this time. Jeans would be a stretch, but she would at least know what I was talking about, and able to direct my guards to the correct place to procure what I had asked for.

In the meantime, I returned to the transport. When my guards arrived with Septa, she did not disappoint. Thirty minutes later I stood in front of a mirror staring at my new outfit. A black Stetson hat, that I hadn't even thought to ask for, sat upon my ebony hair, which hung loose and curly beneath it. Above the open collar of my red, long-sleeved shirt, my neck was circled by a silver choker, and silver earrings hung from both ears. I took shallow breaths, adjusting to the tightness of my deep blue Rocky Mountain jeans, which were tucked into black snakeskin boots. Now all I needed was the belt.

Covered with sequins, the gold buckle arrived a few minutes later.

I laughed and shook my head. "Well it's...certainly elaborate, but not quite what I had in mind."

The guards appeared uncomfortable. "Don't worry, I should have been more specific. Kavra?" He had walked in laughing at the sight of the sequin belt. "Do you mind helping them, please?"

"Sure thing." He took my guards outside and explained what I was asking for.

A half-hour later, I was handed a wide western buckle, on a black belt, much more appropriate than the last one.

I left the ship and was surprised to find Kavra, in a white, long-sleeved shirt with the top few buttons undone, waiting for me outside. His blue jeans, I was willing to bet, were as tight as mine.

I smiled before asking, "Where do you think you're going?"

"Following my leader. What kind of a second would I be if I let you go in there without backup?"

"Okay, you can walk down there with me, but I want you to stay outside."

"I don't understand."

"This is a small town," I replied. "The chances of two completely different strangers walking into the bar on the same night are next-to-none. If I need you, it's great you're dressed for the part, but for right now, let me go in alone."

"My necklace," I touched the silver chain, "has been implanted with a transmitter." I handed him a small earpiece. "You will be able to hear everything going on while I am in there."

This late at night, the bar was the only place open. My guards followed me to the parking lot before dispersing to ensure all the exits were covered, and they would have easy, quick access into the building if necessary.

A typical, tired dive, the half-burnt-out flashing neon arrow blinked above the Sportsman Lounge's roofline. From inside, various neon beer signs lit the outside windows, and a tattered Pepsi poster adorned the entry.

The door had been propped open by a wooden stool that looked like it hadn't been used for anything else in quite a while. Plastering a smile on my face, I stepped into the smoke-filled room.

On my immediate right, against the wall, were two arcade games, which no one was playing. Between groups enjoying a couple of pool tables in the back, and pairs scattered amid round tables throughout, I counted about thirty or so people. Music drowned out a majority of the voices; a country song, though not one I could hope to identity. On my left, in the center of the space, a row of eight stools stood beside the bar, of which only three were occupied.

Shortly after I settled onto one of the vacant bar seats, a lady who appeared to be in her mid-thirties slid over from behind the bar. "Howdy. I've never seen you around here before."

"Passing through," I replied.

"Well, what can I get 'ya?"

I glanced behind her. A chipped mirror hung over a sink, in desperate need of cleaning from all the smoke in the air. Nine fountains lined the back counter, each offering a different brand of beer. The lowest wooden shelves were filled with glasses. Bottles of gin, rum, and hard liquors lined upper shelves, offering a relief from solitude. "How about a Beam Me Up, Scotty?"

"Sure thing, honey."

As she poured my drink, my eyes wandered to the dance floor on the opposite side of the bar. Fifteen or so people moved in lines across the floor, with varying degrees of uniformity. I watched in fascination. Though I had been taught various forms of dance, from countless planets across the empire, this group dancing proved entirely unfamiliar.

"Here you are," the bartender said as she placed the drink in front of me.

Ignoring the crack in the glass' side, I fished in my pocket for a twenty dollar bill, and placed it on the counter. "I don't suppose you get many visitors?"

She shrugged. "Close neighbors sometimes."

"Do you know a Ryan?" I asked, trying to make the question as casual as possible.

"Afraid not. What does he look like?"

I described him.

"Oh wait, do you mean Brian? I must not have heard you right. Sure, he's lived in these parts about two years."

Since the start of the resistance, I thought.

"He's nice enough, not disliked by anyone, but rather quiet; keeps to his own company."

"Oh? What kind of company?"

"A group of friends; he's here with them tonight. I used to try to get him to notice me, but after I saw the girl he was with…" She motioned over to one of the tables by the dance floor.

A familiar-looking svelte blond, drinking beer, laughed at something the man beside her had said. As my gaze traveled to her grinning companion, my breath caught.

Not the individual I had asked about, but her companion had sandy brown hair. Standing, he would reach six-foot-one, and in the light his eyes would appear more gold than brown. I knew who he was, because his was another face I had seen every night before closing my eyes, his picture posted on my "most wanted" wall, directly across from the bed.

The bartender sighed. "That's Kyle. Handsome isn't he?"

"You're telling me."

"Brian's the one on the dance floor. He sure loves to dance."

I picked up my drink and took a sip as I searched the floor. Ah, there he was, near the front of the line. Slowly sipping my drink, glad I'd taken a pill to prevent the alcohol from affecting me, I waited for an opportunity.

When the song ended, Ryan took a seat while Kathleen and Darin took his place on the floor. I turned back to the bartender. "Does Mr. Brian have a usual beverage?"

"Yep."

"I'd like to buy him a round of whatever he's drinking."

She returned the smile I hadn't realized was on my face. "Sure thing."

I watched as a waitress delivered the drink, and Ryan looked up surprised as she pointed me out. He waved uncertainly as he accepted.

My own drink in hand, I sauntered over to the table. As I reached a chair beside him, I tossed a strand of hair back over my shoulder. "May I?"

"Please." He indicated the chair beside him.

"How are you this fine night?" I asked, settling into the offered seat.

"Pretty good," he replied, trying to figure out who I was. "And you?"

"Fantastic," I said, drawing out the word.

He gave up. "I'm sorry, who are you?"

"Chris," I replied. "I'm new to these parts, and noticed you alone over here while your friends were on the floor. Thought I might introduce myself."

"Well," he said, taking a drink, "I certainly like your way of saying hello. I'm Brian."

"Pleased to meet you." *At last*, I added silently.

"How long have you been here?" His speech was slurred, and the smell of alcohol clung to his breath.

"I've been coming and going," I lied. "House-hunting at the moment."

"Why here? If you don't mind me asking."

I shrugged, figuring out answers as I went. "A complicated story, but to make it simple, I came into some money and decided to disappear for a while. Figure out my next steps, you know? And besides," I added, "beautiful out here."

"I don't know. It's hot; hundred degrees yesterday."

I tilted my head and took a breath of smoke-filled air. "I don't mind the heat. I had enough cold in…Chicago."

"Chicago, huh?"

We spent the next few songs talking about the weather, the area, and other mundane topics.

Until we were interrupted by a voice asking, "Who's your friend?"

I turned, heart beating too fast, and looked up into Darin Hoyle's eyes.

"Chris, I'd like you to meet Kyle and Kathy."

I ignored the lie, and shook hands in turn with Darin and Kathleen. "Glad to meet you both." *If you only knew.*

Darin and Kathleen, whom I had now placed as another face on the empire's most wanted list, sat down with us. I waved at a waiter, and flashing a handful of twenties, ordered a round of drinks for everyone to a chorus of thank yous. Not much of a plan, but I hoped keeping the drinks flowing would ensure people kept talking.

To my surprise, several rounds later, Darin asked, "So, Chris, since you are planning to move here, what do you think about those Rockies?"

I looked at him, wondering if he was less intoxicated than I originally thought. The answer was a fact few Setians would know. "Well, I would have to say I hate them, since they are one of the chief rivals to the Diamondbacks."

"You're a baseball fan?" he asked.

"No," I replied, "my brother was."

"So," Ryan asked, changing the subject as the waitress brought yet another round for everyone, "you said you were wealthy, huh? How wealthy?" Clearly alcohol had muted his social filters.

"Wealthy enough." An idea hit me. "Nothing extraordinary, but well, I've always been a kind of car collector."

Ryan sat up straighter. "What kind of cars, exactly?"

"Well," I replied with a smile, "my favorite is a vintage 1957 Corvette. White with red interior, and all original, except for the engine, which has been altered with a few…special upgrades."

"No way!" Ryan said. "You're playing with me."

I shook my head. "No really. In fact," I added, "do you want to see it?"

"Wait, you mean, it's here?" he asked with a look of awe on his face.

"Of course," I grinned, "wouldn't drive anything else." I sounded excited even to myself. "Do you want to see it?"

"Heck yeah!"

"I want to come too!" Darin sounded equally enthusiastic.

"Sure thing. I hate to admit this, but I love showing off my car. It's parked on the left side of the building." I bent my head down to ensure my security detail would hear my voice in the microphone. "Want to head outside?"

Both men were on their feet before I finished with the question.

"Guess so."

Kathleen and I followed at a leisurely pace, the excited boys in front of us.

"A real '57," I heard Ryan say, as if he were a kid being handed a new toy.

Darin cracked some joke a few seconds later, and we exited the building laughing amongst ourselves.

"It's over there," I motioned.

I inhaled, breathing smoke-free air for the first time in hours, though my lungs claimed it had been much longer.

As we came around the corner, Darin asked, "So where's the—"

"Don't move!" Thirty men surrounded us. I put up my hands.

"What's going on?" Darin demanded.

Kavra appeared. He grabbed me, jerking me out of the line of fire.

My men moved in, forcing our captives to the ground.

"No!" Kathleen screamed. "Help!"

Two men, who had been in the front of the building, came running at her call. "What the hell?" one of them asked when he took in the scene.

Before I could come up with an answer, two suited officers, not usually listed among my guard, stepped forward.

"FBI!" they said, flashing their badges.

"I took the liberty of calling in some of our people working for the investigation division," Kavra whispered in my ear. "I thought it might make things go more smoothly."

"Nice," I replied.

As the two agents diffused the locals, I turned back to the captives and surrounding guard. Darin, from his position facedown on the deteriorating asphalt, demanded an explanation.

"Hello, Darin," I said, dropping all pretense of not knowing who he was. "You know, it's not nice to lie." I turned to the other two. "Ryan, Kathleen, great to finally meet you."

"You're the aliens?" Kathleen said, half-asking, half-knowing.

"Sorry, guys," I ignored her question, "it would seem I forgot the car after all. But," I added, "it would be my pleasure to offer you an extensive tour of the fastest, and most technologically advanced, ships of the empire."

"Ships?" Ryan asked, the alcohol clearly affecting his ability to connect the dots. "Space ships?"

"Yep," I replied. "Kasar's to be exact. Today is your lucky day!"

Once bound, Darin, Ryan, and Kathleen were placed in transports and taken back to the ship. "They are not to be harmed," I ordered.

Now early-morning in standard Setian time, I received a transmission ordering me to Kasar's ship.

"What's the expression?" Kavra asked from beside me. "Time to face the music?"

I smiled. "The only one who will be facing anything is Jetreal."

We flew directly to Kasar's ship, where he waited for us on the main deck.

"Dehartra—" Nicholas began, but he was interrupted by Jetreal.

"You deliberately disobeyed me!" he shouted. "I'll see you demoted for it. Demoted, and if I have anything to say about it, which I assure you I do, infested. Look at your ridiculous outfit! Both of you. Making you a member of this empire was a mistake on the council's part. You will—"

"Jetreal!" Kasar commanded sharply. "Cease!"

He laughed, wiping his slobbery mouth crudely. "You can't protect her this time! She deliberately disobeyed a superior commander, and it would seem that Kavra did as well. Two down, one to go."

"Jetreal! Quiet, or I shall have you punished for the same crime you accuse Dehartra."

"And what is that?"

"Disobedience!"

"Kasar," I said calmly, "allow me to speak."

He nodded.

I told him of the call we had received from Lukare 15, and my subsequent argument with Jetreal. "He dismissed the information. My instincts demanded investigation."

"She violated a—" Jetreal tried again.

"I found him."

"What?" Kasar asked.

Pausing between each word, I repeated myself, "I found him."

"You found Ryan? Ryan Shore?"

"Yes, and a bigger prize." I smiled.

Slowly, Kasar smiled back.

"I have, in the belly of your ship, the number one Earth resistance leader."

"You captured Darin?"

"Yes."

Indignant color drained from Jetreal's face. "Darin?"

"Yes. I found Darin Hoyle. He's being transferred to a holding cell as we speak, with two of his top commanders, Ryan Shore, and Kathleen Law.

"Kasar, I would like to inform the council that I could have gone back to bed, as ordered by Jetreal, but instead decided to capture the Earth resistance leaders."

News of our success spread. Jetreal was executed by the council for his insolence, and failure to command.

Three days later, I was summoned to appear before the council.

As I entered the now-familiar chambers, I gave a low bow.

Vektor addressed me first, "Greetings, Dehartra."

"Greetings, Councilor Vektor."

"I assume you know why you've been summoned?"

"I assume nothing, Councilor."

Vektor nodded. "Always the perfect answer." He cleared his throat. "The council finds ourselves in a quandary."

"Quandary?"

"You're very young." He shook his head. "Yet your record is unrivaled. I suppose there is only one thing to do."

"Forgive me, Councilor. I don't understand."

"Fellow Councilors," Vektor addressed the room, "at the age of fourteen, this extraordinary woman devised a plan that won the Battle of Trests. At seventeen, she won the Battle of Palta. At nineteen, she assisted in a major victory in the Seltas Galaxy, and was promoted to the third-highest rank. Now, at twenty-one, she has again proven her worth and leadership by successfully capturing the Earth Resistance leaders, an act her superiors proved unable to do."

He drew a deep breath. "It is the judgment of this council, and my personal honor, to bestow upon Dehartra the rank of councilor, and grant her all the rights and powers that come with such an esteemed title."

"Councilor?" I was stunned. "Surely, Councilor Vektor, Kasar is next in line."

"The victory was yours. As were all of the victories I have listed. You have earned the right to sit upon this governing body." He stood from his chair and turned back to those seated among the crowd. "I give you Councilor Dehartra."

"Thank you," was all I could manage.

The emperor, though his rank among the other councilors was known only to a few in the room, stood. "You will return to Earth, Councilor Dehartra, and assist in the final conquest of Setian Colony 428. Following that, you'll be in command of the impending attack on the Lorid home defenses."

I gave a bow before him and said, "Yes, Councilor."

Kavra also received a promotion for the capture, to second-in-command of the military behind Kasar.

Setian Empire tradition was to hold the highest-ranking of our enemies in captivity so they could see the fall of their people, and their people could see them in our power. They were often paraded as war prizes, a demonstration of the futility in resisting.

When the war was over, it would be up to me to decide their fate.

Chapter XXV

I DID NOT HAVE TO wait long. After the capture of Darin, Kasar was granted permission to send in our forces in full, public style. With a force of twenty thousand, augmented by existing humans already under our command, Setian forces destroyed the Earth's military. The American president, who had been infested two years before, calmly instructed people to stay in their homes and wait for instructions from the nice military men, who would eventually come to collect them. In three weeks, we had the entire planet under Setian control.

Dominance established, with minimal humans in hiding, Kasar issued orders for ground troops to land and begin building pools on the surface. These additional guards joined those already present, patrolling from house to house, gathering the civilian population. After assuring their frightened charges they were being led to safety, troops took captives to underground caves, and into Setian pool complexes.

Three weeks after the invasion began in earnest, Kasar provided a formal report, via holographic conference, to the council. Over ninety percent of the planet's inhabitants were under our control.

He further requested the honor of my presence before he destroyed the final resistance members. En route to Earth, from the council chambers on Setianta, it came to light particular members of the rebellion had worked closely with the Lorids, the only major unassimilated species left on our side of the galaxy. From undercover contacts among their ranks, I learned that leaders of the Earth rebellion might know critical information about the Lorid home defenses. While it would be easier to simply infest the ranking leaders, personal pride dictated I break Darin myself.

As I approached the planet, my first order of business was to place an official call to Lukare 15.

His holographic image appeared before me. He bowed and said, "Councilor Dehartra."

"Rise," I told him. "Lukare 15, I would like to thank you for the information you sent, concerning the rebel leaders' location. You took a great risk, which proved successful. For your contribution to this capture, I hereby award you the title of Harars 5, and offer you a commission of your choosing."

"My...Councilor," he stumbled. "This is an honor." He seemed to shake himself. "Thank you, Councilor."

"What commission do you choose?"

"I would like to serve at the Lorid front, to help in preparations for the battle to come."

I nodded. "It will be done. Congratulations, Harars 5."

When I landed on Setian Colony 428, I was escorted to the pool area recently built above ground. Kasar greeted me with a smile.

"Congratulations, Kasar," I said, my smile matching his own. "What a glorious day for the empire."

He placed his hand on my left cheek, raising my gaze to his, before kissing me softly. "For you, I would do far more."

Recognizing the same resolve and determination, shared so perfectly between us, I answered, "And you shall. It's good to see you, especially on such a joyous occasion. However, I believe we have some business to attend to."

"As you wish, Councilor."

Approximately thirty cages, each containing about twenty prisoners, surrounded the pool. Darin and his top three commanders had been placed on an elevated platform closest to the pool's edge, as Kasar did love to show off his prizes.

Darin was thinner than I remembered, but physically unharmed. As I looked into his golden eyes I saw the intelligence responsible for him being the leader. Even chained in a cage, he could be mistaken for no one else. Only in his mid-twenties, but he possessed tired eyes that could have belonged to someone twice his age. This young man, like myself, had been forced to grow up far too quickly.

In the cage with Darin were Ryan Shore, Damon Deval, and Kathleen Law. Ryan and Damon were in their early twenties, and had both fought bravely, but one look revealed they had lost their spirits during the past few weeks of captivity.

I ordered the prisoners removed from the cage.

Once before me, I greeted, "Hello, Darin."

"Who are you?" he asked.

"Forgive me, I forgot we were never properly introduced."

"Chris," he cut in, "the name means nothing to me."

"Chrissa, actually, though my full name is Councilor Chrissalynn Dehartra Kasar."

He said nothing.

I turned to Kasar. "These three," I pointed to Kathleen, Darin and Damon, "have information vital to the empire. I shall take the two young men, while you do what you wish with the girl. Use any method to gather from her. But beware, my sources suggest the upper level leaders may have been injected with *curine*."

"Curine? So they can't be infested?" Kasar asked. "How is that possible?"

"Lorids provided doses for each of them."

Poisonous to Setians, curine had been developed by the Lorids, and could linger in the body for months. However, the drug was not widely distributed due to harsh side-effects, and was generally administered only to warriors who risked direct contact with our kind.

"We shall have to procure answers from alternative means," Kasar said, with an excited glimmer in his eyes.

"I expect a full report of what she knows, particularly information concerning the Lorid defenses on their home world."

I turned again to the rebels. "One of my commanders is interested in an improved human body. Send this one," I pointed to Ryan, "to the Lorid war front with the curine caution."

Kathleen stood beside Ryan, and at my words, grabbed his arm.

Darin straightened and met my gaze directly for the first time.

Kasar's guards stepped forward.

Kathleen refused to loosen her grip.

Without needing to be told, three more guardsmen stepped forward and broke her hold on Ryan, who was taken to a ship. He went without resistance, while Kathleen fought to break free, before being completely overpowered.

I turned to two cages that had been set apart from the others. "Tell me, Kasar, were all these prisoners members of the resistance?"

"Yes, Councilor."

"Line the prisoners in front of the pool."

I waited as my orders were carried out. Forty-three people. The eldest appeared in his early sixties, while the youngest girl couldn't have been more than thirteen.

Signaling several guards to step forward, the highest ranking asked, "Councilor?"

I pointed to a girl who looked to be about sixteen. "Kill her."

"What?"

Two of my own guard stood behind me. With a slight motion, the guard who had offered the objection screamed as his flesh evaporated, leaving only a pile of ash where he had once stood. I turned to the next guard and repeated the order.

The girl disappeared where she stood.

"No!" Darin screamed. He ran toward me, but was shackled, so our men had little trouble knocking him to the ground.

"I want him alive," I warned.

Three more of my men stepped forward and together, they secured him.

"No," he yelled. "She was a child!"

Kneeling, I leaned down to lightly place a hand on the back of his head, and ran my fingers through his hair until he calmed enough to speak.

"Is it true?" he asked.

"True?"

"Do you serve them of your own free will? You are not a host? You're...human?"

"I'm free, but I am not human. I am Setian, and I will show you why." Turning to the guard standing in front of the line of prisoners, I ordered, "Kill them all."

A high-pitched screech deafened my ears as lasers singed the air. Bodies did not fall to the ground, instead being incinerated where they stood. Smoke filled the air, choking the lungs of all those who dared to breathe, and burning the eyes of those who attempted to watch. Where once forty rebels had stood side-by-side, there was now nothing; not a soul in sight.

Kathleen's ear-splitting scream pierced the resulting silence. More guards stepped forward, holding her to the ground beside Darin. As I glanced back his way, I found him sobbing.

"Why?" he asked again and again.

"I am the daughter of the Setian Empire, and rebellion is not to be tolerated." As he lay crying, I turned to my guard and ordered all other prisoners to be infested immediately. Finishing my instructions, I ordered Kasar to expedite things on Earth, and join me at the front line of the Lorid War. I wanted him by my side as I conquered the empire's greatest foe.

I had Darin and Damon taken to separate cells aboard my ship, and chained to their beds to ensure they would not attempt to harm themselves. After giving brief orders, I left Earth for the Lorid battle front.

Chapter XXVI

Three days into our journey, the *fun* began. Due to the curine in their systems, it would be impossible to infest them, and know their minds, for many months. Besides, when I gave this information to the rest of the council, I wanted absolute credit, so the poison gave me an excuse to break them myself.

For the first session, we planned *neptal*, which was performed by placing neps, a cluster of needles, into sensitive nerves.

Damon and Darin were both removed from their cells and brought to the torture chambers. The white walls were covered with numerous devices, practical storage that also added to the patient's psychological terror. For this particular day, two tables had been placed near the center of the square room, featuring unbreakable straps made of an expensive metal from the Palta system. Guards stripped them from the waist up, and forced each onto a table. Their arms and legs were spread to the corners and chained down with the metal strips. Additional straps were place at their knees, the bend of their arms, and over their foreheads and chin to keep their heads still during the torture. Past prisoners had injured their necks from jerking their head.

"Hello, Darin," I greeted softly. "How are you today?" When he did not answer I chided, "It's rude not to answer when a lady speaks."

"You know exactly how I am."

"And you, Damon? How are you today?"

He also refused to answer.

"Okay, gentlemen, here's how this works. You can talk, or you can scream; I don't really care which. However, before this is over, you will tell me everything you know about the Lorid home defense system. You have the choice to begin speaking, and you might have a good day, or don't, and we can begin." When they remained silent, I sighed. "Have it your way."

I turned to my guard. "Would you ask the inquisitor on duty to attend Damon? I'll treat Darin myself."

Less than a minute later, the inquisitor walked in and took a seat beside Damon. I picked up the first nep and inserted it into a cluster of nerves at the base of Darin's neck. The inquisitor did the same to Damon.

Darin bit his lip, pain instantly showing on his thin face. I placed a second nep on the opposite side. He screamed.

"Tell me you wish to talk, and they will be removed immediately," I informed him.

He managed to stop screaming, but said nothing.

I ran the tip of my finger gently over the veins of Darin's left wrist. "Such smooth skin for a male," I said softly. "Do you know how many nerves run through a human hand?" Fear touched his eyes, but other than an involuntary jerk against the straps, he did not respond.

"Careful, you'll cut your wrist."

As I had warned, a trickle of blood slipped down his right hand. I took another nep and placed it in the center of his left wrist. His screams filled the room. After I placed three more in the same wrist, tears filled his eyes.

Noting Damon also cried out—my focus such I saw and heard nothing beyond my patient—I turned to one of my assistants. "Hand me a vial of sectra 4-D12."

Pulling the stopper on the clear liquid, I moved to Darin's other wrist. "Seeing as you have already cut yourself, we might as well do this." I placed a few drops. It took mere seconds for his blood and the chemical to mix.

Darin shrieked, breaking into a sweat while attempting desperately to jerk his hand away. The erratic movement impacted his other wrist, in which the neps were still embedded, intensifying his pain.

"That discomfort is from a tiny, shallow cut. Imagine how it will burn injected into your veins?"

I removed the neps from his left wrist and neck, easing his pain. "Shall we try this again?" I asked. "Darin, how are you today?"

"Peachy," he answered through gritted teeth. He had bit his lip so hard a trickle of blood ran down his chin.

When he flinched as I approached his face with a damp cloth, I assured him, "It's only water. I am going to wipe the blood away." I touched the cloth to his lips as gently as I could, using the other side to wipe away his tears. "Better?"

"Yes," he admitted softly, his voice strained.

I ran my fingers down his cheek in a comforting touch. "Tell me, Darin, what do you know about the Lorid home defenses?"

"Nothing."

"You're not very good at lying. However, we can start with a simpler question. It's my understanding you have held audience with Supreme Commander Darcoth, of the Lorid Sovereignty. Is my information correct?"

He avoided my gaze.

In a softer tone, "I only wish to know if he's as noble as the stories claim."

"I've met Darcoth."

"Is he everything they say?" I asked, genuinely interested in hearing a firsthand account of the esteemed commander.

"He is," Darin replied, awe in his voice. "The way he described battle strategies, and some of the surprise victories, was amazing. Ideas I'd have never even dreamed. He likes to take risks on nothing more than an unexplainable hunch, and somehow manages to come out on top."

"Protective of his people?"

"Oh, yes. He would rather risk his own life than another's." Darin looked up. "Have you never met him? I would have thought empire leaders would meet on occasion."

"Other councilors, yes, but I've personally never had the pleasure. I look forward to doing so someday, and I hope to be the one to offer him an honorable death."

Silence fell and I moved the subject forward, keeping my voice sugary. "I want to know about his inner defenses. Are you going to tell me?"

"No," he said firmly.

"How about you, Damon?" I called across the room.

"This one," the inquisitor answered, "is not talking either."

I turned back to Darin. "Tell you what. I am going to give you both a night to think about it. We will begin again tomorrow."

After a restful night, the following morning I had Darin and Damon brought back to the interrogation room, and strapped to their respective tables. "How are you doing this morning?"

"Better than last night," Darin answered.

"Are you ready to give me the information I require? I promise it will be a lot less painful if you do."

"No," Darin said. "I will not tell you anything."

"Okay," I answered. "We are going to try a different approach." I took a thin blade off the table behind Darin and moved it into his field of vision. Without warning, I cut sideways into the muscle of his upper left arm.

He hissed.

I made a matching cut across his right arm, followed closely by two cuts on both sides of his upper chest. None of the incisions were deep, barely enough to draw blood to the surface. Soaking two cloths with sectra 4-D12, I held them over both of his arms and squeezed.

"AHH!" he screamed. "Goddamn it!"

"Don't curse, Darin. It's very un-hero like."

From across the room, Damon matched Darin's curses with screams of his own. I poured more of the solution directly onto the cuts. After I had exhausted the efficacy of topical application, I filled a syringe with the powerful liquid.

"Darin, look at me."

He did.

"This," I held up the syringe, "is going to hurt. You can't imagine how much this is going to hurt. You do not want this in your veins. Tell me about the Lorid inner defense systems, and any other vital information you have, and this needle will not touch you. You have my word."

He looked at me through his tears. "Please," he whispered.

"Talk to me."

"I can't."

I nodded sadly. "Here it comes." I reached for his arm and injected the harsh liquid into his bloodstream.

It took only a few seconds before he whispered, "It burns."

I nodded. "There's an antidote. Tell me what I want to know, and I will give it to you."

Liquid fire spread throughout his body. He jerked, attempting to escape the terrible sensation. "Oh my god!" he cried out.

Damon also screamed across the room, but neither man expressed a willingness to trade information for relief. I let the drug run its course.

When both men had stabilized, I had them returned to their cells with the promise we would continue the next morning.

Not that they were able to rest. Alternating between bright lights and loud music, they were awoken several times, in hopes that sleep deprivation would make them more willing to entertain conversation the following day.

Frustrated by the lack of progress, I spent the rest of the night in the command room changing perimeters of the Lorid battlefront. I rearranged commanders, and added troops to the inner rim. The emperor had expressly ordered we hold the line between the two armies, and not attempt to advance.

The next day both men awaited my arrival, however this time I had ordered only Damon be strapped to a table. Darin had been restrained in a chair, giving him a clear view of the other man.

Darin spoke first. "How are you?"

"I'm very well today, thank you for asking."

"That's good to hear, but I'm not going to tell you anything."

"Yes, you will," I replied. "I would love to play for a few more days, however, I am running low on time, and the information you have is important to the coming battle. Therefore, we're going to try something different."

I walked over to the table where Damon waited.

"Where is Darcoth planning to attack?"

Neither answered.

Selecting a simple knife, I cut Damon across the chest deep enough to draw blood.

"How many new ships have been accumulated by the Lorid military since their defeat in the Keif system last year?"

Silence.

A deep slice down Damon's right arm.

"What are the names of Darcoth's top military advisors?"

An arc into Damon's right cheek, below his eye.

"What are you doing?" Darin screamed. "Stop!"

"Every time you refuse to answer, Damon will be punished."

Darin stared, his eyes brimming with rage, and horror.

"Tell me about the Lorid defenses."

I grabbed a vial of sectra 4-D12 and turned the bottle over Damon's chest. Liquid splashed, causing so much pain, Damon couldn't even gather the breath to scream.

"He'd rather die!" Darin said in anguish. "We'd both rather die than tell you."

"Darin," I said softly, kneeling down so I gazed up into his golden eyes. "I am going to tell you three things. First, every time you do not answer my question, Damon will suffer. Second, he'll experience more pain than you can imagine in a hundred lifetimes. And third," my voice was reduced to a harsh, slow whisper, "he will never die."

Pity niggled my soul as Darin stared into my cold expression.

"Are you a monster?"

"No, but I'm willing to commit monstrous acts to protect the empire. I'll do anything to win this battle, Darin. Anything. And there are fates far worse than death."

BY THE END OF THE night, I had acquired the information I sought, and provided it to my captains. Defenses were destroyed, prisoners taken, and the Lorids were forced to question whom they could trust among their own people. When members of an army and government no longer have confidence in each other, it becomes difficult to effectively fight a war.

Darin had confessed the information I sought, but I desired to break him completely. I ordered their wounds be tended, and over the next few weeks, both were taken care of by the best of our physicians.

When the doctors reported their return to full health, I ordered formal attire sent, and commanded their presence for dinner. When I arrived, Darin and Damon sat in one of the ship's elegant ballrooms. Gold plates and crystal champagne flutes sparkled under diamond chandeliers in the dark red room.

I had to walk clear across the space to reach where they were seated. My heels were silent on the carpet, so they did not notice my presence until I had nearly reached the table. As Damon saw me, in a fitted red dress, very different from my usual black attire, his body stiffened. Darin turned to find me standing directly behind him.

"Thank you for joining me, Gentlemen."

Damon nodded while Darin remained utterly still.

I took a seat next to them and the first course was brought.

"You'd best eat. You must be starving." I watched them exchange confused glances as I ate my meal in silence. After a moment's hesitation, they devoured theirs as well.

When finished, I ordered them to follow me to one of our computer rooms. I had the computer create a 3D map showing all the major planets and systems, with the ones the empire controlled in red, and all those free in blue.

Every system containing a major species, with the exception of the Lorid's, was in red. As the map surrounded the two young men, the computer inventoried all the planets and species belonging to the empire.

"Why are you showing us this?" Darin finally asked.

"To illustrate the power of the Setian Empire, and convince you no one is coming to your rescue," I answered. "There's simply no one left to do so."

After instructing guards to return them to their cells, I met Nicholas at the command center. "Nice to see you."

"Agreed, but I'm curious to know why I was summoned."

"I've been working on a few projects behind the scenes. Since they're finally in place, I wish to share them with you. The information is confidential, and I didn't want to broadcast over any channels, even encrypted."

He leaned forward with interest as I laid out recent events. Slowly, his eyes lit up. "Excellent news, Chrissalynn. What do you require from me?"

"Accompany me to the home world to address the council. My forces are ready; everything's in place. All I require is the okay from the other councilors."

"Of course I will go with you. But who will stay here if we both leave? I like my second well-enough, but to leave him in charge of the Lorid front?"

"Kavra will be in charge while we are gone."

"Kavra? He's in the Fultra system."

"He left two weeks ago," I replied. "He'll be here by tonight; we can leave tomorrow."

"Perfect."

Later that night, Kavra arrived, and as I had instructed, he left his main fleet behind. He immediately took a transport to my ship. As he stepped out, I ran up and embraced him.

"Hey, Chrissa." He hugged me back.

"I'm glad you're here," I said, his presence comforting. My plan was falling into place.

He released me and I walked with him into the guest quarters.

"So," he said, as he slid onto a chair beside the bed, "what's going on?"

"Nicholas and I are taking a short trip. I am leaving you in charge. Please stay on this ship, and run things from here, so hopefully the Lorids won't notice the change."

"Do I need to do, or be aware, of anything special?"

"Hold the line, and don't lose any ground. Nothing fancy until I return."

He nodded.

Business complete, we ended up lying down and talking into the night.

"What are you really doing tomorrow?" he finally asked. "Don't tell me it's an errand. This battle is too critical to leave if it weren't important."

"Battle? What battle? Our current orders are to hold these lines, yes, but make no move to strike. Again and again I implore the emperor for permission to attack, to let me lead this army like it should be led, but he will not hear of it. Tomorrow, I'm going to plead my case in person.

"Yes, I could have had some Harars hold the front as easily as you, but I don't trust them. Besides, if everything goes according to plan, you'll want to be here. Trust me."

"Always," he replied.

As I drifted toward sleep, I tucked my body next to his and rested my head on his chest, listening to the steady rhythm of his heart as he slipped his arm around me.

More asleep than awake, he asked, "Chrissa, you're not about to do anything stupid, are you?"

"Not if I can help it," I said back softly, before falling asleep.

THE NEXT MORNING, I RETURNED to my chambers and changed into traveling clothes. After saying goodbye to Kavra, I took a transport to Kasar's ship.

Three battleships accompanied us on our journey home. Nicholas and I spent time planning and strategizing for upcoming battles. I stayed in my old room, perfectly preserved. The pink walls stood in complete contrast to the darker shades on my own ship.

Four days later we arrived. Our ships landed in the suspended docking bays, and we journeyed to the council chambers.

We had both changed into black suits for the occasion, mine paired with a crimson shirt, while Nicholas wore a white. Together we reached the building, handed over our IDs, and were allowed into the chambers. I had called ahead and requested my fellow councilors be present when I arrived. As I had been the only member off-planet, everyone was there as I walked into the room, Kasar at my side.

Nicholas gave a low bow before the council.

I simply said, "Councilors."

"Greetings, Councilor Dehartra," a tall woman sitting on my left, Councilor Reta, said. "Your message sounded urgent."

I smiled. "Emperor, and fellow council members, I have called you here today regarding a matter of the utmost importance.

"Emperor, I have come to plead with you. My ships are in place to strike against the Lorid world. The commanders are eager, and the planet is covered from every angle. Everything is ready to go, except for your agreement. I have come to tell you all of this in person, and to ask for your consent to start the final siege."

The council was seated in the front half of the circular room. Directly in front of me, Emperor Hidford, occupying a human host, stood. A reasonably tall man at six-foot-one, he had closely cropped blond hair and harsh emerald eyes.

"Councilor Dehartra, how many times must I tell you? Fighting the Lorids is suicide. Their forces number our own, and their weapons are equally advanced."

"Give me a chance. I will win the battle."

"Impossible!" he yelled. "Your job is to keep the Lorids at bay. You cannot expect to win in a full-fledged war."

"But—"

"No!" he said firmly. "The Lorid commander Kimle is brilliant. While you've gotten lucky a few times with your unusual strategies, you're no match for him."

I exchanged a glance with Kasar.

"Interesting," I said, turning back to the emperor, "that you should mention Commander Kimle."

"Why?"

"Kasar, if you would…"

He walked toward the door.

"Where—"

"He'll be right back," I assured. "Tell me, Emperor, could Commander Kimle be turned?"

"Impossible."

Footsteps. I turned to the door.

"Members of the council, Emperor, may I present Commander Kimle."

With bright red fur, and three eyes fixed on me, the Lorid commander walked into the silent room. After a brief bow to the council, he kneeled before me. "Councilor Dehartra."

"Commander. Thank you for joining us today."

I turned back to the emperor. "As you can see, it is clearly not impossible. Neither is my victory."

Hidford glared as though his hatred could sear my skin. "How?"

"We grabbed his wife and daughter, and he, like a cliché hero, came running, handing us not only himself, but all his troops, to save their precious lives." I shrugged. "Sometimes basics work best."

I cleared my throat and turned back to the commander at my feet. "Thanks to Kimle's assistance, three-quarters of the Lorid outer defense systems have already been infested, and those who remain soon will be. The inner rim is ready for our next push."

"Wait," the emperor said, "have you been inside of the battle front?"

"Yes."

"Despite my direct orders not to leave your post?"

"Your orders, Emperor, were to stay at my post, the Lorid battle front. I stayed at the front, only pushed those boundaries deeper than you imagined."

"You once again deliberately disobeyed a superior commander?"

"Again?" Marina, a fellow counselor asked, from the emperor's left. She had sat on the council for upwards of twenty years, and so had the unquestionable authority to challenge, "What do you mean, again?"

Taking Marina's invitation, I put a point on his objection. "Would you be referring, Emperor, to the incident where the recently *executed* Jetreal ordered me to remain in my room during the takeover of Colony 428, instead of capturing the leaders of the Earth Resistance?"

"That doesn't change the fact she disobeyed an order. As I've said, she's gotten lucky."

"Lucky? No battle in the history of this great empire has ever been won without some measure of luck. Your orders, as with Jetreal's," I drew breath, "are wrong."

When no one spoke, I continued, "No battle has ever been won by your judgment or leadership, Emperor. You have ridden on the backs of others, claiming their credit. You always play the safe card, and avoid risks. Every major battle, in the past twenty years, has been won by myself, Nicholas, or Kavra. You're weak, Emperor Hidford, and unfit to rule this council. Your orders will result in an eternal stalemate. Mine will win the war."

Marina spoke, "Kasar, Dehartra, Kimle, would you please step outside?"

We consented, leaving the chamber. I dismissed Kimle back to his duties, then Nicholas and I sank into black chairs lining the corridor.

"The words needed to be spoken," Nicholas encouraged.

"Tell me again when we both live through this."

"You did want an adventure, didn't you?"

I couldn't help but smile. "With certain death assured. They're the best kind, you know?"

"So Kavra informs me."

We waited for what felt like years, the infernal hall clock chiming merrily with the passage of each new hour.

At the end of the fourth hour, the door to the chamber opened, and we were called inside.

As we stood to enter, Kasar whispered, "Do you regret it, Chrissa? What I did to you?"

"No, I do not." I kissed him, a light brush of the lips, and turned to enter the chambers with far more confidence than I actually had. The emperor was notably missing. A good sign.

"Councilor Dehartra."

"Councilor Vektor," I replied back.

"I trust there is no need to inform you how dangerous your words were, or how easily you could have lost your life."

Could have. Another good sign. "No, Councilor."

"You are also aware, for standing with you, Nicholas could have lost his life as well?"

"I am aware."

"Tell me, Dehartra, can you defeat the Lorids?"

No hesitation. "Yes. As I've won every other battle to which I've been assigned."

After a pause, he gave a slight nod. "The emperor was right about one thing. Luck must live on your side," I let out a breath I did not know I had been holding, "because we find your claims to be correct. The emperor is being executed as we speak."

My breath caught.

"And it is my pleasure," Councilor Vektor continued, "to bestow upon you the title of empress of the Setian Empire. Empress Dehartra, you have the council's assent to begin the final assault on the Lorid home world at any time you wish."

I stood speechless for the second time in my life. "Empress?" I stammered.

Councilor Revdran smiled. "So you are capable of emotion. I was beginning to have my doubts." He laughed, a joyous sound. "Congratulations, Empress Dehartra."

"I… Thank you, Councilors. I will not fail you. The attack upon the Lorid home world will begin soon, and bring glory to the Setian Empire."

Kasar whisked me out of the council chambers. Once outside, he took me in his arms and literally swung me around the opulent hall. "Chrissa, Chrissa, I am so proud of you! Empress. I have never been more proud." He put me down gently.

"Soon, Nicholas," I replied. "Soon we shall defeat the last of our enemies, and you shall rule by my side."

A few days later, we docked back at the Lorid battlefront. Kavra waited for me with an exaggerated pout. "Aww, you mean I don't get to keep your bedroom after all? Your kitty and I had finally worked out an arrangement."

"You did not sleep in my bedroom!"

The grin he could not stop from spreading across his face was one I knew well.

"You're a sight for sore eyes, Kavra."

He pulled me into his arms. "Glad you're back, Chrissa. Was worried there for a while."

"Safe and sound," I replied. "Talk with me?"

"Absolutely." He offered his arm and I took it gladly. We walked into my room, finding the bed unmade. He had slept in my room!

Before I could remark, he beat me to it, "You said an adventure with certain death assured. I thought I might as well get comfortable."

I smiled. "They're the best kind, you know?"

"Wouldn't miss it for the world," he answered. "So, who'd you kill?"

"What do you mean?"

"You haven't been this giddy since you got Jetreal torched. Who'd you kill this time?"

"You helped me kill him, thank you very much."

"You, me, there's no difference."

I shook my head. "I'm changing the subject now. What did you do for my war while I was gone?"

"Not much, sadly. Read the daily reports, played some board games with the computer. In other words, boring on my end."

"Not for long."

He looked at me.

"I wouldn't be so fast to leave if I were you."

"What's going on?"

"Well, I thought I'd start a fight."

"The emperor finally gave you permission? Thank goodness! I thought that coward would never come around."

"He did not give permission. But I'm going to start a fight anyway."

"With who?"

"The entire Lorid fleet," I said in a quiet, matter-of-fact voice.

"You're joking?" One glance was all it took. He groaned. "Death assured."

"The *emperor*," I paused, "did not give me permission."

Kavra tilted his head with a strange look on his face. "What do you mean?"

I stared at him, fighting to keep my smile from reaching dramatic proportions.

"What exactly did you say to the emperor?"

"That he was unfit to rule, and rode the backs of others to power."

His jaw dropped. "You're serious. You got the emperor executed?"

I couldn't stop the smile.

"Who's the new emperor?"

"There is no *emperor*."

"You're the empress!"

In an instant, I was in his arms.

"This…" He spun me around. "This is the happiest day of my life." He drew back enough to see me, his mind grappling with this news. "I'm going to throw a party. I'm going to hire the best artist for your portrait. I, I…I'm going to tell everyone I slept in your bed."

"No, you're not!" I shouted playfully.

That night was as happy as I'd ever been.

Plans for the upcoming attack moved swiftly. With both Nicholas and Kavra by my side, and help from existing Lorid hosts, we infested the rest of the outer fleet. Ever so slowly, Lorids fell victim to Setian infestation, their own leaders luring them to captivity.

Damon was now held on Setianta, while we waited for the curine to disperse from his system, allowing infestation, I dined with Darin frequently, and allowed him unrestricted access to the ship's vast archives. He had a keen interest in learning about the empire and its history. I was happy to provide the information he sought.

Darin failed to notice how, over time, he became more willing to comply with my desires. His compliance and, furthermore, his ignorance of this compliance, convinced me it would only be a matter of time before I would own him completely.

Nightly, Nicholas, Kavra, and I met to discuss the daily reports. Infestations rose steadily. Soon only a scattered group of uninfested Lorid defenses remained.

The last battle would soon be fought.

Chapter XXVII

One night, I invited Darin to my private chambers. Against the black leather vest I'd provided him to wear, his skin appeared pale from the lack of sunlight. His attire matched my own black gown, which was floor-length, and lined with crimson lace.

The jewels I wore, ornate when compared to the plain gold band on my left ring finger, sparkled in the dim light of the glowing glass rocks. At a table set for two in the room's center, a vase of two dozen red and black roses provided the backdrop for our waiting meal. Darin sat down across from me as I poured the champagne. We enjoyed a private dinner, and talked quietly about nothing important.

Once dinner was cleared, I stood slowly and moved to his side of the table. I ran my hands over his bare arms before moving my lips to his, offering a soft kiss. He remained still under my caress.

When I pulled back, Darin asked, "Why are you doing this?"

I knelt before him. "Because you're mine, Darin; body and soul."

"You can never have my soul."

I gazed up when, to my surprise, he moved his hand and touched the left side of my face with the tips of his fingers.

"You look sad, Chrissa."

"There was a girl I once knew," I answered, not knowing why. "I wonder if, in another life, she would have been as brave as you."

"What happened to her?" His voice was soft.

"The same thing that happens to all who become a part of the Setian Empire." I shook my head. "Understand, Darin, soul or not, you belong to me. I am giving you a choice. Stay by my side, and in my bed, or return to the torture chambers. Your call."

His eyes shifted around the room, but his body betrayed him.

I stood and reached for his hand. "Come with me, Darin." I smiled. "Please."

He rose and allowed me to lead him into the bedroom, where crimson blankets covered black satin sheets. Soft music played in the background.

"Dance with me, Darin."

He paused briefly before taking me into his arms. The music grew louder as we swayed, our shadows dancing along the walls. At the heart of the music, Darin twirled me in a tight spiral, and then brought me back into his arms.

"Where'd you learn to dance?" I asked.

"My mother."

"She taught you well."

"Thank you. You're not bad yourself."

"I've had many instructors over the years."

He twirled me again. "Were you born into the empire?"

"No."

"How did you become…"

"I was raised the daughter of a Setian commander."

We swayed as I closed my eyes and placed my head against his shoulder.

"You're beautiful." His words were hushed as though constituting a confession. "It's hard to believe someone so beautiful could be…"

I pulled back and met his gaze, his golden eyes so different than the blue of Nicholas' or Kavra's.

Kavra. The thought caused me to pause.

Even as empress, I would never be free to have the one my heart called for. Kavra was Kasar's equal. Far different from this slave, whom Kasar would never view as a threat to his possession of me.

Pushing past the thought, I again pressed my lips to Darin's. He kissed me back, and chaste gave way to deep and passionate.

"Come, Darin." I backed away, unzipping my dress and letting it fall to the floor. "I won't hurt you—not here."

He threw his shirt to the floor, climbed into the bed, and pressed his body to mine.

Chapter XXVIII

One day, as my plan of infesting the Lorid defense system was nearing completion, I received an unexpected call from one of my advisors. I took the holographic communication in a private chamber adjacent to the main command room.

Harars 12 awaited me. "Councilor Dehartra."

"Yes, what is it?"

"I regret to inform you...Well, you see..."

"What is it?"

"Forgive me, Councilor. Two Lorid commanders, Defret and Pert, have discovered our plan and managed to escape. We've blocked all communication, but have been unable to locate them. We believe they are headed to the Lorid home world in an attempt to warn Commander Darcoth."

"What!" I yelled. "How did this happen?"

"I don't know, Councilor."

"This could ruin everything! The entire plan hinges on surprise until its completion. Everything will be undermined unless these men are found!"

"We are doing everything within our power to find the escapees."

"Have you found them yet?"

"No."

"Then clearly you are not doing everything."

I turned as the door opened behind me. Darin walked in. When he saw I was in a meeting he gave a bow and said, "Apologies, Councilor. I shall return another time."

"No," I said, an idea dawning. "Don't leave."

I turned back to my holo-conference. "Allow me to ensure I understand," I said to Harars 12. "Two Lorid commanders, Defret and Pert, have been infested, and are on their way to their home world as we speak. Once there, they shall attend a private meeting with Commander Darcoth and infest him. Is this correct, Harars 12?"

A confused silence fell. I rushed ahead to fill it. "Correct?"

"Yes, Councilor Dehartra," the man said, following my lead.

"Good," I replied. "Everything is going as planned."

Two nights later, I received the news I had been hoping for. I called Darin to my room, and opened a bottle of his favorite wine. We drank most of the alcohol before falling into bed.

The next morning, I untangled my nude frame from his.

As I tied a robe around my body, Darin turned to his side. "Are you going to tell me why you were so happy last night?"

I finished tying the black satin in place, and sat on the bed facing Darin, petting Aurora absentmindedly. "I received excellent news. For the past few months, our troops have been secretly infesting the Lorids stationed on the outer defenses of their home world. A few days ago, two commanders learned of our plan. Every ship in my fleet searched for them, unsuccessfully. However, as the escape pods reached the home world, they were blown out of the sky," I paused before adding, "by the very people they were hoping to warn."

It took a moment for the story to sink in. Darin turned from me and sat up on the opposite side of the bed. "No," he said. "You told me those commanders were infested!"

I glanced at Darin with a look of pity. "You know what's strange, Darin? The only person I told was you. Did you think I was unaware you've attempted to send messages to the Lorids before?"

His eyes cast downward.

"Oh come now, Darin," I said softly, "do not fear. You have served me well this day." I rose and left the room in silence.

A few weeks later, I was called into a command room to find Kasar awaiting my arrival.

"Empress Dehartra, the last of their outer defenses have been destroyed, and their fighters infested. The entire Lorid army stands at your command, with nearly a thousand ships between them and us. Thanks to your manipulation, and careful maneuvers to ensure absolute secrecy, the Lorids don't have a clue what is going on."

"Darcoth may not realize his entire army is at my command, but he knows some of them are. You never did give him enough credit. He, like his people, is cunning and strong, but they know the odds are against them.

"What do you say to standing by my side as I contact him, and demand the immediate surrender of his people?" In response, Nicholas took a step beside me.

After dressing for the occasion, I sent a priority message to the Lorid's home planet. A half-hour later, I faced the Lorid leaders.

"Greetings," I said. "I am a representative of the Setian Empire. Nearly a thousand ships await my orders to attack. I'm offering you a chance to surrender, and an opportunity to save the lives of your people. You are outnumbered, and all but defenseless. You're defeated. Now I implore you, for the sake of your citizens, to accept your defeat."

"You may have us outnumbered, but we are by no means defenseless," a Lorid replied. "There are not that many ships in the entire empire. I believe you are lying."

"Actually, there are more than a thousand ships, but you are correct in that a majority of them are not meant for war. I was referring to the Setian warships I command, along with a majority of your own forces, which now answer to me." I watched the screen as the Lorid's top military commander stepped to my right side, opposite Kasar. "As I was saying, a thousand ships await my orders to attack, unless you will surrender now, of course." In contrast to the severity of my message, I smiled.

As our link abruptly ended, a handful of inner defense system ships rose to meet us.

"Give the order to attack," I said to Nicholas, who practically radiated with excitement beside me. "I want every last one of those ships annihilated; no survivors. Destroy any ships that attempt to flee. Do what you will with any resistance fighters, but leave Darcoth for me."

Kasar gave a low bow and turned to carry out my orders.

I stood on the bridge of my command ship and watched the slaughter. Our fleet came from the far side of the planet like a black cloud of death. Several hours later, I received a message, and once again found myself facing a holographic image of the Lorid military command center. Only this time, instead of facing our enemies, Kasar waited to greet me.

"The planet has been taken. Darcoth and his commanders await their fate at your hand. The greatest, and last empire victory is yours."

"No. The greatest and last Setian Empire victory," I paused, "is ours."

We shared a smile.

"I shall contact the council to advise them of our success. Send my sub-commanders to prepare the planet for my arrival. Also send troops down to the Tuvorian planet and make sure it's secure."

He bowed and promptly cut the communication.

We had won, but the job was far from done. Within a few weeks, Setian pools would be built, and the infestation process would begin. While I had overseen these tasks countless times, in my new role as empress, for security reasons, it would not be safe for me to step onto the planet until infestation was complete.

Unfortunately, not all of our war problems were solved. We had successfully taken the Lorid's planet, but a few ships managed to escape. They existed as rebels now, scattered throughout the galaxy. More of a nuisance than actual threats, but on occasion they would take out a supply ship, or free one of their own. Reports indicated a number of Earth humans had also been freed by these rebels.

Despite these minor setback, commanders worked diligently to destroy the last of the resistance, and transform the Lorid planet into a land more suitable for our cause.

When infrequent reports of rebel gains were brought to my attention, my gaze fell to Darin. His expression usually stayed neutral, but every once in a while I saw the faintest glimmer of hunger in his eyes. The slightest shimmer of hope.

Chapter XXIX

THE TUVORIANS WERE A MINOR species on a planet within the Lorid defenses. Cannibals in the most uncivilized sense of the word, despite having a sophisticated culture, and valuing old-fashioned family units.

While they cared deeply for their loved ones, the species could not resist the smell of blood. Much like vampires of human legends, these creatures needed blood to survive. Therefore, if one is harmed, others nearby often go into a frenzy. Control is hard to learn, and especially difficult for the children. There are times when stronger children will harm those they love and care for, drinking blood with a thirst that's never satisfied.

Lorids were the first to discover the Tuvorians. Everything went well between the two species until one day when the Lorids witnessed an incident. No one really remembers what the accident was, but it left several Tuvorians hurt. The Lorids ran to help those harmed, but they arrived to a sickening sight.

Tuvorians were lying atop fallen friends, basking in their blood. The sight horrified the Lorids, who reported the incident to the ruling leaders of their home world. An order was issued for the Tuvorians to be abandoned to their depravity, and the planet guarded to prevent them from leaving and spreading their bloodthirst across the galaxy.

When my empire defeated the Lorids, we sent several well-armored troops down to the Tuvorian world. I wanted to know if the blood lust was real, or an attempt to hinder what might be a superior species. My commander spent several nights on the planet, and reported they were indeed as bloodthirsty, and as helpless to control themselves, as our newly defeated foes had claimed.

Curiosity won, and I journeyed to the planet with a vast personal guard, wanting to observe them for myself.

I witnessed an older child attacking its mother when the thirst for blood overtook him. After watching the two struggle, I ordered my guards to separate them. With the help of a portable Setian water source, which after my experience with Kavra I had instituted as necessary for all off-ship missions, I had one of my trusted Setians transfer himself from the mind of his host to the Tuvorian teen.

After ordering the room to be cleared of everyone except my guards and the Setian, Nara 246, I explained my test. "I am going to fill this room with blood, and I want you to overcome this creature's craving for it. If you cannot control his hunger, you will die."

I took a knife from one of my guards and sliced lightly down my right arm. With my personal guard on either side, I flexed, encouraging the blood to run down my arm. Nara took two steps forward before halting abruptly. The guards on either side of me tightened their grips on their weapons.

Nara's body visibly relaxed and he turned to address me. "I'm in control, Councilor Dehartra."

"Well done, Nara. How does your host feel?"

"He wants to thank you for stopping him from hurting his mother. And he'd like to speak to you, if you'll allow."

I nodded consent, and his host spoke. "I do not understand how this creature can resist my cravings, for he experiences them as I do. I might have killed my mother, and I love her very much. I never could have lived with myself if I had harmed her."

"Your species needs help with self-control. Your population dwindles because you, for lack of a better way to put this, eat each other. My people have an incredible sense of control, but lack the pleasures of life. They are blind, deaf, and forced to live inside a pool; an existence which we have found to be not acceptable. I believe we can help each other, and bring our two societies to a peaceful arrangement.

"We would treat you as members of my empire. This arrangement would not only give you the control to stop harming your loved ones, but also the opportunity to leave this planet, and see the universe that has been denied you by our mutual enemies, the Lorids.

"In short, I offer a peace treaty, and ask that you speak to other members of your community about forming this union."

He smiled. "Counselor Dehartra, what you offer us is a great gift. I will speak to my people. I am sure this alliance will be eagerly embraced. The chance to leverage the self-control of your people, and save our species, is much too good an offer to pass up. I thank you once again for saving my mother's life."

I issued orders and Nara removed himself from the creature, returning to his former host. The story was spread, and my offer was taken to Tuvorian leaders.

A few hours later, the Tuvorians agreed, and a formal alliance was created. Several of my high commanders were called to begin the voluntary infestation process. The moment Setians entered the minds of the Tuvorians, their cravings decreased, and their frenzies stopped. Darin had been down on the planet with me, and seemed to be looking at this transformation with new eyes.

Over the next few weeks, Darin witnessed an entire population rush for the newfound control we offered. They were educated about the wider galaxy, which had been denied them. Hosts befriended Setians, and formed a union of friendliness rarely found within other species, even when the hosts were voluntary. By joining with the empire, the Tuvorians found a freedom they had never even dared to dream about.

Chapter XXX

About the time the Tuvorian situation was stabilized, one of my subcommanders informed me the Lorid home world was ready for formal inspection. Based on my earlier orders, the leaders had been held and awaited their sentences. I was faced with the choice of killing them outright, or giving them as new hosts to my top commanders. Even in defeat, these leaders served as a symbol of hope to their people, or so I was informed. Hence the question of whether their slavery, or their death, would be more effective in crushing the people they had served so valiantly.

Seeking advice, I called two of my top intelligence agents, and we spoke for several hours alone in the solitude of my private chambers, where the soundproof walls provided absolute security. With us was my top psychologist, who had studied the affect leaders held over a defeated nation.

Our decision made, my orders were dispatched. I instructed Darin to dress in his finest, and report to the ship dock, where he would accompany me down to the Lorid home world, along with several members of the Setian Council who had arrived to participate in the celebration.

Once assembled, our entourage boarded a private craft to the newly conquered planet.

I studied Darin carefully. The sorrow in his eyes was well-hidden; only one who knew him well would be able to truly see the hurt beneath the surface. The Lorids were the last hope of resistance, and now Darin saw firsthand how defeated they were. The streets were filled with the sounds of triumph and celebration. The Setians had won the war, and the Lorids no longer existed, except for a faint echo inside their own minds.

We entered a seven-story building, which had once been the planetary defense center. Where Lorid symbols had once shone proudly on green and white walls, Setian symbols now hung from red and black surfaces. We had won, and soon their world would be like all the others; a land stripped of all signs of hope or resistance.

My advisers and I approached the commanders waiting to greet me, with Kasar at the head of the line. I met him with a warm smile, and allowed him to kiss my hand softly. This victory was to his glory as well as mine.

"Congratulations!" I announced, after I and other councilors had greeted each commander in turn. "You honor the Setian Empire, and your ancestors, with this victory. You will be rewarded greatly, in both this life and the next." They bowed, and I nodded in acknowledgment. "Take me to the captives, and we shall see what is to be done with our heroic rebels."

As my advisors and I moved into an elevator, I motioned for Darin to join us. We were taken to the fifth floor, and led into a dimly lit room with no windows. Fifteen guards surrounded the door where the six defeated leaders were being held. I entered the room surrounded by my own personal guard. One look at the prisoners confirmed my orders had been followed; apart from looking somewhat thin, they had not been harmed.

"Which of you is Darcoth?" I asked.

A middle-aged Lorid with a powerful build and intelligent eyes stepped forward, blinking from the sudden spill of light that flooded the room from the opened door.

"You have fought valiantly, worthy of the fame you have gained through the many years of this war," I addressed him. "But alas, you have lost. This game must be played out to its final end." I spoke in a quiet, revered voice.

"Yes," replied Darcoth, "it must be finished."

We shared a lingering glance of understanding.

"Your underlings will face a crowd of loyal Setians, now in Lorid hosts, who have proven themselves worthy. However, you shall be given a more dignified choice." I turned to one of the guards who produced two weapons: an ancient blade, and a highly polished laser gun.

"I have but one question. Are you a member of the famous Setian council, sent here by your peers to witness my death?"

I leaned forward so only he could hear. "I am the reigning Setian Empire Empress Chrissalynn Dehartra Kasar. You have been a worthy opponent. I believed it only right we meet before you die."

He gave a nod of consent. "Your personal presence means more to me than anything I could have hoped for. I would be honored if you would assist me in ending my life with your Setian blade."

I nodded. "It is Emperor Dehartra's weapon, borrowed from the ancient archives." I took the simple blade by its black hilt. Turning the sword slowly to the side, I offered it hilt first to Darcoth, who took it from my hand.

"Heavy. Fit for an emperor," he glanced at me, "or an empress."

"Is there a ritual you would like performed?"

He shook his head.

"Dervik Darcoth, Lorid Sovereignty Commander, you have been found guilty of resisting your rightful sovereigns, the Setian Empire. For these crimes, the sentence is death by Setian blade."

I placed my hands over Darcoth's, and together we turned the blade.

"With your death," I spoke the ancient words as the blade sailed forward, sinking into the center of his chest with a sickening sound, "we forgive you for your sins."

The blade cut through muscle and bone alike. Darcoth's eyes glossed over, his lips opened at the sudden pain. I put my hand against the left side of his face. "Go, with our forgiveness. Be at peace." I used my other hand to twist the blade deeper. Darcoth gave a low moan in the otherwise silent room.

His body fell with a thud.

I withdrew the heavy blade from Darcoth's chest, and the guard to my right handed me a white cloth, which I used to carefully wipe the blood from the blade. I placed both the sword, and soiled cloth, into a black case, which would be returned to Setianta.

Gathering the remaining commanders, we exited the building where a crowd of Lorids, now slaves within their own minds, had been brought to witness the death of their leaders.

"My dear Lorids, you have fought bravely and well. Your species will always be respected within the empire you are now a part of. Try not to think of your new lives as tragedy, but the inevitable beginning to the evolution of a new species; a species where our strengths are combined. Together, we shall create a new order of rule within this vast galaxy. Together, we can turn your loss into a gain, for both our species.

"In saying this, I regret you have yet to accept graceful defeat, or see the potential our empire presents. Instead, you look to your idealized leaders. You cling to false hopes and dreams, instead of accepting your new circumstances. Due to your insistent rebuff of reality, and continuous fighting in the hope your former leaders rise, I find no choice but to destroy those leaders."

I changed to a note of triumph. "Now, having delivered that message to those newly assimilated, I speak on a happier note. My fellow Setians, this is a day of great victory! Your hard work and dedication has brought us glory. Today, the last of your great enemies will die. Congratulations my fellow Setians! Long live the empire!"

The crowd cheered as Lorid leaders were dragged, one-by-one into the crowd, and executed by Setian's in Lorid hosts.

Our enemies were at our mercy. We had won the war.

By chance, I glanced at Darin. Tears ran down his cheeks, likely imagining the turmoil Lorid hosts were enduring, being forced to harm loved ones. This is what I had been waiting to see. The last of his rebellion crushed by the reality of this new world.

He caught me staring, and for an instant, I lowered my emotional shield, allowing him to see what lay underneath my stony exterior. He saw a sadistic joy. The unending thirst for power and strength.

I turned to the crowd as the last of the executions were carried out. These commanders, dying as bloody blobs of flesh in dirty streets, would never become the revered saints my advisors feared. They would be forgotten, as though they'd never existed.

Chapter XXXI

After the celebration concluded, the councilors left for the home planet. Leaving the administrative detail to those who enjoyed it, I was focused on reviewing security reports when one of my commanders interrupted.

"Councilor!"

"Yes, Commander?"

"We have received a call from one of the councilor's ships."

"I'm aware they wish to call a vote for the open position, but does it have to be—"

"Their vessel was attacked by a human rebel ship," my commander cut in. "They managed to get away, and traveled a distance, before the commander ordered a pause to regroup and assist the injured. While they were stopped, the enemy ship appeared. They're being boarded as we speak."

The blood drained from my cheeks. "How many councilors are on the ship, Commander?"

"Five."

I took a deep breath to clear my head. "What commander would have been stupid enough to..." My heart sank. Fear filled me as it had not done since I was a child. I only knew of one commander who would stop to save lives as opposed to racing for the safety of the home planet.

"Kavra's ship?"

"Yes, Councilor Dehartra."

"Transfer the call to my private chambers, and contact the nearby Setian commanders to make them aware of the situation. Order them to my location. Tell Kasar to meet me in my chambers immediately."

Nicholas entered my room, a serious expression on his face, just as I pulled on my councilor's robe. "I assume I will be standing behind you as you make the call?"

"Yes," I replied. "You shall stand on my left."

The door opened once again and Councilor Revdran walked into the room, wearing identical robes. He had chosen to join me after the celebration, as we had not had a proper visit since prior to me joining the Lorid battle. "And I," he stated, "shall stand on your right."

Determined to face whatever threat awaited, we walked together toward my private communication alcove, where we'd soon see a 3D image of the councilor's captors. As the men stepped beside me, it seemed strange to have Councilor Revdran in Kavra's usual place.

"Councilor Dehartra," the computer's voice cut through my thoughts, "are you ready to receive the transmission?"

I closed my eyes and pictured Kavra lying on the floor, blood pooling around his lifeless body.

"Dehartra."

My eyes flew open at the sound of Kasar's voice. "Transfer the call."

The air shimmered and we stood facing two human men. They both looked young, no older than twenty-five, and thin.

"To whom am I speaking?" I addressed them.

"I could ask you the same question," the taller of the two replied.

"Councilor Dehartra," I answered. "Also Revdran and Kasar."

"I am Commander Jones, and this is Sub-Commander Taylor. We have taken control of this ship."

"What can we do for you, Commander Jones?"

"I have a list of demands, and if they are not met immediately, I will destroy this ship, and kill all those who are on it."

"What demands?"

"We want ships. Ten of your best, cleared of all troops and handed over to us. We also demand two hundred *feeders* upon each of the ships, and the kitchens to be supplied with rations enough to feed a thousand people."

"Ships, weapons, and food," Kasar stated. "These are your demands?"

"Yes." The commander nodded. "Bring them to our location, and leave. If I even suspect you are trying something stupid, I'll start killing the men and women on this ship immediately. Do you understand?"

"Yes, Commander, I understand. I will bring what you request to your location, and we will meet face-to-face. However, if you so much as harm one person on that ship, you get nothing. I'll be there in five hours." I waved my hand. The computer cut the communication link.

"We cannot possibly give them ships," Councilor Revdran protested.

"Of course not," I answered.

"What are we going to do?"

"Simple," I replied.

I glanced at Kasar. He nodded.

"I will meet with them at the rendezvous point, and establish a new set of demands." I turned to the councilor. "Would you please consent to remaining on my ship throughout the negotiations?"

He nodded, not attempting to hide his confusion.

"Good. Please excuse me, gentlemen. I am going to get some sleep. Wake me when we near our destination."

Darin waited for me in my chambers, sitting in a chair by the glowing glass, reading a book, Aurora in his lap. I found it interesting that while she tolerated everyone, Aurora most preferred the two humans.

As I entered the room, he closed the cover, gently set Aurora aside, and rose to greet me. "Hello, Chrissa." His eyes caught the glint of gold on my robe. "Why the formal attire?"

"Kavra's been captured," I informed him, and relayed the details of the last half-hour. At the end, I added, "Don't worry, they'll get nothing from this."

"What will you do?" Darin asked. "Half the council..."

"Can be replaced, if necessary."

"And Kavra?"

I allowed my eyes to close.

A mistake.

I opened them to find Darin had closed the distance between us.

"Could you replace him as well?"

"Yes."

"Liar."

"Careful, Darin. You forget your place."

"And you," he challenged, "have a heart. You care for Kavra, as much as you are capable of caring for anyone."

"Love is a luxury I cannot afford."

"Do you love him?" Darin asked, an edge to his voice I could not quite place. "Was he your lover?"

I don't know why I answered, "No, Nicholas was."

"Kasar? But I thought he raised you."

I cast my eyes to the floor. "He did."

"And Kavra?"

You are mine. Nicholas' words echoed across my memories. *Kavra will be safe, as long as you belong to me.*

"Safe," a rare truth fell. "He was safe, as long as I..."

Darin's hand touched my arm, causing my stiff frame to jerk.

"Leave, Darin."

"Chrissa—"

"Go."

He left without another word. I removed my council robe and slipped into a thin, black satin gown.

Darin's voice stayed with me as I lay upon the bed. *Could you replace Kavra as well?*

I closed my eyes and fought my way to sleep, but not to peaceful rest.

Kavra lay injured against his destroyed ship, in the center of a Paltian forest. His breath was shallow and unsteady. Blood gushed from his side.

"Stay with me," I begged. "Kavra please, please don't leave me."

Tears streamed down my face as his eyes lost focus. I looked to my left. An open coffin waited beside us. I stood from Kavra knowing I would see his sister's young, peaceful face inside, as Kavra once had.

The black dress clung to her thin body. Crimson jewels sparkled against the dim light, reflecting dazzling colors across the room. Faceless creatures stood on either side, clearing a path. When I reached the coffin, I looked down to gaze into her peaceful expression. My own face stared back, eyes closed in death's eternal grasp. Startled, I jerked back, a shrill scream falling.

"CHRISSALYNN!" A VOICE SHOOK ME from my dream. My body jerked up, but Darin's strong hands held me in place. "Chrissa," he said again, "you were dreaming."

Real tears wet my face. "No," I whispered. "Memories. Mine…and his."

"What?"

I looked around the familiar room and took several deep breaths. My racing heart slowed. "How far are we from the rendezvous point?"

"Twenty minutes. I was coming to wake you."

I took a few more deep breaths. "Thank you. I am going to shower and prepare for the meeting. Please inform Kasar to be ready to accompany me within the hour."

"Command would like to know if you want more ships to head to this location?"

"No. We should have more than enough firepower to deal with the situation."

Darin left to inform Kasar of my orders. I took a quick shower, and put a chain with a gold cross around my neck, before once again donning my formal robe.

Dressed, I spun the simple gold ring on my left hand, which glistened in the glass rock's light.

My sister wore this ring every day until she died, Kavra's voice echoed. *I want you to have it.*

"Councilor?" Darin interrupted my thoughts.

"Coming," I replied. I left the room, Darin following a few steps behind me, and entered one of the main communication rooms where Kasar and Revdran awaited.

"Computer," I said, "open communications with Kavra's ship." Once again, after a shimmer, I faced Commander Jones.

"Commander, as you can see, we have brought ships."

"Yes," he stated, "but not in the required condition."

"Let me explain what is going to happen, Commander. One of my ships is being cleared as we speak. When the total evacuation is completed, shields will be dropped, and you will be allowed to scan to ensure all personnel have been removed.

"When you agree the ship is in fact empty, you and I shall meet face-to-face upon it. We will each be allowed two guards to accompany us. There, and only there, will we discuss the finer points of your demands. I will see you in thirty minutes." I cut communications before he could reply.

"I hope you know what you are doing," my fellow councilor replied.

"The empress always knows," Kasar offered.

A half-hour later, I faced the commander in the flesh. We met on a ship belonging to Nicholas' fleet. Two couches faced each other, and I took a seat, sinking into the soft pillows, as I motioned for the other men to do the same. They looked surprised at the setting, as though they had expected a barren room with uncomfortable chairs.

Commander Jones, and Sub-Commander Taylor, took their seats beside another man with dirty blond hair.

"Welcome. May I ask the name of your third companion, Commander?"

"This is Sub-Commander Burns," he replied.

"May I offer any of you refreshments?" I indicated a bar. "Some tea, or perhaps a glass of wine?"

The commander looked startled. "No," he replied.

"Water?"

"No, thank you," he refused again.

"Well, I do believe I am going to partake. Kasar, would you mind opening a bottle of wine?"

"Certainly, Councilor Dehartra. I have your favorite."

"Good." We waited as Kasar opened the bottle. "Computer, music please, something from Earth? Mozart perhaps?" I glanced at Commander Jones. "Unless you have a different preference?"

"No," he answered.

Music played in the background. "Better?"

None replied as Kasar handed me a glass of wine. "Thank you," I said. "Are you sure you and your men won't join us? It's an excellent vintage."

"No, thank you," Jones replied again. "Look, what is going on here?"

I took a sip of the red wine, allowing the sweet fragrances of cherry and oak to fill my senses before gently placing the glass on the table to my left. "Well, gentlemen, I was hoping we could enjoy the evening, but since you insist upon business, I am willing to oblige."

"That would be best," the commander replied. "I don't understand why our demands have not been met."

I sighed. "Because they're not going to be met, Commander."

Silence followed, as though no one in the room had understood what I'd said.

Finally, Jones asked, "What?"

"You have two choices. The first option is you can order your men off the Setian ship immediately. You will be allowed to re-enter your own ships, and run as far as you can. At the end of twenty-four hours grace, you will be considered as much a threat as any other rebel ship."

"Do you not understand?" Jones asked. "I will kill everyone on that ship we have taken, and at least two have been identified as Setian leaders! I will kill them—"

"Option two," I cut in. "You refuse to leave, in which case, you and all of your men will die."

Silence followed again.

"Oh, forgive me, if you wish to join the empire, always an option as well. Any number of Setians would be proud to share the mind of the leader who managed to capture one of our esteemed commanders." I took another sip of wine. "Are you sure you don't want any? It truly is...exquisite."

"Are you not understanding?" Commander Jones asked in disbelief. "I *will* kill them."

"No, Commander, it is you who fails to understand. Those men would be proud to die in service to their empire. They will die with full forgiveness, and travel from this realm to one of eternal glory." I touched the cross hanging from my neck. "Heaven, if you will."

Jones cleared his throat. "What would your men say if they knew you were willing to throw their lives away so casually?"

"Those men will say they are honored to die for the empire." I sweetened my voice. "They will die for honor. They will die for glory. They will die for me."

"You?" the commander asked. "Who are you?"

Jones was about my age, but staring into his wide eyes, he seemed decades younger. "Councilor Deharta," I finally replied.

"May..." His voice was only a bare whisper. "May I ask you a question, Councilor Dehartra?" He seemed younger with every word, panic slowly filling his eyes. "What...if you were human, and had captured a Setian ship. What would you have done?"

I stood and walked to the bar, where the open bottle of wine sat. I grabbed a new glass from the cabinet and filled it halfway. Returning to the sofa, I placed the crystal in front of the captain.

"Have a drink with me, Mr. Jones, and I will answer your question." I touched our glasses together and we both took a sip.

"If I were you?"

He nodded.

"If I were human, had come upon a Setian ship, and had managed to take control? I would have immediately killed everyone on board, wiped the computer's memory, taken the ship, and proceeded to run to the farthest hiding place I could find, hoping I had not killed someone important enough to send the entire empire after me. That's what I would have done, Commander."

"The Lorids," he replied, "warned me that making demands was pointless."

"And they are correct. They are a wise species; you were ill-advised to ignore their warnings."

"You would let them all die, wouldn't you?"

"I never lie about death, and I will pull the trigger myself if needed." My voice was soft, the statement a simple matter of truth. "In fact, should you choose to live, the first thing I will do is order the execution of the pilot who failed to evade you. He will die in shame and, in our belief system, be sent to a type of hell for his crimes."

"Wait, I thought in death you forgave your kind?"

"Only if they die in service to a Setian cause. If they die by execution, they are forever damned." Silence followed as I finished my glass of wine. "Your decision isn't that complicated. Death, life, or infestation? Choose, and I'll take care of the rest."

"I could order this ship blown up," the naïve man said. "We would both die."

"You can't," I replied.

"Oh, yes—"

"No!" I cut him off. "First, because you have shown your fear. Second, because you are *human*," I said the word as though it were dirty, "and that is not the human way. Third, I chose this ship because it has the best shielding in all the empire. There is no known technology that can break through its shields." I gave him a pitying glance. "Your ship and men will be destroyed. Now, are we done with idle threats?"

A heartbeat of silence passed before he nodded.

"Choose one of your two assistants, and send them back to our ship. A task force of my guards will accompany them. When it has been confirmed that you've killed no one after our initial conversation, your men will be allowed to leave. Twenty-four hours of safe passage will be granted to your ship."

"And if anyone has been killed?"

"I would pray they have not," I said. "Computer, open communication to the captured ship."

I turned to the young humans as the image appeared before us. "You're up," I advised Jones. "Choose your words wisely."

He talked to the man on the opposite side of the image, instructing him to allow our people on board, and to follow our directives. The other human questioned him, to which Commander Jones replied, "If we want to live, we have to do this!"

"A last piece of advice," I said, when the communications were cut. "Kill the man who questioned you. Next time, no one will."

Twenty minutes later, their people had disembarked from Kavra's ship. Jones, Taylor, and I sat on the couch, working on a new bottle of wine, when a knock sounded.

Kasar rose and opened the door.

I turned to address the visitor, but my words died in my throat. Kavra stood tall, draped in a navy robe, a perfect match to Kasar's. I rose to go to him, but a slight movement from Kasar stopped me.

He was right. Showing affection in front of the enemy was never an option. Both men remained by the door as I turned back to Jones.

"Are you ready for your last lesson?"

His eyes searched mine.

"When you accept a role of leadership," I explained, "you must also face the consequences of your mistakes. You have my word that your ship will be given free passage to run. However, you will not be offered the same courtesy. You, or your sub-commander, must remain here and pay the price for your failure. The choice lies solely with you."

"What?" Commander Jones exclaimed. "You said we would be released!"

"I said your ship would be given the chance to run, yes. I never said you both would be on that ship when it left. Now, you try my patience, Commander. Choose, yourself or your comrade, before I infest you both."

A moment passed before Jones said, "Me."

"Your choice, to sacrifice yourself, is the reason your kind will fall. And you'll live to see it, Commander. That is a promise."

"I'm not leaving him," the other human declared.

"You will," Jones replied.

"No, I…"

"She will infest us both!"

After several minutes of arguing, the sub-commander returned to the human ship and left, leaving its captain with me. Kasar and Kavra led Commander Jones back to my ship, and into one of the rooms that hosted a Setian pool.

"Wait!" He stopped in his tracks. "I was number one on my ship. Don't your laws allow me to ask for death?"

I considered the question. "Is death your desire?"

He gave no verbal answer, only nodded.

"If you were a top-level leader, death would be an option. A mere captain, or commander, is not of sufficient rank to qualify.

"Come now, it won't be so bad. Think of this new life as an opportunity to learn. Who knows, you may even form a positive relationship with your chosen Setian. Many do, in time."

"Other human leaders were granted death. They died as heroes instead of facing slavery."

I looked at Kavra and could not help but laugh.

"I'll let you in on a secret, Jones. Computer," I called to the ship, "find Darin and tell him to come here immediately."

"Yes, Empress Dehartra," the computer replied.

"Empress!" Jones exclaimed.

I smiled.

He looked at me in a new light. "The other commander wore a matching robe."

"Yes."

"He is part of your council?"

"You had five councilors on the ship you captured. Five councilors, and the empire's second-ranking military commander in your grasp. Their death would have been a devastating blow to our morale. However, it did not happen, thanks to you."

We both turned as Darin walked into the room. "Hello, darling," I said in a cheerful voice. "I'd like you to meet the man who captured Kavra. Commander Jones, meet Darin Hoyle, one of the true leaders of your rebellion."

"Darin?" Jones said. "You're…alive?"

"My lover," I informed.

Darin did not respond, other than to avoid the gazes of those around him.

"I personally captured the leaders of whom you speak. There were no heroic deaths. No self-sacrifice. They chose life, Commander, and your great leader is a willing slave."

I turned back to the others.

"He's seen enough."

When Jones was led away to be infested, I dismissed Darin, and motioned for Kavra to follow me.

When we reached my chambers, my suppressed emotions rose in a wave of fury. I slapped him hard across the face.

He reeled, then turned back to face me.

I slapped him again. "You stupid, horrible, dim-witted… What were you thinking?" I screamed at him. "What the hell were you thinking? You almost got yourself killed! You stupid, fucking idiot!" Hot tears rolled down my face as he pulled me into his arms, sobbing against him.

"I'm sorry, Chrissa. I was stupid. I thought…it doesn't matter. You're right, I was an absolute idiot."

My body shook as I pulled back enough to meet the pale blue of his gaze. "If I had lost you, I don't know how I'd survive." I shook my head. "If I'd been forced to give the order that ended your life? No, I wouldn't. I couldn't."

He looked startled. "Chrissa, what are you saying? I thought you didn't..."

"You're the heart that beats in my chest, William," the words ripped from my lips, tumbling forth, "and I was forced to make a decision that could have ended your life! How could you?"

Kavra fought to draw a sharp breath, his expression shifting from surprise, to a reflection of deep regret. "I'm sorry, Chrissa, I never meant to scare you."

I buried my face into the fabric of his shirt. "I can't live without you. Please don't make me. Not again. Please, William..." My words gave way to incoherent sobs.

Wrapping his arms around my body, he carried me to the bed. "I won't," he promised, holding me as tears continued to fall.

Chapter XXXII

The next morning I awoke alone to the sound of pounding on my door.

"All right!" I called. "What's so damned important?"

The door opened and four of my fellow council members walked into my room. Two had chosen the form of human men, while the other two held Lorid hosts. One of the Lorids, Councilor Lindis, stepped forward first.

"Empress," Councilor Lindis addressed me.

"Yes, Councilors?"

"First I would like to thank you for finding a solution to our dilemma. Your brilliant and fast thinking shows, yet again, we were right in choosing you to lead us."

"Thank you, Councilors. Your gratitude is much appreciated but, I assure you, entirely unnecessary. Any Setian would have done the same."

"Yes," Councilor Lindis replied. "However the point, Empress, is the situation never should have happened in the first place. Someone must pay."

"I agree. The pilots responsible will be executed shortly, along with Sub-Harars 14, who was on duty in the control room."

"We are aware. However, after much discussion, we have decided, considering the severity of what happened—nearly half of the council's lives were at risk—the death of a sub-commander is not enough."

I sighed. "Fine. I'll kill Harars 3 as well."

"Insufficient."

"What are you asking, Councilors? Everyone responsible is being punished."

"The ship was Kavra's," Lindis said.

The room went silent.

"Would you care to repeat yourself?" I said in a low voice. "Be very specific, Councilor."

"Kavra was in charge," he clarified, with far less confidence. "Therefore he should be held responsible."

"Kavra is the second-highest-ranking military commander on record, and one of the key players responsible for the Lorid victory. His pilot fell into a random trap, a situation that could have happened to anyone, and you believe Kavra should be killed for it?"

"He was in charge, and ultimately responsible for the mistakes of his men. He should be punished accordingly."

"Because he was in charge?"

"Yes!" Lindis replied.

"Would he have disobeyed, had you ordered him to return to the home planet immediately?"

"What?"

"If you had ordered Kavra to flee to safety, would Kavra have disobeyed you?"

"I am a councilor."

"Exactly. You're a councilor, and one of the highest-ranking on the ship. Therefore, the person ultimately responsible for half the council almost losing their lives…is you."

"But I was not in charge, Kavra was."

"You're a councilor, yet you claim Kavra was in charge. How is this possible, Councilor Lindis?

"If any of you," I motioned to the rest of the councilors, "had taken command of the ship, per your rank, you would have reached the home planet without being boarded. However, since you failed to do so, I must believe you agreed with Kavra's choices.

"Is there one of you who should be charged for not taking command when you disagreed with Kavra's decision? Or should I tell the executioner to prepare for all of your deaths?"

"All of us?" Councilor Byde questioned.

"You have stated that whoever was in charge should be punished. I agree. Which one of you, Councilors, should have taken charge? Name someone, or I will order all your executions."

They looked at each other.

"Give me a name."

Lindis gave me the one answer I had not expected. "Councilor Vektor."

"Pardon?" I asked, taken off-guard.

"Councilor Vektor is the one who takes charge in your absence. He should have taken command."

"Yes," Councilor Byde jumped in as the other two nodded in agreement.

"You should leave now, Councilors."

Lindis looked like he was about to argue, but seemed to think better of it. The councilors filed out of my chambers as Darin walked in.

"Darin, summon Kasar, now."

Five minutes later, Kasar was inside my chambers. I told him of the council's demand. "I didn't even know Vektor was on Kavra's ship."

"They fear you."

"What?"

"If the council members on the ship had died, Kavra, myself, and two of your other closest allies would have been promoted to the council. Combine this with your friendship to Revdran and Vektor, and seven of the thirteen council members would have been loyal solely to you. You scared them, so now they are going after your power base."

"How do I save him?"

Kasar looked me at me with a rare display of sadness. "I don't think you can, Chrissalynn."

"Vektor wasn't in charge; it could have happened to anyone."

"Nevertheless, the council has made a declaration that someone should be punished, a decision I happen to agree with. If you choose not to kill a member of the council, the blame will fall upon Kavra. I don't believe it is possible to save them both."

"Vektor is one of the reasons I achieved my success. I would not be empress without him. I can't..."

"You must choose."

I looked at Kasar's stern expression. "If they force me to kill Vektor, I'll take all their lives."

"Yes, you will."

I looked at him with a mixture of horror and fascination. "Execute the councilors?"

"You have the right to demand the life of the highest-ranking Setian. Kill them all, Chrissalynn."

My voice sounded childlike as I stared into his eyes. "And Vektor?"

"A necessary sacrifice." If it had been a film, the sky would have been gray, and thunder would have shaken the building as the cold wind howled. But in space, there was only silence.

I stared at him, considering. "Call the guards. Have each of the involved council members taken into custody, and inform the executioner to prepare for a series of private executions. Send Kavra to me."

Nicholas nodded as he turned and left the room.

A few hours later, the remaining members of the Setian Council had come aboard my ship, summoned from Setianta. I informed them what was about to happen, and was greeted with a tense approval.

Tessersa, my maid, helped me dress formally for the occasion. After she left, I stared into the golden mirror before me. The eyes that stared back were harsh despite the artful touch of cosmetics. As though they had forgotten the warmth of joy, or happiness.

"Lovely," a deep voice startled me out of my trance. My eyes remained on the mirror as a tall, handsome man joined my reflection wearing a black suit. I remained motionless, allowing him to walk slowly toward me until his hands were on either side of the carved chair in which I sat. "Beautiful, Empress, but you don't need me to tell you that."

"Kavra," I whispered, "who am I?"

His left hand touched my bare shoulder. "You are the Setian Empire empress, and Nicholas' chosen heir."

"I do not want to do this. If I am the empress, why do I have to? Vektor is…" I struggled with the words. "He was my teacher," I finally said. "If you had—"

"Chrissa, listen to me. Vektor had nothing to do with this. You don't have to kill him. You're empress, and forgiveness within this empire is found both in death, and in you."

My eyes remained on the mirror, staring into the reflection of his eyes. Kavra was right, I could save the councilor. But…

After a deep breath, I explained in a firm voice, "It does not matter if they were the ones who ordered the ship to stop, or not. What matters is that they have demanded a life in payment, and the debt must be paid.

"By attempting to blame you for their own failure, they admit their unworthiness to hold the rank of councilor. That is unacceptable behavior, and those men, yes even Councilor Vektor, proved themselves unfit for the Setian Council."

I turned away from the mirror and looked directly into the depths of Kavra's eyes. "They will die today, and I will sign their order of execution, because our traditions require me to do so."

Kavra pulled back with a strange look, as though seeing me for the first time. The same expression that crossed Darin's face every time he stood witness to one of my more horrific acts; surprise, with a touch of fear. A countenance I had never expected to see grace Kavra's usually proud, brave features. "You are everything we had ever hoped for. A true daughter of the Setian Empire."

"I am what you and Nicholas made me to be."

"Councilor Dehartra," came a call over the communications system.

"Yes."

"The council members are ready. They await your presence."

"I'll be right there."

I turned my attention back to Kavra. "Shall we finish this?"

He gave me a sad smile, turned, offered me his arm, and together we walked to my formal conference room.

"Councilors," I greeted. "I welcome you."

"Thank you, Empress Dehartra, Kavra." The reply came from Councilor Iselita, who occupied a tall human female host. "I did not expect to see you both here."

"I'm not," Councilor Revdran said. "I'm usually surprised to see them apart."

"I am but a student," Kavra replied, "learning from the best."

"Ah, yes," Revdran said, "we must always continue to learn."

"Yes," Iselita agreed. She turned to Kavra. "A nasty business, this. Yet it seems you might benefit."

"Benefit?"

"The open council positions," Revdran clarified. "You must have realized that, after this mess, you're as good as in."

"I assure you, Councilor, I take no pleasure in these affairs."

"Okay," I cut in. "We are all here. Let's finish this."

We walked into an adjoining room with stark white walls. Guards surrounded the condemned council members. Of them, only Vektor had requested the privilege of taking his own life.

"You can't do this!" Councilor Lindis called as we entered the room.

"Yes, we can," Iselita said. "Orders have been signed by all the non-guilty council members, and approved by the empress."

"You four will be executed by the guards immediately. Councilor Vektor will be allowed to take his own life."

Executioners stepped forward and forced the councilors to their knees.

"No!" one of them screamed. "You can't do this!"

"Councilors," I spoke to the room, "you have been found unfit to sit on the Setian Empire Council. For your failure, by imperial decree of the loyal members of the Setian Council, you shall be executed."

The executioners aimed their weapons as I spoke the ancient line, "May your sins haunt you for all eternity."

Their bodies were incinerated, leaving only Councilor Vektor standing between the guards, and amid small piles of ash.

Kavra stepped forward, handing the ancient blade of Dehartra hilt-first to Councilor Vektor.

"Thank you, old friend," Vektor said softly.

"The sword was on loan for the Darcoth execution," Kavra told him.

I stepped forward to speak, but Councilor Vektor preempted my planned words, "It has been an honor, Empress Dehartra, to serve and die under a ruler worthy of the ancient title. May your name live forever, and may my death further serve to honor the glory of the Setian Empire. Be proud, Chrissalynn. You truly are the perfect Setian."

I nodded, my eyes completely dry, and put my hand over Vektor's. This was the man who had made me a member of the empire. The one who had promoted me to the council, and ultimately, proclaimed me empress. Every victory of my life had been shared by this man.

"Councilor Vektor, of the Setian Empire," I said in an empty voice, "with your death," the blade sank into his flesh, straight through his heart, "we forgive you for your sins."

He died less than a minute later, his blood covering my hand as I withdrew the blade.

Kavra stood with tears in his eyes.

"Thank you for your attendance, Councilors. Escort his body back to the home world, and bury him in a place of honor."

"Yes, Empress Dehartra," Councilor Iselita said.

"Is there any other business at hand?"

"No, Empress. Not at this time."

Without another word, I left the room and walked toward my chambers.

"Chrissa!" Kavra's voice called out as I reached the door, and he followed me inside.

"Kav, please don't." I stared at the floor.

He gently reached under my chin and lifted my face up to meet his eyes. Leaning forward, he kissed me tenderly before pulling me into a tight embrace and crying silent tears.

My own eyes remained completely dry.

Chapter XXXIII

I AWOKE IN THE MIDDLE of the night to what sounded like thunder. Aurora stood beside me on the bed, pink fur sticking straight out. I opened my eyes to someone coming through the door to my chambers.

My captain stepped forward and gave a low bow. "Forgive me, Councilor. Our ship is under attack."

"Attack? Who is attacking us?"

"We initially brought a huge fleet, but in the last few days, current events took us by surprise, and we've dropped to only a few ships. I believe the rebels have found us, but I don't think they know who is on this particular ship."

My mind raced. We had fallen into the same trap? What the hell was going on? "How many ships are attacking us, Commander?"

"Nine as of right now. We can disable some, but we do not have enough power to defeat them, nor enough speed to lose them. They are asking to speak with the commanding officer."

"Let me think."

"Forgive me, Empress, but we must answer now."

In all my years of ruling, I'd never made this caliber of mistake; now in an instant, everything was falling apart. The majority of the remaining council was on my ship.

I advised my commander I would be on the bridge shortly.

He came back with an idea I had not thought of. "I do not believe they know someone of your rank is on this ship. If you allow your commander to handle the situation, we may all be saved. Do you think they'll bother to take prisoners if they are aware the highest-ranking of their enemies sits within their grasp? They'd want you dead, not captured."

"The rules of command are clear, but your rank has always been the exception. Councilors are replaceable. An empress is not."

"I killed councilors for doing as you suggest, for failing to take command."

"We are meant to protect one of your rank at all cost. It has always been our way. Allow someone else to take the fall. They know they have found a high-ranking ship, but your face has never been made public, and so they have no idea you're here."

I considered his recommendation briefly before giving a slight nod. "Do it."

After my commander gave an official surrender, I entered my private codes into the core computer, and sent a distress signal to all Setian ships in the area. Surrender would buy us time. I only hoped it would be enough.

I changed from my robe into a plain uniform, one that might be worn by a janitor.

Finally, I moved Darin to a cell. When he questioned me I simply said, "You are, and always have been, my prisoner."

The look in his eyes told me there was more he wanted to say.

I smiled. "There's no time."

To my surprise, he pulled me to him and kissed me passionately while holding me for what might be the last time. "You won," he said.

"No. I could only claim victory if I could have had you without emotion. I lost, Darin." I paused and tried to harden my heart for what was to come. "I'm sorry."

With those words, I closed the cell door, and turned to see Kavra standing behind me. I gave him a nod as I reached into the left hidden pocket of my uniform, and handed him a sheet of paper, folded neatly in half.

"Why do I think I know what this is?"

"Because you do."

"Chrissa, no. You can't possibly."

"Yes, I can," I replied in a firm voice. "You of all people know the laws. Take it, Kavra, and see it done. I must get to the command room."

"Chrissa, I cannot do this, and you cannot want it."

"Kavra," I sighed, "we are children of the empire, condemned to our fate. For honor, for glory, my orders stand."

"Chrissa, please! You are asking me to... It will kill you."

"Emotions cause people to make mistakes, that prevent them from getting what they deserve. Carry out my orders."

"What did we do to you, Chrissa?"

"Empress!" I said sharply. "I am Empress Dehartra, and you, Kavra, will carry out my orders as is your duty. Do you understand?"

Silence followed before he finally said, "Yes, Empress Dehartra, I understand."

I turned from him, eyes dry as I hurried toward the bridge.

There I found my commander bound and gagged, lying on the floor with bruises forming where the rebels had beaten him. They were asking him, over and over again, who was on his ship. Who was he protecting. Demanding the Setian in his brain to leave, in hopes the host would be willing to talk.

A Lorid, appearing to be in charge, promised to spare the life of everyone, and even release the ship, if the commander would either tell him who the ship belonged to, or leave his host.

The commander hoarsely asked if he had the Lorid's word no one would be killed should he leave his host, so that it would not actually be him betraying the high-ranking official.

The Lorid gave his word.

At this promise, my commander removed himself from the body of his human host.

The Lorids waited for the man to once again gain control of himself.

When he was able to speak, he verified, "We do have your word no one will be killed since he left me, correct?"

When the Lorid nodded, the former host, whose name was Brandon, laughed. "I hold you to your word. The commander has removed himself from me, and fulfilled his obligations to the conditions you set. I am now free, and as such I choose to tell you nothing."

The Lorid took a step back in surprise and asked Brandon, "You were taken voluntarily?"

"Not at first. I tried to fight, but my efforts were futile. I was miserable until I came under my commander's possession. We serve someone who can be as ruthless and cruel as they come, but who would never harm those who obey orders. We serve a person who protects those under her, and now I plan to return the favor.

"You swore an oath to leave quietly if I were released. We have kept our end of the bargain, now go!"

A touching sight. To see one of my own defend me was one thing, but a slave imprisoned upon my orders was altogether different.

As the Lorid stood in shocked silence, a human stepped forward. His eyes held a lifetime of hatred as he grabbed Brandon and knocked him to the ground. "My fellow rebel might have promised you freedom, but we humans do not take orders from anyone; especially them. You are a traitor to your race, and will die an agonizing death, if you do not tell me what I have asked right now!"

Brandon stood his ground and flatly refused to give me up. "Every being on this ship would rather die than tell you anything. And if you knew this person, you would protect them as well."

At this, the young man raised his fist and landed a blow firmly against the left side of Brandon's face. Bones cracked and blood splattered the floor.

I looked away before forcing myself to return my gaze. If Brandon could endure the beating, I would watch it. The man grabbed Brandon's left arm and twisted. Brandon screamed as the bones snapped in two, but refused to tell them the information they sought. The beating continued.

A voice finally called out, "Wait!"

My heart stopped beating.

Chapter XXXIV

Kavra stepped forward. "I'm who you want."

"And you are?"

"William Kavra, second-ranking military commander of the Setian Empire."

The man in charge turned toward Kavra with interest. "Kavra," he whispered. "You captured the leaders of the Earth resistance, did you not?"

Kavra nodded. "Ryan, Kathleen, Damon, and Darin."

"Yours is a name I know well."

"I've not yet had the pleasure of learning yours."

"Mathews," he replied. "Thomas Mathews, captain and fourth-in-command of the Lorid Earth Resistance."

They grabbed Kavra, who offered no resistance.

Captain Mathews walked across the room to stand directly in front of him. "You have no idea how long I've waited to have one of the famous Setian commanders in my grasp."

"Lords," Kavra corrected him. "We are known as Setian lords."

Without warning, Mathews hit Kavra hard across the face. No blood spilled, but Mathew's handprint lay clearly across Kavra's skin as he pulled his arm away. He then proceeded to beat Kavra, ribs breaking from the force with a sickening sound. Another man joined in.

Kavra could not suppress random moans of pain.

My heart broke with every sound.

Kavra, my Kavra, was taking the cruelty that should have been mine to endure.

Tears fell as I glanced at the ring encircling the finger of my left hand, the plain gold band glistening in the dim light.

In too much pain to stand, Kavra lay on the ground as the beating continued.

There was no reason for this abuse, no information to be learned, only cruel and pointless brutality. My mind wandered back to the last time Kavra had lain in such agony, dying on Palta. How he had fought for each breath, and the fear that had clutched my heart as I begged him to stay with me, just stay with me.

He cried out as another blow landed on the left side of his face, painting his lips red with blood.

"No," I whispered, but my voice was tight in my throat, and no one heard me.

They picked Kavra up, dragging him by his arms, to take him to their ship.

My voice was wrenched from my throat, a cry that rose straight from my heart. "No! He's not the one you want!" All eyes turned to me. "Leave him alone."

I stepped forward and turned not to Mathews, but to the Lorid by his side. "Are you in charge?"

"Yes," he replied.

"What would the life of the Setian who killed Darcoth be worth to you?"

"What?" he asked, confused by the question, especially coming from what appeared to be a low-ranking crew member.

"Do you know the name of the Setian who killed Commander Darcoth, and led the final conquest of the Lorid home world?"

He looked at me intently as he answered, "Dehartra."

"What would the life of Dehartra be worth to you?"

"A great deal."

"The lives and freedom of all the people on this ship?" I asked. "Including Kavra's?"

"We have the ship," Mathews cut in. "Let's take them all."

"Silence!" the Lorid commanded. "Dehartra would be worth this ship, and all those on it."

"Do you swear to allow this ship to go free, and all its member to leave with their lives, if I give you Dehartra?"

"There is no way in hell I'm giving up Kavra," Mathews protested. "He was responsible for the demise of Earth, and besides—"

"Silence!" the Lorid warned again, anger in his voice. "You Earthlings, and what you think you know. This soldier is offering a member of the council. It is not a deal to be refused."

"Besides," a second Lorid spoke, "Kavra had a role in the attack on Earth, but Dehartra was the real leader behind your planet's demise, as for our own. Humans, never taking the time to search for the power behind the mask."

"You have my word," the head Lorid promised.

"No!" Kavra managed to step away from his captors and ran painfully to my side. He jerked me around to face him, grabbing my arms tightly, ignoring the various guns pointed in our direction. "Don't do this Chrissa."

I learned forward, close enough to whisper for his ears alone, "No matter what happens, make sure Nicholas takes his place as emperor. Accept a council position, and rule by his side, as you would have mine. Promise me you'll help him finish what I have started, for only you can act as the balance to his power. Promise me."

"Chrissa, no."

"For the good of the empire, promise me."

"Chrissa."

"Say it!"

He pulled back to look at me, tears in his eyes, which fell as he nodded. "I promise."

"Okay," I whispered, tears threatening my own vision.

He finally lessened his grip enough for me to take him into a tight embrace. "Kavra, it's okay, just another adventure." I raised my hand to wipe a tear from his cheek. "Our favorite kind."

With a deep breath, I pulled away from Kavra, and announced, "I'm who you want."

I took a step toward Captain Mathews, but Kavra grabbed my arm and spun me back to face him.

"No," he said, "she's trying to protect me."

A lifetime of training was betrayed as his name escaped on a sob. "Kavra, it's my turn."

"No," he said with such force it made me cry even harder. "No. I promised you on the day we met, I would live to serve you."

"Then serve me," I whispered, though my voice must have carried like a scream in the awed silence of the room. "Let me go. Kavra, please, I have lived my life for the honor of this empire. Let me die the way I have lived: as a servant, a daughter, and an empress."

"How, Chrissa? How can I let you go?" he wondered aloud in a strangled voice.

I stared into the eyes of the only man who had ever seen my soul. When I finally found the strength to draw a steady breath, I kissed him with all the passion I possessed, trying to convey all the words that would never be spoken, and all the truths which would never be told.

His arms came around me, and still, the room remained shocked into silence.

When he pulled back, his blood stained my lips. I stared into his eyes and said, "You know how."

"I love you, Chrissalynn"

"I love you too, William. Always have." My tears had not stopped, and I made no effort to slow them. "Kavra, I..."

"I know."

I choked out the words, "It's just another adventure."

He stared back at me, his eyes screaming what he could not voice. He shook his head. "With certain death assured."

"They're the best kind, you know?"

"Yes, they are."

"We wouldn't have it any other way." I offered a smile, and my tears finally stopped. I slowly stepped back away from him until only his hand was in mine. "You can let go now," I said softly.

His own tears finally subsided, as he caught my gaze and slowly, ever so slowly, raised my hand to his lips. He gave a gentle kiss, and the slightest of bows.

After a quick smile at Kavra, I turned back around to the Lorid in charge. "I'm who you want."

Captain Mathews glanced at me, uncertainty plain on his face. "What rank do you hold?"

"If I said anything lower than a top military commander, would you believe me?" I returned his stare with blank, cold eyes, which told him nothing, yet everything. The contest seemed to prolong into a battle of wills.

"Who are you?" he finally asked.

"I am the leader of the Setian military forces, responsible for the demise of both the Lorid and Earth resistance, and the highest-ranking member of the Setian Council. As empress, I am the most decorated member within this vast and all-powerful empire. And I am ready to face my destiny."

Chapter XXXV

"The rest of my story you have witnessed with your own eyes," I said to a silent courtroom, listeners clinging to my every word. "I was taken into custody, and promised a hearing. The charges brought against me were those of murder, rape, and treason.

"In response to the first charge: As empress, I am responsible for every action taken by every person under my power. All the deaths committed by them can be traced back to me. I am most certainly guilty of massive and multiple murders, in every degree.

"As to the charge of rape, I also plead guilty. That man here with us today," I motioned to Darin, who sat in the stands to my right, "is living proof of my pleasures.

"But in response to the third charge, I profess I've never committed treason. I served the Setian Empire faithfully, as I was raised to do. I will die proudly, in service of my empire, to ensure it shall never die. My death will become legend, and result in Kasar becoming the new emperor, with Kavra by his side.

"You may take my life, but in doing so, you shall grant me eternal forgiveness and glory. Your children will one day gaze upon my portrait as they walk blissfully toward their Setian masters."

"Tell me, Dehartra, do you have anything else you would like to add before your fate is decided?"

My eyes were drawn to the second floor rail, where Darin watched. He kept his eyes locked with mine, not caring who saw as I answered, "What's done is done. I offer no excuse for my actions. What little has gone unsaid," I focused on Darin's eyes as if they were my entire world, and he did not look away, "was never meant to be heard."

"You may step down."

As two armed men reached for me, the man presiding over the hearing glanced to where I was staring and inquired, "Commander Darin, is there anything you would like to say?"

There was a moment of silence before Darin said, "No."

Hearing his voice, I finally found the courage to look forward, and walked steadily down the rows of seated people to the double doors. Surrounded by no fewer than fifteen men, I was taken back to my cell, a room with solid wooden walls, a dirt floor, and only a tiny window where a hint of artificial light could shine through. Six hours later, my inevitable sentence was delivered. I would die by their hands, and my legacy would be immortalized. As the hour of my execution drew near, the door opened unexpectedly, and Darin walked in.

Chapter XXXVI

Darin sat in the cell where Chrissa had placed him, anxiously awaiting his fate. After pacing the confined space for twenty minutes, he succumbed to fatigue.

Damn it! What is going on out there? Is there a fight?

Potential pictures of Chrissa flashed through his mind. Her blood splattering the walls. Chrissa's body being dragged as those of her enemies had been dragged before her in the past. Darin opened his eyes. No, he did not want to see those images. What the hell was taking so damn long?

The lights in the cell were neither bright nor dim, but a medium level, like the light produced by an evening sky after the last rays of sunlight had faded. He heard voices, but they were distant; a low, indistinguishable mumble.

Is Chrissa all right? What are they doing to her?

His thoughts were interrupted by the sound of many thudding footsteps outside his cell. The door flew open and three men stepped into the room. Expecting a rescue party, Darin was unprepared to find himself roughly grabbed as he attempted to rise from the bed.

"Wait!" he said as they forced him to the ground.

The men were human, so he switched to English and tried again.

Two men hit him on his left side, turning his plea into a gasp of pain. His arms were grabbed roughly.

"Wait! I am a prisoner, from the rebellion!" Darin shouted to seemingly deaf ears. A heavy boot was placed on his left ankle and he grimaced in pain. "I am a Setian prisoner, from the Earth resistance!"

He was dragged down the hallway.

"Please," he pleaded with his captors as they moved toward the bridge. Darin searched for Chrissa, but she was nowhere to be seen.

Instead, he found Kavra.

"Where is she?" Darin asked, oblivious to the men surrounding him.

"He's a prisoner," Kavra told the guards, ignoring his question. "A former leader of the Earth resistance. We had him here for interrogation."

The guard finally turned his attention to Darin. "Are his words true?"

"Yes!" Darin replied.

They started prodding him out of the room, with only slightly less force than before.

He walked with them until they reached the door directly beside Kavra. "Where is she?" he asked again. Kavra stared at him blankly. "Is she alive?" Darin demanded. "Damn it, tell me!"

"Yes," he finally replied, "They took her aboard their ship."

"Their ship?"

"Yes." Kavra paused, staring at him. "I… Tell her."

"I will," Darin replied, before being ushered through the door to board the other ship.

The rescue ship he boarded had been designed for defense and power, not luxury. Darin took in the dull features, and poorly-dressed crew. He could not understand how this ragtag group had managed to capture the empress.

He was taken to the bridge where a Lorid and human captain stood side-by-side, quietly discussing their victory. On a large screen behind them, he watched the empress' ship leave, carrying five members of the council to safety.

"Hello, stranger. You are safe now, and the fiends will no longer harm you, but I am curious to know who you are? Obviously someone of importance, considering you were being held on the empress' ship. Did you know she was the empress?"

Darin took a deep breath. "My name is Darin Hoyle, and yes, I knew she was the empress."

"The Darin? As in the former high-commander of Earth's resistance? They said you were captured and that you, along with all those who fought with you, were killed."

"Most were," Darin replied, "but a few of us were taken prisoner and held."

The human commander gave Darin a genuine smile. "Commander Darin, I am honored to be in your presence. You are a hero, and legend among the rebels. Your courage at the beginning of the war inspires those fighting today. I can think of no greater pleasure than to give you back your freedom.

"We are on our way to headquarters, where the empress shall be tried and executed. Once there, you will be free to move about as you wish, but it is my sincerest hope you choose to meet with the council, and consider once again leading your people to freedom."

The rebel headquarters were on a barren planet in the outskirts of a place nicknamed the Shallow Galaxy, because of persistent coarse sand and rocks, no tree had ever graced the surface of its planets, only sickly, yellow grasses. The headquarters complex was encased in a glass dome, which provided oxygen, and other such necessities of life.

The Indoctrination

Darin was welcomed as a hero, and given the best quarters the rebels had to offer, which paled in comparison to the luxurious surroundings Darin had grown accustomed to. The walls were a dirty off-white with wooden floors, and a bed covered with a worn blanket.

During the trial, which spanned the course of five days, Darin sat quietly in the back listening to Chrissa's story. She sat proudly on a straight chair in the wooden box, hands shackled, as her telling spun a spell over the courtroom. Some of her story Darin knew, but other parts, such as how she came to the empire in the first place, were a surprise. Sad fascination brought him back every day, as she recollected the major events of her life, leading her to the disdain of her enemies.

On the second night of the trial, one of the rebellion leaders came to see Darin. "I have no doubt the empress will be put to death, but I'd like to give you a chance to testify against her. Her cruelty is legendary, and I can't imagine what she put you through."

Darin looked at the young man before him. "I appreciate the gesture, but I cannot and will not testify against the empress. Her story is to be told as Chrissa sees fit. Even helpless, and in the chains of your power, she is the empress. I fear her wrath."

"There's no reason to fear her. She will never leave this planet alive. If I had my way, she would already be dead.

"What really happened between the empress and yourself? Why do you call her 'Chrissa'?"

He paused, but continued when Darin gave no answer.

"You were a prisoner of war, and held by the empress herself. Yet you refuse to testify against her. I find this peculiar."

To this Darin replied, "If you do not fear her, you're a fool."

The man left in disgust, leaving Darin to his thoughts.

In formal scenarios, Darin had always addressed Chrissa as "councilor," but when they were alone, he was one of the few allowed to use her real name.

Watching Chrissa in court chambers, surrounded by her enemies, was difficult. His strong, beautiful Chrissa sat abandoned by her empire. A commanding leader, who could bolster troops' failing courage with her mere presence, she'd been contained, but not entirely humbled.

She told the good and the bad of her life, with no excuse for her actions, admitting to every act she'd committed. What unfolded was a surprising tale of loss, despair, and triumph, relayed with an utter lack of emotion, as her training dictated.

There was no doubt in anyone's mind the empress would be sentenced to death. When Chrissa was taken from the courtroom for the last time, Darin stood by the door. Though she should have been bowed under the weight of defeat, dressed in the dirty uniform she had on when she was captured, the empress walked from the assembly with her head high. Just as she didn't show emotion, neither did Chrissa welcome pity.

That night, Darin rose to a knock on the door.

He opened it to find a young man standing on the other side. Three deep scars ran down the side of his left arm as though scratched with a three-pronged blade. "Rob," he greeted.

"Darin," the man replied. "God, Darin, it's really you." The man pulled Darin into an embrace. "When I heard they'd found you, I wanted to come see you immediately, but I was off-planet and couldn't make it back until now."

"You survived capture?"

"I got lucky," he replied. "God, I'm sorry you didn't."

"Come in," Darin said, motioning Rob inside.

"Thanks." The two men settled onto the cot.

"I've been watching the trial via hologram," Rob said. "She certainly is an evil thing, isn't she? All those people she killed. I hope someone has at least given her a good beating when the Lorid's backs were turned," Rob prattled on. "Who does she think she is, acting so mightily?"

Darin had heard enough. "What do you mean, who does she think she is? She's a decorated commander, and Setian Empire empress. You would do well to remember that."

"What?"

Darin didn't respond.

"Look, you've been through hell, but you have to know she can no longer harm you. You're free, my friend; no more cells, and rotten food. The bitch is our prisoner. She'll be dead in a matter of days."

At Rob's words, Darin became angry—very angry. "She didn't give me rotten food, and she certainly did not keep me in a cell!"

Rob stared at him, mouth agape.

"This apartment," he informed his friend, "is the size of what was my private bathroom. My bed was covered in silk."

"You were found in a cell."

"For my protection!" Darin shook his head. "She put me in the cell so the enemy ship would not think I was one of her troops. She was protecting me."

"Enemy ship? Don't you mean your rescuers?"

Darin said nothing.

"My god, if I didn't know any better, I would think you are defending her. Darin, she's evil."

"You know nothing about her."

"Are you telling me you..." he searched for the word, "support her now?"

"No," Darin said quickly. "All I am saying is..." His eyes searched the air in frustration. "I don't know, okay? But she doesn't deserve all of what you said. She's harsh, and cruel at times, but not evil."

"Yes she is! They are all evil, Darin. You taught me that!"

"A lot of them are," Darin replied, his voice operating on a much calmer level than before. "Chrissa can be a cruel, heartless woman. She kills indiscriminately, and without a conscience. However, at other times...at other times she is an inspired leader." A slight smile crept onto his face. "Oh yes, she can lead. And protective, god is she ever protective of her people...I have never seen her match."

"Umm, Darin?"

Darin shook himself and turned back to Rob. "Yeah, sorry."

"No, it is okay. So, I guess your captivity wasn't as horrible as I'd imagined."

"Only at first."

"I've been listening to her testimony. Darin..."

"What?"

"Rape was on the list of crimes. Yours."

Darin said nothing.

"Don't you at least hate her for that?"

"Yes," his voice was a whisper as he stared intently at the floor, "and no. At first, but not later. She never hurt me, not during sex." He sighed, a slight blush heating his cheeks.

"Oh."

The two remained in awkward silence.

"Rob look, we've been friends since we were six years old. But, well, I've been with her for a long time. It's not an experience I can simply brush off, my friend. A part of me agrees with you, she's wicked. But being here, away from her, I don't know how to feel. Some of what I experienced was horrible, yet other parts were exhilarating."

"Are you saying you were willing?"

He drew a harsh breath. "She's a beautiful woman. Well, maybe, perhaps. I," his volume increased, "I don't know, okay? I...don't know what happened. I was a prisoner, but I swear being her prisoner was better than being anywhere else free."

The two looked at each other as though across a vast and deep ocean.

"I'm sorry, Darin. Truly sorry for what happened."

Darin smiled bitterly. "Not your fault. Our own mistakes, Ryan's, Kathleen's, and mine, resulted in our capture. I'm the one who should be sorry. If we'd been more careful, events might have turned out differently."

"Don't be so hard on yourself. The Setians would have found us eventually, with the same result. I only wish we could have gotten the three of you out."

"Doesn't matter now. We can't change what happened."

"True."

The two men picked at pointless bits of conversation for several minutes before Rob excused himself. Darin locked the door behind him, and lay down on the ratty bed, the conversation replaying.

Chrissa's eyes haunted him. His proud, brave empress reduced to a defeated prisoner at the mercy of those who felt nothing but hatred toward her. The realization brought tears.

He was free, and alive to see the rebellion he had started bring down their greatest enemy. Finally safe, without fear of torture or pain, yet his heart ached for the woman who had been the cause of his suffering. Who had stolen everything he loved. Taken his body and soul, and crushed every dream.

Chrissa could not cry, so he cried for her, but even exhausted from his tears, sleep would not come.

Releasing a frustrated sigh, Darin left his room, and after taking the elevator down, stepped outside to the artificial environment. Wandering aimlessly, he ended up at the dome's outer shell, staring out at the vast unknown beyond, until he realized someone had come up behind him.

"Sorry," Darin said, turning to leave.

"Don't be," the man replied. "I didn't mean to interrupt you."

"You didn't." Darin turned to get a good look at who he was talking to.

"I'm Darin." He offered his hand to the mid-twenties man in faded blue jeans and a plain white t-shirt.

"I know," the man replied, offering a firm handshake, but not his name.

The younger man came to stand alongside Darin, looking out as he had been. "My parents went to dinner one night. When they came home, the front door had been broken to pieces, and the babysitter was dead in the living room. Found shaking in my bed, and unable to speak, I spent months in therapy while my parents and investigators tried to figure out what had happened."

He sighed. "When I finally managed to tell them, I was informed what I had seen was impossible." The man shook his head. "They declared that my mind had been so traumatized, I refused to see what had really happened, so I'd created an alternate reality.

"For five years, I went to counseling sessions at least three times a week, until I finally stopped talking about what I had seen, and started telling them what they wanted to hear."

In the silence that followed, Darin said, "I'm sorry, I'm not sure I understand."

The young man looked directly at Darin. "Do you know what they said, when I told my parents my sister had been kidnapped by an army of men, who came in ships that could not exist? Can you imagine what they thought of me, when I told my parents my sister had been kidnapped by aliens?"

Darin gasped. "You mean...you are..."

"James," the man replied. He shook his head again, his voice unsteady. "For the past eight years, I have fought against the empire. Blamed them for taking away the one person I ever cared for. Yet all this time, the person I hated, the person I have done everything in my power to destroy, was the same person I was fighting for." In a voice so soft the night itself tried to swallow his words, he said, "The empress is my sister."

"Oh my god," Darin whispered, as softly as the confession had been made.

"What do I do?" James asked.

After a lengthy silence, Darin gave the only answer Chrissa could live with. "Nothing. You do nothing."

"What?"

"James, I have been with Empress Dehartra for many years, and I swear to you," Darin stated, no longer knowing if he was lying or telling the truth, only that this needed to be said, "that woman is not your sister." Darin fought to keep control of his words. "She stopped being your sister the day she stepped onto that ship. She kills without remorse, and no one, not even those few she loves, are above her loyalty to the empire. If you loved your sister, think of her only as she once was."

"But..."

"But nothing," Darin said sharply. "Your sister is dead, James. She gave her life to protect yours, and there is no more to be said on the subject. You have no sister." These last words were spoken slowly, placing emphasis on each syllable. He placed a gentle hand upon the younger man's shoulder, and squeezed. "She's going to die for what she has done."

Darin walked back to his apartment, and later had no recollection of how he had gotten there. All he knew was somewhere between the lobby and his room, tears fell once again. He fumbled with his keys to open the door, and by the time it closed, Darin was sobbing. Chrissa was going to die, and there was nothing anyone could do to stop it. He felt helpless, scared, and utterly alone.

Exhausted, he finally lay back down and cried himself to sleep, dreaming of the warmth in Chrissa's arms.

Chapter XXXVII

Darin entered my cell, and before I could find the words to ask, he kissed me with a passion that stole my breath. Pulling me into his arms, he whispered words of comfort in Setian. I shook my head against his chest, but allowed him to hold me.

"Chrissa, I needed to tell you…no one defeated you."

I pulled back from his embrace and looked at him, confused. "Of course not," I replied. "I could have left the ship to safety. I brought my own downfall by allowing emotions to cloud my judgment; an act my training taught me never to do."

Darin leaned back enough to see my face, but did not remove his arms from around me. "I lost too, Chrissa." His voice trembled. "You may not have been able to rule my mind, but…" He took a deep breath. "I fell in love with you. You are a tyrant, murderer, and the love of my life." Tears rolled down his face. "You may not have broken my mind, but my heart shall die with you."

"Darin," I soothed, "do you think I am afraid to die?"

"I don't know," he whispered brokenly.

I gave a soft laugh and pulled back enough for him to see my smile. "Look at me, Darin." I shook my head. "I am not afraid. Not at all. Instead, I'm proud to go to the glory of my Setian ancestors, both in this realm, and the next. My name will live immortal." I widened my smile. "I am not scared, Darin. I only wish I could ease your pain. This is my fate. I walk willingly into its arms."

Darin searched my face. "Is there nothing I can do?"

I smiled. "Tell Nicholas I am sorry for what I had to do. Tell him…" I took a deep breath. "I hope I made him proud."

"I will."

"And tell Kavra not to blame himself. Tell him this was an adventure, with certain death assured. Tell him I wouldn't have missed it." I took Darin's hand in my own and turned it palm-side up. Placing the golden ring I always wore into his grasp, I instructed, "Give this back to Kavra, if you can."

Darin moved the ring to his left pocket and held me close in silent comfort.

As the hour arrived, seven guards walked into the room. I stepped away from Darin.

Two of the guards grabbed me, jerking my hands behind me so harshly I could not suppress my surprised yelp of pain. A third guard took a coarse rope and bound my wrists, cutting into my soft skin. They pushed me to my knees as they pulled the rope tighter. Someone slapped my right cheek.

When I turned back, the ropes loosened as the guard who had been tightening them was knocked to the ground by Darin.

"There is no need for this!" Darin screamed. "It takes seven of you to control one girl? She's not even resisting! How dare you treat her this way? She is your most revered enemy, and you can't even give her the dignity of a proper death? How dare you!"

One of the guards stepped forward and tried to reason with him. "Darin, we're doing our job. We are taking this fiend away to—"

Darin hit the man. He fell to the ground, blood splattering the dirty floor as he dropped to his knees. Darin hit him again.

Two of the other guards stepped forward, when Darin pulled a knife, held it at a guard's throat, and shouted, "No!"

The rest of the men froze, unsure of what to do as their hero lost control.

"She's not evil!" he screamed at them. "She is Setian's Alexander the Great! Their Julius Caesar! Yes, she killed many for the goal of ruling, but so did they, and we don't call them monsters! We call them remarkable, kings, even heroes. How dare you treat her this way!"

"Darin!" I cut in, moving slow so not to startle him.

His eyes were wide, and he searched the room.

"Darin," I said softly again, my voice cutting through his panic as he turned those wild eyes on me. "You don't want to harm these men."

"It shouldn't be like this. You deserve more."

"I stand at the hour of my death, and the Earth Resistance Commander is here to honor me. No Setian could ask for more."

"They don't honor you!"

"But you do," I pleaded. "You're a hero to these men. Don't ruin what you gave your life to create."

His breathing became uneven, and tears streamed down his face. "They will hurt you."

"No, they won't." I glanced at the guards, who seemed too stunned to respond. "They were going to, but now they won't. You have seen to that, Commander. I'll walk out this door, and these men will simply follow." I gave the men a questioning look, and they nodded. "Say it out loud."

"We will follow," they affirmed in broken unison.

"Your hand is shaking. Give me the knife, Darin. Please?"

He looked at me as though unsure of what to do, or where he was. "Darin, look at me," I demanded. He did. "Who am I?"

"You're, you're...my empress."

"I am. Now I am ordering you, Darin Hoyle, hand over the knife."

Hand trembling, he moved the knife away from his prisoner's throat to place it into my steady hands.

The man on the floor immediately got up and moved away, blood pouring from his nose.

Hilt-first, I handed the knife to one of the men behind me, then reached for Darin's shaking hands. I pulled him into an embrace, and kissed his brow lightly. "It's okay," I whispered. "Everything will be okay."

He moved to kiss me, and I let him, a soft, chaste caress. "You deserve better."

I smiled softly. "Thank you, Darin. It has been an honor, but I have to go now. I have to go."

Turning, I walked toward the door, the men parting before me as though transformed from a group of barbarians to a magnificent personal guard.

When I reached the threshold, I glanced at Darin for the last time, and said simply, "I love you." A phrase that betrayed every value I had ever upheld.

In response, Darin's voice filled the room. "Empress Dehartra," he said in perfect Setian, "with your death, we forgive you for your sins."

I drew a sharp breath, and turned to end the legend I had become, knowing the indoctrination was finally complete.

Epilogue

CHRISSA'S STORY ENDS HERE. SHE did not live to see the battle that followed. Setian ships arrived minutes too late to save her life. They came in a colossal force—every ship in the empire—with Nicholas in charge of the fleet.

No surprise, considering the extent of their search, they found the rebel camp, and discovered the empress was being held there. What followed was no battle, but a slaughter. The base was only loosely defended, most of the rebel forces out celebrating the defeat of their greatest enemy.

High-ranking rebel commanders were killed, and most others were enslaved, but their consequence came too late. Chrissa had already died at the hands of her accusers, from a poison that had done its work far too quickly. Nicholas knelt beside the sterile table on which she lay quietly, unable to touch her. For the first time in his life, he faced defeat.

Darin entered the room quietly, and sat down near her waist, gazing upon her relaxed face, beautiful even in death.

"She was the empress," Kasar whispered.

"She should have seen this—this victory over the rebels who killed her. This victory belongs to her." Darin kissed her still-warm lips, as if the coldness of death itself feared to touch her.

"Kasar, I have spent the last few years in the personal care of the empress. Today, you have destroyed what was left of the organized resistance I began. My legacy has ended, while hers has begun. I ask you to take me with you. Allow me to help finish what she started." A pause. "She..." Darin's voice seemed less controlled. "She asked you to forgive her."

Nicholas looked at her as though she could hear him. "Chrissa. Oh Chrissa, there was nothing to forgive." He turned, finding Darin's eyes as though seeing him for the first time. "She was mine, you know. She was always mine."

Darin accompanied Chrissa's body to Setianta, where she was dressed in a black silk gown covered with black and red jewels. Her ebony hair was curled and arranged to frame her face. Thus composed, her body was put under guarded display for two days.

Darin sat in a chair near Chrissa's body on the second day when the glass doors opened.

Councilor Kavra stepped inside, carrying a small crate with holes in the top. Dressed entirely in black, he walked to the body and, setting the case off to the side, knelt on one knee beside his beautiful lady. Kavra gently took her cold hand in his, and kissed it, before pressing it tightly against his face, his entire body shaking.

Darin allowed him a few moments before gently placing his hand on the councilor's shoulder. When Kavra did not push him away, Darin squeezed tightly, and stood in silence until Kavra's tears were spent.

"Was it painful?" Kavra asked after a deep breath.

"No. She went to sleep and never awoke."

Kavra shook his head, gasping deep, harsh breaths as he struggled for composure. "You couldn't speak against her, could you?"

Darin gave a sad smile. "No...I didn't even want to." He paused before saying, "She spoke of you, at the end. She called it..."

"An adventure?"

"With certain death assured." Darin offered a slight smile.

Kavra nodded. "They are the best kind, you know. Her favorite." More tears ran down his face.

Darin reached into his left pocket and removed a golden ring. "She wanted you to have this."

Kavra took the ring and nodded. "I gave her this after she saved my life on Palta."

"I never saw her without it."

"When I was with Nicholas, on some battlefront years ago, he described this young girl he had decided to raise as his own. Yet, when I arrived on his ship, out walks this enchanting beauty with eyes that stole my heart. From that moment, I knew I was lost. Her every desire would be met, even if it cost me my soul.

"The day she became empress was the best day of my life. She...was my best friend, the light of my life, my soul mate, my love." Kavra paused. "Chrissa was a star; the brightest in the sky, the most awe-inspiring, and the quickest to burn out. She was my world, and Nicholas was hers. But..." The councilor reached into his left pocket and withdrew a piece of paper, folded neatly.

Darin took the sheet from Kavra's hand and opened it.

In Chrissa's elegant handwriting, Darin read: "By order of the Setian Council, Darin Hoyle, former Earth Resistance leader, is to be executed immediately for crimes against the empire. Signed this day, the 45th of Apresta, by authorization of Empress Dehartra of the Setian Empire." Her signature stood clearly against the whiteness of the page.

"She was the daughter of the empire before all else."

The Indoctrination

Several heartbeats of silence followed before Darin finally asked, "Why am I alive?"

Kavra looked up at the taller man. "Because I loved her too much to kill the last piece of her heart that was human."

Standing, Kavra shifted the small case to Darin's feet before walking away. From inside, came a rumbling purr. Darin smiled for the first time in recent memory.

On the third day, Empress Chrissalynn Dehartra of the Setian Empire was carried though a massive crowd of mourners. Two torches were lit, one held by Darin, and the other by now Emperor Nicholas, with Councilor Kavra standing between them. They lit the funeral pyre, and stood side-by-side with tears running.

As the flames consumed her mortal remains, a commander stepped forward to inform the new emperor that the last remaining rebel ship had been captured. The empress had won the final victory.

Her ashes were divided between three bottles. One was spread over the waters of the Setian home world. Another destined for the oceans of the Lorid home world, her most famous victory. The final bottle was placed in an inner pocket of Emperor Nicholas' black jacket.

When the ceremony was finished, the emperor boarded his ship, and issued orders to travel immediately to Setian Colony 428. A driver waited as he stepped off the ship, but the emperor dismissed him with a wave of his hand.

"This trip is personal," he told his usual guard. "I must do this alone."

He got behind the wheel of the red mustang convertible, and headed down the California coast. The cold bite of the wind on his bare face helped tie him to reality as his mind wandered down a path all but forgotten, yet his hands seemed to know the way as if he had been there only yesterday.

Nicholas found the forgotten beach he had been so fond of years before. He had to climb over the jagged rocks, down a narrow path in order to reach his final destination. The sand under his feet was smooth and untouched as he walked slowly toward the ocean, the sea welcoming him home.

Watching the ocean's currents, he recalled his former human host's love of the sea, and for his intelligent, and spirited child. A love to which he should have been immune, yet had endured in his Setian heart, and brought him back to Colony 428 with a new host, to claim the child as his own, when his rank would allow him to do so without question.

Reaching down he allowed white foam to tickle his fingers. Taking a deep breath, he straightened and reached into the inner left pocket of his billowing jacket to withdraw the bottle of ashes.

Stepping deeper into the ocean, without regard for his clothes, he opened the corked flask and flung her ashes into the sea. The sun set as waves carried her away.

He reached into another pocket, and withdrew a black satin cloth, which he unfolded with utmost care. Within lay a jet black shell, still smooth to the touch after all these years. In the center, a splash of red in the shape of a rose.

"My princess," he whispered through his tears, as he tossed the shell into the sea after her ashes, "my daughter."

Nicholas stepped back, and stood on the dry sand of the beach, gazing into the sunset, which held the perfection normally found only on a postcard. Clear cerulean blue slowly changed to an elaborate array of oranges, reds, pinks, and purples before finally fading to utter and complete darkness.

Thanks & Acknowledgements

I WOULD LIKE TO OFFER a special thanks to a few people who both assisted, and supported, me throughout the creation of this novel.

First, I would like to thank my long time writing mentors, Kate and Mike, for instilling within me a passion for storytelling, and reminding me of that passion when it was needed most. In addition, my appreciation to members of the Watling Street Writers group of St. Albans, who helped shape the direction of this story, offering both support and critique along the way.

To my family, for their never-ending love and support. With special thanks to my husband, parents and grandmother.

To my fabulous content editor, Melissa, who worked above and beyond, tirelessly reading through draft after draft, assisting me in making this story the best it could be. You've kept me straight through this entire process and gave me the courage to stay true to the story. I love working with you and appreciate all that do!

Also to my second editor, Tara, your willingness to work with me, challenge me, and passionately debate the various aspects of this story has helped me to become a better writer. Also for teaching me the mysterious ways of science-fiction, and her patience in helping me navigate through the genre and story.

Finally, to my amazing cover designer, copyeditor, and formatter, Skyla, who takes the jumbled pictures in my head and consistently turns them into beautiful covers. Your work is nothing short of marvelous! Thank you for being my friend and mentor on this journey.

About the Author

K.L. BONE IS THE AUTHOR of the bestselling Black Rose Guard dark fantasy series, The Rise of the Temple Gods fantasy series, and a stand-alone science fiction novel, *The Indoctrination*.

Bone has a master's degree in modern literary cultures and is working toward her PhD in literature. She wrote her first short story at the age of fifteen and grew up with an equally great love of both classical literature and speculative fiction. Bone has spent the last few years as a bit of a world traveler, living in California, London, and most recently, Dublin. When not immersed in words, of her own creation or studies, you'll find her traveling to mythical sites and Game of Thrones filming locations.

Follow her at: www.klbone.com
On Twitter: @kl_bone
Or on Facebook: https://www.facebook.com/klboneauthor

Read on for a preview of *Black Rose*,
the first book in the Black Rose Series by K.L. Bone.

Chapter I

FOR THE FIRST TIME IN *over six hundred years, Mara dreamed of the sea.*

She walked beside the ancient wall, her feet sinking into the sand. Mara was reluctant to face the water that foamed in soft waves behind her with an elegance held only by the sea. Above her, the sky was painted in pinks, oranges, and reds. The sun slowly rose on the distant horizon, as though emerging from the ocean's deep blue waves. When Mara finally turned, the scene, so vivid in her mind, was even more beautiful to behold. Taking a deep breath, Mara could taste salt on the tip of her tongue. She closed her eyes and took several steps forward, allowing the damp sand and salt to saturate her pale skin as she welcomed the first rays of the rising sun.

Reaching the water, she lowered her hand, allowing the foam to wash over the tips of her fingers. She knelt upon the beach while the wind bit at her full-length royal blue gown. While Mara kneeled at the water's edge, a shadow fell over her face. She did not need to look up to know who had joined her. "Phillip."

"Hello, my lady." *His voice was deep and gentle, the way it had sounded ages ago.*

"Is it my time, my lord? Have you come to take me away?"

His bronze hand came into Mara's view, raising her chin to meet his crystal blue gaze. "Do you truly wish it?"

"Every day." *Her usually strong voice came out soft and unsure.* "I have much to atone for."

He stared at her, and sorrow dimmed his striking eyes. "You know you cannot stay here."

"Why not? It should have ended, all those years ago." *The wind teased her hair softly behind her.* "I should have followed you into the sea."

"Do not say such things, my lady. You must go back. He needs you now."

"Needs me?" *she whispered, confused.* "He has not needed me in centuries."

"If you do not find him, he will surely die."

With those words, the dream changed. The cooler purple hues of the sky spread, swallowing the lighter pinks and reds throughout the clouds. Darkness crept from the water to fill the sky, which changed again, from purple to gray. The ocean's depths rose, in ever-increasing waves, before surging in a high wall, which reached to blend with the darkening sky. Finally, the water and sky turned pitch black as the ground beneath Mara's feet transformed from soft sand to unrelenting stone. The sun dimmed to a single flame, the only light visible in the pervasive darkness. Mara once again stood trapped inside those dark, horrifying chambers.

She closed her eyes, but was unable to block out the young woman's voice, begging for the release of the man Mara knew would be atop blood-soaked sheets. Her eyes opened, against her will, and she saw him there, lying nude across the bed. A beautiful woman lay naked beside him, terrible in her wild beauty, a bloody, silver knife clutched in her left hand.

"No!" Mara screamed as she was pulled from the dream in a violent jerk. "Edward," she called out the one name she had not spoken since the night Phillip had died. "Where are you?"

She hugged her knees to her chest, shaking from the dream's impact. Forcing herself to draw a series of deep breaths, Mara turned to glance at the clock. It would be after midnight at the Ciar Court—crazy to call this late.

Disregarding propriety, Mara rose from the bed, and grabbed her phone from a desk in the room's left corner. She dialed a number she knew by heart, despite rarely calling it. Moments later, the Ciar Court Guard's secretary greeted her.

"I need to speak with Captain Edward," Mara announced without preamble.

"I'm sorry," the young woman replied, "the captain is away on assignment."

"Then patch me through to whoever is in charge of the guard while he is away."

"Do you mean Sub-Captain Jake?"

"Yes! Jake, Garreth, whomever Edward left in charge."

"Umm, I'm sorry." The woman did not sound nearly apologetic enough for Mara's taste. "Sub-Captain Jake gave orders not to be disturbed."

"Tell Sub-Captain Jake it's a pretty woman on the other end of the phone."

"I believe he's with a pretty woman," the secretary replied, "which is the reason he asked not to be disturbed. I apologize, ma'am. I can either take a message, or you are free to call back tomorrow."

Mara sighed. She would have to do this the hard way. "Tell the sub-captain Mara Sethian of the Black Rose needs to speak with him. He can come to the phone, or I will get on a flight and knock down his door."

"Did you say, Black Rose?"

"Yes. Captain of the Black Rose, to be more precise."

"Oh," the woman said, sounding much younger than she had over the past few minutes. "Right away, Captain. I will get him right away."

The line went quiet as the call was transferred. Approximately thirty seconds later, a rather tired-sounding male voice answered. "This had better be important."

"Jake," Mara said, "when exactly did Edward get the crazy idea to make you his second?"

A telling silence spoke volumes before Jake's answer. "He ran out of other candidates for the job."

She laughed. "Yes, I figured that is what it would take."

"How are you, Mara?"

"Depends, Jake."

"On what?"

"Where's Edward?"

"All these years and the only thing you want to know is the location of another more powerful, and better looking, man? I'm hurt."

"You're right, Jake. Where are my manners? How are you? And do you happen to know where your better-looking half is?"

Jake's turn to laugh. "I am doing rather well. Edward was sent to deliver some messages to the Arum Court." He paused. "Come to think of it, he should have been back by now. Did you ask for him when you called?"

"Yes."

Jake's voice took on a far more serious tone. "Wait. You actually called for Edward? What happened? You never call for Edward."

"Sometimes I do."

"No. You have never called for Edward. Not once in six hundred years. You ask about him, but you never actually speak to Edward. What the hell is going on?"

Mara paused before answering, "A bad dream."

"A dream?"

"If you hear from him, call me, no matter what time of day."

Jake gave a slight gasp. "Must have been a terrible dream."

"Let's say," she replied slowly, "it was as deep as the sea."

Chapter II

Lady Sandra walked down the Arum Court's halls. The main, upper palace walls were generally painted in deep reds or royal blues, but as Sandra descended, the vibrant shades gave way to faded, darker tones. The lower levels ran deep underground, built in blocks of black stone, and enchanted to withstand the ravages of time. A light chill filled the air, causing Sandra to shiver in her thin blue shirt.

The man walking by her side was Regald, captain of the Arum Court Guard, who had served as her bodyguard for several years. Tall with pale skin, short golden hair, and green eyes, he wore a long-sleeved crimson shirt with a black rose upon the single left-side pocket.

"So," Sandra asked the captain as they descended the darkened hallway, "do you know why King Mathew has ordered us into these…" she searched for the word, "charming chambers today?"

Regald hesitated before answering. "No, my lady. I am afraid I have no idea."

She looked at him in surprise. "Does this worry you?"

Regald gave the slightest of nods. "I am not normally excluded from the king's plans."

They were ushered through a tall wooden door and into a circular room featuring torches burning sporadically along the stone walls.

"Line the perimeter," a younger guard called to the arriving crowd. "Please, everyone, backs against the wall."

Sandra took several paces into the musty room and stepped to her left. The rough surface behind her back was damp, prompting her to step forward to keep her blouse from touching the stone. "Do you see Darek?" she asked, inquiring as to the whereabouts of her fiancé.

Regald glanced around the room as he moved to stand beside her. "I do not, my lady."

"Hmm. I wonder if he will arrive later."

Her gaze traveled the room, barren of furniture, save for a single table standing at its center. Thick, silver chains lay upon the top. As her gaze traveled downward, she realized they were bolted to the floor.

Sandra's eyes shifted back to Regald's warily. "What is this room used for?"

With an apprehensive glance at the table, he explained in measured words, "Once this room was used to punish prisoners, but it has not served in such a capacity for more than a century. I have no idea why the king would want us down here."

An uneasy feeling settled over Sandra as she glanced through the crowd's nervous, silent faces. She again searched for Darek, but the crown prince was nowhere to be found.

A soft click drew all eyes to the left. Guards led a tall, pale-skinned man into the circular room. Legs shackled together, he moved in a slow shuffle with his arms bound behind him in thick chains. His shirt had been removed, and his hair hung loose around his shoulders in long, dark strands. As his face came into view, a murmuring rose through the crowd.

Beside her, Regald whispered, "By the gods."

"Who is it?" Sandra kept her voice quieter than the soft hum surrounding them.

The man was directed to the table by four figures covered completely in midnight-blue hooded robes. They guided the unresisting man to its sleek surface, expertly transferring him from portable bonds into the thick, silver chains. Once secured, his body lay taut across the table, the metal cutting into his wrists.

The guards stepped back as twelve more hooded figures entered the room, each wearing deep red robes. Their movements flowed seamlessly together as they stepped forward to form a circle around the restrained man. The four in blue stepped back toward the wall.

When one of them moved past Regald, he asked, "What is going on here, Kala?"

"King's orders," the woman replied.

"What? Do you have any idea who that man is?"

"Do not insult me, Regald. He is captain of the Ciar Guard."

"Then what, in the name of all that is sacred, is he doing on that table?"

"I do not question the king's orders, Captain. I merely carry them out."

He looked back at the man chained to the table. "You do understand they will come for him, don't you?"

"I am not afraid of our sister court," came her curt reply. "And if you interfere, you will be chained right beside him."

"Might be worth it."

Kala met his gaze with blazing golden eyes before resuming her route, one that eventually stopped on the opposite side of the room.

Sandra looked closely at her captain, noting that despite his stiff posture, she could see the color draining from his face. "What is going on?"

Regald shook his head. "He is Edward, captain of the Ciar Royal Guard."

"Why would the king order him harmed? Will this not anger the Ciar Court?"

"Yes, it will. However, I fear it won't be the Ciar guards who come for that man."

"I don't understand. Who will come for him, if not his own guard?"

Regald either did not hear, or chose not to answer, as his attention returned to the twelve hooded figures. Moving in unison, they had closed around the table in a tight circle and then, as one, tossed back their hoods, revealing twelve women, with matching black hair, held by silver bands. Their reflective, catlike eyes were a green so light they could have been considered yellow, with black, vertical slits where a round pupil should have been. The prisoner remained stoic.

The women raised their arms, each revealing the black handle of the whips they carried. Designed to inflict maximum pain, each of the wrapped grips had three leather straps attached to the main handle, with a sharp, triangular piece of silver on each tip. The jagged edges of metal would tear skin from bone when dragged across the prisoner's vulnerable flesh.

Sandra's gaze traveled back to Regald, who motioned for her to remain silent with a curt gesture. She turned forward. Her eyes scanned those whispering around her before turning back to the room's center. Inadvertently, she caught the gaze of the man lying on the table. His eyes were jet black, the darkest she had ever seen.

The room spun. Sandra closed her eyes to steady her vision and found herself standing in a rose garden. Red and violet flowers surrounded her, climbing the rockery walls to blossom in beautiful clusters of royal colors. A full moon, high above, reflected in the calm waters of the pool before her. The image showed she wore a thin, royal blue gown. Her black hair curled in luxurious waves, framing her face and flowing down her back. A gold chain, with a white, rose-shaped diamond, nestled at the hollow of her neck, visible in her gown's plunging neckline. A smile graced her crimson lips, extending to her rouge-tinged cheekbones.

Behind her stood a man, his white shirt open at the upper chest, and silver buttons below that twinkled in the moonlight. The top of the shirt should have been laced together, like something out of the Renaissance, but instead the silver strings hung loose on either side, leaving his pale throat bare to the cool night air. He stepped closer to Sandra, and placed his arms around her. Her smile widened as a mild gust sent ripples through the previously still water, distorting their reflection.

The ripples slowly spread, and with them the moon's reflection vanished, changing the pool from blue to black. For no apparent reason, she tipped forward, her thin frame tumbling toward the water. Anticipating a shock of cold, she closed her eyes, but instead of water, hit stone.

"Sandra?" Regald's deep voice pulled her from the vision. "You don't have to watch this." But his delivery came too late. The whips rose high in the air before crashing simultaneously onto the restrained man. When they pulled back, blood streaked his skin. The prisoner was silent, but Sandra knew he would not remain so for long.

Searching her broken memories for anything about the man chained to the table, Sandra found nothing tangible among the scattered pieces.

She closed her eyes again and this time lay on the stone floor. Smooth beneath her fingers, but also cold. She tried to rise, to push herself up, but something crashed into her, knocking the wind from her lungs, keeping her pressed firmly to the floor. She held still before attempting to see her surroundings again, this time raising only her head.

A man and woman cavorted on a bed near the room's center. Topless, the woman's pale skin glowed, luminescent in the darkness. Her black hair danced around her in wild curls. The sweet music of her laughter carried upon a summer breeze, like the ringing of bells only angels should be pure enough to hear. She tossed her curls to the side, revealing the man beneath her.

Lines of blood streaked his chest. The beautiful creature lifted a thin, silver blade, cruel intent lighting her eyes. Sandra's gaze followed the bloody lines from the man's open chest to his face, where she stared into his dark gaze.

Whips whistled through the air, again pulling Sandra from the strange vision. The room had fallen to utter silence as the chained man gave a deep moan. Sweat poured from his skin, mixing with the ever-increasing blood now streaming from the table.

She searched her memory, but no answer came. The whips struck again, and this time, he was unable to suppress his screams. Sandra's heart cried out at the sound. Another scream shattered the room, and she had to resist the urge to scream with him. She closed her eyes, only to see the same man, being slowly cut by the blade of a woman Sandra had never seen before.

The whips again rose in the air. Without thought or understanding, she took several steps forward then broke into a run. Before the guards could react, Sandra reached the table and threw herself across the injured man. Their trajectory set, brutal whips crashed against her back, cutting through her blouse and sinking into the thin flesh of her back. Her high-pitched scream rang through the room, echoing down the halls, before finally reverberating back toward her with a living force of their own.

Blood oozed across her back, running down to mingle with the blood of the man tied beneath her. Her back burned, like it had been lit on fire. A second stroke came down upon her, the guards having moved into the motion before realizing what had happened. The second blow tore past the ragged tatters of her shirt, pulling more flesh from her body. Her vision swam. The pain was nauseating.

Regald bolted to her side. "Sandra," he whispered in horror.

She heard his voice as though from a distance. "No more," she said as the world dimmed. "No more."

Chapter III

SANDRA WRITHED IN AGONY. THE lines of ruined skin burned with fire from the antiseptic, which had been slathered over the open wounds before her back had been bound in thick, white bandages. She moved to rise from the bed, where she lay facedown, but thought better of it as searing pain answered each muscle contraction. After taking several breaths, she tried again, this time moving more cautiously.

Once in a seated position, Sandra met the deep green of her fiancé's eyes. At over six feet tall, Prince Darek was a handsome man. His skin held a healthy bronze tan, which matched his sandy brown hair, a shade darker than blond. He wore a pair of black slacks with a royal blue shirt, closed with buttons that coordinated with the simple silver chain worn loosely around his neck.

"Sandra," Darek began, uncrossing his arms and leaning forward on the upholstered stool, his elbows on his knees. "What? Why?" He shook his head, unable to continue.

"I don't know," she answered. "Darek, I really don't know." Embarrassed to not have an explanation, she lowered her gaze before asking, "Is he still alive?"

"Yes. He was returned to his cell after you fainted." A hint of anger entered her fiancé's voice. "You threw yourself over him, and you don't know why?" He rocked back and slapped his hands on his knees, frustration evident on his face. "I know you can't remember much of your past, but this..."

"Look, Darek, I don't know!" Her voice sounded strained. "I don't know what I saw. I don't know who he is. I don't know why I threw myself over him." She jerked upright, and immediately regretted it, hissing in pain.

"Look, stop," the prince soothed. "Lie back down and rest. I'll send a healer in to give you something to help with the pain." He stood swiftly and walked toward the door.

Sandra lay quietly on the bed. When she managed to settle into a bearable position, she closed her eyes, but did not find the quiet dreams she longed for.

Instead, she stood in the same garden, the roses so vivid their sweet aroma engulfed her. A light breeze slid across her skin, moving her hair in its gentle breath.

Sandra opened her eyes and stared across her fiancé's room. She could still smell the roses.

Find Black Rose *and other works by K.L. Bone wherever books are sold.*

Made in the USA
Las Vegas, NV
17 November 2021